Praise for *When the F*

Rhonda Dragomir's debut novel is not to b[...] with research, and a tender love story. So [...] and some stories last a lifetime. *When the Flames Ravaged* is one of those unforgettable stories.

 –DiAnn Mills, bestselling author and winner of two Christy Awards,
 writer of the 2023 ECPA Christian Fiction best-seller *Facing the Enemy*

When the Flames Ravaged is a story of hope in the midst of tragedy that doesn't shy away from hard spiritual questions. The depth of research is evident and small touches will drop the reader right into wartime America. Dragomir's debut is quite the satisfying read!

 –Erica Vetsch, author of the Thorndike and Swann Regency Mysteries

How do we prevent our faith from growing as cold as next morning ashes when a fiery tragedy upends our lives? Rhonda Dragomir's skillfully drawn protagonists explore this difficult question in her page-turning novel. The emotional depth in this story deeply touched my heart—definitely a five-star story!

 –Johnnie Alexander, bestselling, award-winning author of
 Where Treasure Hides and *The Cryptographer's Dilemma*

Every emotion you've ever sought to experience between the covers of a book Rhonda Dragomir delivers with her stunning debut novel, *When the Flames Ravaged*. Not only the romance between the unlikely hero and heroine, but also the "aw"-inducing family moments remind us God is in the business of bringing beauty from ashes.

 –Denise Weimer, historical romance editor, author of *When Hope Sank* and The Scouts of the Georgia Frontier Series

Rhonda Dragomir's characters are so richly crafted they burn into our hearts and become "people" we remember long after we've read, "The End." Fiction can surpass self-help books when it's well done, creating a psychological road map for delivery from hopelessness and despair to faith and trust. *When the Flames Ravaged* is such a book.

 –Dr. Deborah Maxey, Ph.D., Licensed Professional
 Counselor and award-winning author of *The Endling*

A DAY TO REMEMBER

When the Flames Ravaged

RHONDA DRAGOMIR

BARBOUR
PUBLISHING

When the Flames Ravaged ©2024 by Rhonda Dragomir

Print ISBN 978-1-63609-786-2
Adobe Digital Edition (.epub) 978-1-63609-787-9

This book is a work of fiction. Names, characters, places, and incidents are either products of the
author's imagination or used fictitiously. Any similarity to actual people, organizations, and/or
events is purely coincidental.

Cover Design by Faceout Studio

Published by Barbour Publishing, Inc., 1810 Barbour Drive, Uhrichsville, Ohio 44683,
www.barbourbooks.com

Our mission is to inspire the world with the life-changing message of the Bible.

Member of the
Evangelical Christian
Publishers Association

Printed in the United States of America.

DEDICATION

*This book is dedicated to the victims of the Hartford circus fire,
especially Bill Curlee and Raymond Erickson, Jr., and to everyone
whose efforts have made July 6, 1944, a day to remember.*

Chapter One

A wiry roustabout removed his sweat-soaked cap and mopped his brow. "She's a beauty, ain't she?"

"Yep. She sure is." Hank Webb didn't know the man, but he shared the sentiment. His eight-man hammer gang had pounded on the tent stakes in perfect rhythm, each sledge landing one second apart. More than a square mile of canvas had been rolled out, its sections laced together with rope. Elephants, their ears flapping under the heat of the relentless July sun, had strained in their harnesses to pull up the big top. The Ringling Brothers and Barnum & Bailey Circus tent had risen to life like a hot air balloon shot with helium.

American flags topped each center pole and undulated in the late morning breeze, causing a lump in Hank's throat. The 1944 outdoor season had started on June 6th, the very day Allied forces stormed the beaches at Normandy. Those men hadn't sacrificed in vain because American life still thrummed. In Hartford, its heartbeat sounded like midway barkers, the laughter of children, and the trill of the steam calliope.

Hank ducked under the tent flap and inspected the aisle, normally used for patrons to enter and exit, where he and his propmen would deploy the animal chute for the evening show. If the lions escaped, people could die, and Hank didn't need any more of that kind of trouble. He entered ring three and double-checked the fence that caged the big cats for Joe Walsh's act.

A shout rang from above. "Look out!"

The warning came too late, and Hank didn't have time to jump aside. A fifty-pound spotlight tumbled from the center pole and thudded in the sawdust at his feet. Broken glass shimmered and sprayed everywhere.

"Hey! *You* look out." Hank sheltered his eyes with a hand and glared at Russell Segal, the klutz who descended from his forty-eight-foot perch. He stalked to the base of the ladder and confronted the newbie crewman. "You could have killed me."

Russell claimed to be eighteen years old, but Hank doubted it. The boy had giant muscles but a puny brain. He should have attached a safety line to the heavy unit while rigging it. A reckless, dangerous failure—and not his first.

Halfway down the ladder, Russell called, "Sorry. It just got away from me."

When the boy got both feet on the ground, Hank would wallop him good. But Eddie Vermeer—chief electrician and boss of the roustabouts— beat him to it, delivering the boy a sharp slap to his left cheek. Only two-thirds Russell's size, Eddie more than made up the difference with orneriness. Russell massaged the reddening handprint but stood straight and narrowed his eyes. At least he was smart enough not to say anything.

One week—that's all it had taken for Russell to exhaust Eddie's patience. Most able-bodied men were overseas crawling through Normandy's hedgerows and dodging Nazi bullets. Labor shortages had forced the hiring of townies who didn't have a clue what they were doing. Eddie was so hard-pressed he'd even hired a well-built teenager who didn't have the sense God gave geese.

Eddie jabbed a bony finger in Russell's chest. "It don't matter how strong you are, boy. One more goof and you're out. That light was expensive, and I'm deducting it from your pay."

A group of men had huddled together to watch Eddie's outburst with the enthusiasm of servicemen at a Rita Hayworth movie. One carped, "It's the jinx, boss!"

Once the taboo on the forbidden sentiment was broken, others chimed in.

"Cursed!"

"Haunted!"

One crewman, his shoulders muscled from backbreaking work but his belly swollen by too much drinking, leaned against a quarter pole and pulled out a cigarette. "Anybody got a light?"

Russell whipped out his Zippo and sparked a flame.

Eddie knocked it to the ground and stomped the daylights out of it before the sawdust started to smolder. Gesturing to the group, he snarled, "All these accidents are caused by stupid people." Pointing to the offender, who still had an unlit Marlboro between his lips, he said, "The fires in Providence and Portland should make you more careful, but you don't think twice about smoking in here." He drew himself up to his full height, which still didn't put him at eye level with Russell. Evenly, but with menace, he said, "There's no such thing as a jinx."

Russell replied, "But we had to cancel the matinee." The boy had been talking too much with the sideshow folks, who couldn't help telling tall tales. Fear was their currency, and profits were up.

Eddie leaned in so close that droplets of his spittle landed on Russell's cheek. "Our train was side-railed because of this infernal war, and we arrived in Hartford late. There wasn't time to complete our setup. That's it. No curse, no gremlins, and no boogeymen." Swiping off his well-beaten fedora, he slapped it against his thigh. "This jibber jabber about a jinx sets everybody's nerves on edge, and I want it to stop. Now."

With the precision of a military officer, Eddie turned on his heel, strode toward the bandstand, and shouted over his shoulder, "Get back to work." Tension rolled off him like thunder after a lightning strike, and everyone heard the rumble.

The rigging crew resumed their work, but they still muttered. Two years with the troupe had taught Hank one thing—circus folks lived and breathed superstition. They deemed missing a performance extremely bad luck. Nonsense. But Hank couldn't explain the recent string of mysterious fires either.

Russell hovered nearby instead of obeying Eddie. "I mean it, Hank. I'm sorry." He extended his hand like a grown man.

Hank ignored it. "Sorry doesn't cut it. We all have to count on each other, or somebody will end up dead. Next time it could be you."

"Is that a threat?" Russell clenched a fist, and his head cocked to the side.

Hank simply wanted Russell to go away. If he did, maybe the drumbeat in his skull would stop. "You scared me, that's all. Let's buckle down and finish prepping the tent, and then maybe we can go into town for an early dinner."

Turn-on-a-dime mood changes were nothing new for Russell. He grinned. "I'd like that! I'm sick of circus grub." He rubbed his stomach like he'd not eaten for days, but he had scarfed down lunch like a starving tiger only half an hour ago. A job that provided free food might be the only way Russell could afford to eat.

An experienced rigger blocked Russell's attempt to resume his work. The man grabbed the spare spotlight and climbed the ladder. The boy grumbled, but he loped away to help the crew set up folding chairs in the bleachers. Eight thousand people were expected tonight, so they needed the help.

The thick, humid air under the tent, even without patrons in grandstands, made the atmosphere like the Amazon jungle. No wonder the skilled workers had hair-trigger tempers.

Hank glanced at his watch. Five hours until showtime. He should finish his inspections, catch a quick shower, and don his costume and makeup. During performances, Hank dressed as a clown, and his name was on the short list of people being sent on public relations duty to visit a local diner. The circus needed to earn back the goodwill that had been lost by canceling the matinee.

Who wouldn't be cheered up by a clown?

But if goodwill was the goal, Hank should never have invited Russell.

"Evelyn, the boss says you can take care of those clowns at table six."
Darla's guffaw teased Evelyn's lips to smile. They almost did, and would
have, except today had already served up challenges faster than Charlie
plated corned beef hash.

Before she left for work, Evelyn had been assailed by her weeping
niece and nephew, who'd just learned about the cancellation of today's
circus matinee. Bill—Evelyn's brother and the children's father—had
exchanged his tickets for tomorrow's two o'clock show, but it made no
difference to the children.

Then, Evelyn's fingernail had punctured her last precious pair of real
hosiery. A huge run started right below her hem and traveled all the
way into her shoe. A gravy stain hadn't washed out of her apron, and the
five-block hike to work in the oppressive heat wasted all the time she had
spent sleeping on her pin curls.

Not even Bob Hope could have brought a genuine smile to Evelyn's face
today. She loaded glasses of ice and a pitcher of water on her serving tray
and headed to the circular corner booth. Darla would have loved to serve
them. But no, the clowns—real ones—had chosen seats in Evelyn's section.

Four Ringling clowns occupied the curved, red-vinyl bench accompanied by an enthusiastic young man who reveled in all the attention. When
Evelyn drew near, perspiration trickled down her back. The diners fixed
their eyes on her as she set a glass in front of each man. Ice tinkled as
she poured water without spilling a drop. One clown made his eyebrows
dance, another mimed the shape of an hourglass, and a third emitted a
wolf whistle. The fourth merely stared. His white-rimmed eyes and his
crimson, O-shaped mouth made him look perpetually terrified.

Evelyn summoned the authoritative voice she'd learned when babysitting the Johnson twins. "That's quite enough." The offenders straightened
their bow ties and sat at attention, much to the delight of the nearby
children.

"I'm Evelyn, and I'll be your waitress today." One clown offered a snappy salute, and two others waved with exaggerated enthusiasm. On a different day, it might have been funny.

The brawny teenager appointed himself an unofficial translator. "They are mimes, so I'll have to give their orders. I'm Russell."

The youth had turned his back to the clowns, so he didn't see their gestures. One put his thumb to his nose and wiggled his fingers, another rolled his eyes and slumped, and the third scrubbed his hands through his fiery hair until it stood on end. The fourth sat as still as a boulder, but he blinked.

Charlie bellowed through the kitchen window, "Did they come to eat or put on a show? I'm running a diner here."

Everyone sobered up. The adults resumed eating, and only the children kept up their stares and giggles.

The first clown fanned his face with a handkerchief while beckoning Evelyn to guess the meaning of his charade.

She played along. "Hot."

The second clown honked an ear-splitting horn, and Evelyn's empty tray clattered to the floor. Thank goodness, she'd set the pitcher on the table already. Everyone seemed amused except Charlie. The fourth clown deftly retrieved her tray, gave it to her, and brushed her hand with his. Was that intentional? Something in his summer-blue eyes banished the tension from her shoulders.

Evelyn guessed "dog" when clown number one lolled his tongue and panted. Being a waitress didn't mean you were dumb or stuck-up. When she asked if he wanted fries, the clown answered with exaggerated claps of his gloved, padded fingers, prompting more horn honking from his partner in crime.

The shenanigans stole the spotlight from Russell, and he thumped the table with an oversized fist. "That's enough, you—"

He stopped himself, but everyone mentally completed Russell's sentence.

Clowns.

A belly laugh escaped before Evelyn could restrain it. She covered her mouth, but a refreshing lightness infused her soul. She steadied the upset teen with a gentle hand on his shoulder. "It's all right. This world needs all the laughter we can get."

A red flush climbed the young man's neck and settled in his cheeks. He remained silent but spoke volumes with his scowl. Someone should keep a close watch on that one.

The clowns completed their orders with a flair for entertainment. The fourth man simply pointed on the menu to the special—meatloaf on toast points and mashed potatoes, smothered in gravy, with a side of applesauce. His even, white teeth glistened when he smiled, and laugh lines creased his makeup.

Warmth crept into Evelyn's cheeks until their color matched Russell's. If she didn't leave the table soon, she might go up in flames. "I'll place your orders now, gentlemen."

Evelyn headed for the kitchen, but the men's gazes weighed heavily on her back. She could almost see them—three gleeful clowns, a hotheaded teenager with a chip on his shoulder, and an intriguing fraidy-cat she'd like to see without his makeup.

But wasn't that against the clown code of conduct?

Evelyn didn't care.

Hank rubbed his jaw, and his hand came away black. Clown makeup wasn't conducive to public dining. Evelyn waited on other tables, but he couldn't stop admiring her female perfection. Not only was she a beauty—with her heart-shaped face and startling gray eyes—but she was a good sport. Not many women could handle themselves with so much grace under the onslaught of this Ringling trio. Charlie Bell, Blinko, and Happy Kellems often turned intelligent, articulate women into blathering nincompoops.

His guise meant he couldn't talk, but Hank would wrangle more information from Evelyn somehow. He was no skirt chaser, but something about Evelyn stirred him. Perhaps he longed for a connection to a woman not tainted by circus life, but this was more than simple admiration. For the first time in two years, Hank entertained the idea of settling down.

Hartford was far enough away from Speigletown. No one should recognize him even without his makeup.

The rattle of dishes and happy hoots from his companions, all except Russell, announced Evelyn's return. Blinko made a show of sloppy eating, Happy spurted water on his plate like he was the Trevi Fountain, and Charlie Bell watched with mock revulsion. Russell didn't comment, leaning over his plate and shoveling food into his mouth.

Hank pointed at Evelyn and made signs he hoped she'd understand. *You come tomorrow?*

The other clowns nodded yes and clapped.

"Yes. I'll be at the matinee." Evelyn's smile was that of an indulgent teacher with a classroom of hooligans, but her answer was the one Hank had hoped for.

The pointed collar of Evelyn's white blouse sported a round lapel pin with a gold star against a purple background. Not mere jewelry. Evelyn was a war widow. He should be ashamed for thinking it was good news. Pointing to the pin, Hank mimed a trail of tears down his cheeks with both index fingers.

The other clowns stilled.

Evelyn's lower lip trembled.

Hank wrapped himself in a hug and rocked side to side, slowly shaking his head. Then he shrugged and extended upraised hands to her while arching his eyebrows.

"George. My husband. He died in the Bataan Death March."

The fact pierced Hank's chest like a bayonet. What an awful way for a man to die, and what a horror for the survivors. Hank might have been in Bataan, if only. . . Nope. Spilled milk. No crying.

Hank removed his red beret, folded his hands, and bowed his head. His companions joined him, and it wasn't an act. He said a brief, silent prayer for Evelyn and all the women who had been deprived of husbands, fathers, or sons. Even now, good men died under German fire in Europe as they marched beside Sherman tanks through the French countryside.

And Hank wore clown makeup traveling with the circus in Hartford, Connecticut. His throat constricted so much he couldn't have voiced words even if he'd been allowed to.

Russell emerged from his funk. "We're sorry for your loss, ma'am."

Clowning in town was over for the day. The troupers ate their meal in silence like true mimes. After they wrapped up the remnants of their meal, they left payment and a generous tip for Evelyn before scooting out of the diner. Halfway back to the tents, Hank halted like a soldier under orders from a drill sergeant. Blinko ran into him, feigned anger, and knocked his beret off while bystanders snickered.

He'd forgotten to ask for Evelyn's phone number.

Chapter Two

Evelyn's keys jangled as she dropped them in her pocketbook, and she closed the door to the Capen Street house with a quiet snick, having perfected the art of sneaking in after the children were in bed. Her sister-in-law sprawled on the sofa with her feet propped up on the footstool. Fast asleep, poor lamb.

Helen stirred. "Evelyn, is that you?"

"Yes. Hush now. Let me have those toes of yours."

Helen loved nothing more than a foot rub, and she deserved it after long hours on her feet at Pratt & Whitney.

Evelyn picked up a foot, removed the shoe, and massaged the instep with both her thumbs. "How many engines came down the line today?"

Helen moaned an unintelligible answer. Production of the Wasp Major for the Boeing B-50 had ramped up the need for manpower, or woman power in Helen's case. She earned the highest pay among the three working adults in the family, but Bill constantly fretted over the physical toll on his wife. At least she had time off tomorrow to go with the family to the circus.

Evelyn traded feet, and Helen roused. "How was work for you?"

"Same as always. A few clowns but nothing I couldn't handle." Evelyn offered a mysterious smile.

Helen missed it. She replied, although her eyes remained closed. "Bill and I could never afford this place without you."

"I'm glad to pitch in, especially since I had nowhere else to go when George died." Moving in with her brother had saved more than Evelyn's sanity. Since her parents were gone and George was killed in action, it gave her a place to live and a family to cherish as her own. "Times are tight, but together we can make it work."

"Yes, we can. We may be a month behind on the mortgage, but we'll catch up. After the war, maybe we can find a bigger place."

It took three incomes to afford Bill and Helen's homey little bungalow. House prices had skyrocketed in Hartford as people swarmed to town for wartime production jobs. Evelyn's little bed was crammed in a room not much bigger than a closet, but she didn't mind. "Did anything come of Bill's application at Pratt?"

"No, and I don't think it will. If he can't communicate well enough to be a soldier, factory work is out too."

"Does he still talk about being 4F?"

"Sometimes. But his stutter is aggravated by his embarrassment, and he can hardly get the words out. I tell him he's not letting his country down, but he just clams up."

"Well, I'm praying a job opens at P&W. At least that way he'll feel like he's contributing to the war effort." Evelyn's brother worked hard to provide for his family. He had found a second-shift custodian job at the Hartford Accident and Indemnity Company, but the pay was abysmal. At least he could mind the children while Evelyn and Helen worked day shifts.

Maudlin sentiment wouldn't help her brother, so Evelyn turned to a happier topic. "I'm so glad you can go to the circus with the family tomorrow. How did you manage to get off work?"

"It wasn't easy, but I turned puppy eyes on my boss." Helen widened her eyes and blinked several times, wiping away a pretend tear. Droopy Dog couldn't have looked more forlorn.

The women giggled till they were breathless.

"Well, those dishes won't do themselves." Helen sat up, slipped her shoes on, and ambled to the kitchen, with one hand supporting her lower back. Evelyn followed and turned on the oscillating electric fan. The humid air cooled somewhat.

Evelyn's brow wrinkled. "We'll keep Lily and Jamie away from the sideshow, right?"

"Of course. Bill will want to let them go, but thankfully, tickets are extra. I don't want my daughter anywhere near a sword-swallowing woman or a snake charmer. I don't know what the Sam Hill a living skeleton is, and I don't want to." Helen drained the dishwater, got two glasses from the cupboard, and filled them with ice cubes and mint lemonade—the perfect nightcap for a long, hot day, especially when paired with Helen's scrumptious gingersnap cookies.

Evelyn guzzled the cool drink and resisted the urge to groan with pleasure. "I'm surprised Charlie is letting me go. He's stingy with time off when business is booming." His agreement had been more than surprising. Evelyn was shocked. Perhaps Charlie had a heart of flesh underneath his stony exterior.

"I'm glad you're going. It will take both of us to keep an eye on Lily. She doesn't miss a thing." Bill and Helen's vivacious eight-year-old had the imagination and verbal skills of a trained actress.

Evelyn chuckled. Attending the circus with her would be pure joy. "I'll be glad to help."

Helen squeezed Evelyn's hand and said, "Thanks, Evie. Lily loves you like a mother, you know."

"I do." The cookies turned to rocks in her stomach. She might have had her own babies by now if George had lived, but it didn't pay to wallow in self-pity. She should be thankful for the affectionate companionship Bill and Helen offered and the opportunity to enjoy the merriment of the children even if they weren't hers.

"I'm off to bed." Helen emptied the ice and rinsed the glasses before placing them in the sink for tomorrow night's washing. She hugged Evelyn and pecked a sweet kiss on her cheek. "'Night, sis."

"'Night."

Too keyed up to retire, Evelyn took Helen's spot on the sofa and picked up that day's copy of *The Hartford Courant*. It didn't take long to spy the full-page circus ad printed in color. Evelyn studied the images for a few minutes before making an appalling discovery.

She was searching for a picture of a certain clown with fraidy-cat makeup.

A male performer dressed as a lion prowled the hippodrome track growling and snarling at terrified, but delighted, children. A dozen bally girls entered the arena. Dressed in skimpy gold costumes with knee-high boots and Cossack hats, they circled the lion as if to tame him. When Merle Evans, the band director, signaled a clash of cymbals, the lion produced a prop whip. He stole the show, running the girls through a number of catlike tricks and poses. The crowd ate up the role-reversal comedy that served as a prelude to the real show. Joe Walsh and his menagerie—including six adult male lions—would soon occupy the ring. His whip wasn't a prop.

Hank and his men deployed the chute through which the lions would pass, making sure every connection was secure. Getting the ferocious creatures into the ring without their drawing blood was a ballet of its own. Whenever a lion passed, one of Hank's crewmen shoved a board between the bars behind it, both to prevent the animal from turning around and to keep it from attacking the one that followed.

"Hey, Fraidy Freddie, those lions gonna getcha?" A freckle-faced kid with smears of chocolate ice cream on his flushed cheeks leaned over the side of the bleachers and nearly lost his cone altogether. On top of Hank.

Hank froze, swept off his red beret, and clutched it against his chest. He widened his eyes and gawped right and left, making every limb shake as his knees wobbled. The crowd pointed and cackled at his antics. He exaggerated it as part of the show, but Hank's fear of the big cats wasn't faked.

His first night on chute duty, back in '42, the bleachers had been set too close. Spartacus, the largest and meanest of Ringling's lions, smelled fear. When Hank slid the board in place, Spartacus attacked, reaching through the four-inch gap between the bars with claws as sharp as razors.

Hank was too slow, and he couldn't back away far enough to escape a mauling. The lion raked his arm and stomach, scoring deep gashes that had required almost fifty stitches from the circus doctor.

For several shows afterward, Hank had utterly failed in his duties. He tried, but fear won every time. Patrons noticed his trembling hands and hasty exit from the tent before the cats were released from their wagon. "Fraidy-cat," they hooted, and the ridicule had haunted his dreams.

The lead propman wanted Hank reassigned, but the Ringling clowns knew an opportunity when they saw it. They coaxed Hank into costume, with thick padding over his arms and torso as protection, and asked Emmett Kelly to design his makeup. Black covered Hank's lower face, like Emmett's famous Weary Willie, but the white around his lips formed a large "O" instead of a frown. Dark black eyebrows were painted in an exaggerated arch, and three spikes of triangular black eyelashes above his lids added to Hank's look of permanent fright. "Fraidy Freddie" was born, and he was a huge hit with the crowds.

But not with Hank. He wouldn't be recognized if he walked down the street without makeup, but he was tired of hiding behind it. He concealed everything: his real reason for joining the circus, his true last name, and all vestiges of his former life as the son of a beloved Methodist preacher. Henry Frederick Webster from Speigletown, New York, faded day by day as Fraidy Freddie took over.

Which, perhaps, was for the best, because the costume also hid a man wanted for murder. His parents would be spared the shame of watching their son die in the electric chair.

"Hey, Freddie!" A second boy roared and thrust a stuffed lion toward him, and Hank responded as expected. He ran in circles, smacked his head, and hunched his shoulders until they pressed against his ears. Freckle Boy laughed so hard his scoop of ice cream launched off the cone like a cannonball shot from a howitzer. When it landed at Hank's feet, the boy's smiles turned to tears.

Hank did a little dance around the glop and mimed great distress until roars from the real lions reached a crescendo that drowned out the band music. One mighty roar eclipsed them all, and everyone turned toward the entrance to the chute.

Spartacus, King of the Lions, burst into the tunnel—a mass of pure muscle, tawny fur, and sharp, yellow fangs. A propman shoved the board in place, but it was unnecessary. Spartacus thought nothing of retreat. The ferocious beast caught Hank's scent, vaulted to the spot nearest him, and slammed his body against the bars. He took two vicious swats that caught only air. A game for the lion and a delight for the crowd, the nightly encounter was nothing of the sort for Hank.

A crack of Joe Walsh's whip snapped Spartacus out of his bloodthirsty fixation, and he trotted obediently into ring three. The other lions followed, but there could be no doubt which was the crowd favorite. Walsh was either a fool or the bravest man Hank had ever met.

In ring one, May Kovar's act also took place, featuring eighteen big cats—panthers, pumas, and leopards. A kind person, May had offered several times to help Hank overcome his fear, but he always answered with a firm, "No, thanks."

Walsh grabbed Spartacus by his jaws, wrestled them apart, and stuck his head in the gaping maw. Hank could almost smell the lion's foul breath. The crowd cheered while Hank's mouth went dry. The lion tamer paraded two cats around the perimeter of the ring, and they leapfrogged each other in sinuous rhythm.

When Walsh's back was turned, Spartacus leaped upon Brutus, the lion sitting on a tall stool to his left. Their snarls elicited screams from the crowd, but the wrestling was a carefully scripted, highly trained act. Walsh's whip cracked, and he physically separated the writhing animals, commanding them back to their posts. When they obeyed, the screams turned to cheers, accompanied by deafening applause. Walsh bowed, pretending to be humbled by the accolade, but that too, was part of the act. Walsh had an ego as vast as Siberia.

Act over, Walsh herded the lions back down the chute. The performance always sapped a little strength from the lions, and Spartacus growled at Hank but didn't attack. Hank sagged against a patron with apparent relief, fanned his face, and then sat on a surprised woman's lap and demanded a hug. She laughed and patted his back like a kind soul. Hank kissed her cheek, wiggling his lips to leave behind a smear of his red lipstick.

When he tried to kiss the woman's husband too, he elicited a predictable shove. Hank swirled his fists in the air like a heavyweight boxer, bobbing and weaving with fancy footwork. But when the man stood, as expected, Hank fled for the chutes. He and his team made quick work of disassembling them to clear the aisle for patrons, and the performance continued to its next act, the Flying Wallendas.

Hank stepped out into the heavy night air and headed for his break. He wasn't needed again until Display Number 11, the Clown Firehouse. Although still hot, it was much cooler outdoors than under the big top. Instead of entering the performer's tent, however, Hank obeyed a whim and walked around to the back. He stood alone in the shadow cast by the tent, hidden not only from the circus performers, but, seemingly, from the entire world.

Distant and muffled sounds accompanied the orange glow lingering on the horizon. A blood moon was expected tonight, and the superstitious circus folk had grumbled all day about the alleged "omen of death." The moon would appear soon, but for now, a few of the brightest stars peeked through brilliant blue as it transitioned to black. Soon, all the stars now hidden would emerge.

Lost among the company of more than a thousand people who rolled from town to town like a Texas tumbleweed, Hank would remain in hiding. Obscured behind layers of face paint. Confused whether any emotion was genuine because of living among a troupe of performers.

Ancient words from an otherworldly source crept into Hank's thoughts. Like tendrils of a flowering vine, they grew in strength and wrapped around his heart. Mysteriously, they spoke from Psalm 27 in the voice of Hank's earthly father.

For in the time of trouble He shall hide me in His pavilion: in the secret of His tabernacle shall He hide me; He shall set me up upon a rock.

Hank's human attempt to hide had led to this place, this moment. Disappointment, weariness, loneliness. The Hebrew tabernacle had also been a tent—not a place for fleshly entertainment, but a place for worship.

Hank longed to be hidden by God in His tabernacle. Standing not on sawdust but upon a rock. Not a place to be lost but a place for God to find him.

For the first time in a very long time, Hank wanted to be found.

If only he could be.

Chapter Three

Heavy breathing and whimpers woke Hank. He was home—if the circus train could be called such, but so was Russell. After evening shows, Russell often prowled local bars and seedy nightclubs. His berth next to Hank's sometimes remained empty overnight. Tonight, however, he had returned, and he was having a nightmare. Also a recurring event.

Hank checked his watch. Half past four in the morning. Russell's appeal among the ladies must have waned after word got around about that slap from Eddie. Gossip in the circus traveled faster than the horse wrangler's white stallions at full gallop.

A girlish wail erupted from Russell.

Hank shook him. "Wake up!"

Shivering like his bed was crawling with snakes, Russell awakened and sat up, asking in a timid voice, "Hank? Are you here?"

"Where else would I be at this time in the morning?" Hank would rather have been anywhere else, but roustabouts didn't get to choose where they slept. Maybe if he got promoted to being an usher, he could be assigned a different roommate. And Fraidy Freddie could be buried forever.

Russell rubbed his eyes and untwisted his white tank-top undershirt which had bunched up under his arms. "What time is it?"

"What do you care?"

"Oh, man. I just had a terrible dream."

Hank offered only a grunt. He'd rather have his fingernails pulled out than hear about another of Russell's strange nightmares.

Russell told him anyway. "It was the Red Man again." He reached under his bunk and rummaged for a scrap of paper and a pencil. The boy drew a rudimentary face with spiky flames shooting from its skull. Fangs and blood-dripping claws made the figure look more like a demon than a man. "He rides a flaming, red horse. Sometimes he chases me and tries to run me down. I barely escaped tonight. Do you know what it means?"

"No." Hank's one-word answer might staunch the flow of unwanted information.

"I do." Russell reached in his pocket for his treasured Casite Zippo lighter. He rolled the gear, and a small flame flickered to life. A miracle, considering how it had fallen under assault from Eddie's boot yesterday afternoon.

Hands lightning-fast, Hank seized the lighter and snapped the lid shut. "It's stupid to light that in here."

Russell snatched it back and slid his feet into his dirty boots before heading for the exit. "We'll see who's stupid. Just watch yourself today." The car rocked when he jumped out.

What did that mean? Hank reclined in his berth, but sleep wouldn't come. He'd said it many times before, but perhaps tomorrow Eddie would listen.

Something was very wrong with Russell Segal.

———— •┼• ————

Thumps and shrieks. Laughter and yelps. The children were awake, and Evelyn craved a few more minutes of sleep. She rolled over and pried her eyes open. Half past six. She nestled under the sheet—covers would have been too hot—and jammed her pillow over her head.

Soon she struggled to breathe. Evelyn cleared her face but kept her eyes closed and the pillow clamped over her ears. The aroma of breakfast cereal wafted to her nostrils on puffs of warm breath. Jamie was up to his favorite game—Wake Aunt Evie. Evelyn played her role perfectly, scrunching her face and groaning. Jamie chuckled and leaned closer. A tiny, damp hand patted her cheek. Evelyn turned away from him.

The newest feature of their routine involved a task Jamie had only thought of a couple of months ago. He climbed into the bed and snuggled up to her back. Could anything in heaven be more precious than this?

Evelyn turned to him, gathered Jamie in her arms, and gave him an Eskimo kiss. "Good morning, sweet boy. You're up early."

Jamie didn't talk much yet, but he spoke volumes by stroking Evelyn's honey brown hair. What it lacked in curls it made up in softness. He sucked his thumb, and Evelyn gently pulled it out. "Time to grow up, Jay-Jay. You'll ruin your teeth."

Evelyn's heart heated up, and it had nothing to do with the weather. Someday she might marry again and have her own children. But for now? She led an achingly beautiful life, a gift she unwrapped every morning with Jamie.

Heavy footsteps clumped up the stairs. "J–J–Ja . . ." Bill inhaled a deep breath and pushed out his words. "Jamie. Let Aunt Evie sleep. She doesn't have to work today." He held out a hand, and the toddler wiggled closer to Evelyn.

Evelyn plopped a kiss on her nephew's sticky cheek. He tasted like Rice Krispies, sweet in more ways than one. "It's okay. We love our mornings together, don't we?"

"L–Let's go, little man." Bill's burly arms swooped up his son, and Jamie squealed when his father blew raspberries on his bare belly. In all the heat, Helen let her son run around in only a diaper, and another aroma assaulted her nose. That diaper needed changing.

Evelyn sat up and said, "I'll take him."

Bill launched Jamie across the two-foot gap, and Evelyn oofed when she caught him. "He's getting too big for that, Bill!"

Jamie giggled and squirmed with delight.

"Better bulk up, then, S–Sis. You're too s–skinny anyway." He ruffled

Jamie's brown hair. "He wants to join the Flying Wallendas."

Taking Jamie by both wrists, Bill swung him from side to side while Jamie shrieked his glee. In his rich baritone, Bill sang,

> *He flies through the air, with the greatest of ease*
> *that daring young man, on the flying trapeze.*

They headed out the door and down the steps.

As the music faded, Evelyn's smile did too. Bill sang as smooth as glass, but pauses peppered his ordinary speech. She put a hand to her throat to ease the ache.

Bill wanted more from life than slinging a mop, but stuttering had wrecked his plans. One dream had been to follow his buddies—among them Evelyn's husband, George—into the army. George enlisted and died in Bataan. Bill was classified 4F—not qualified for military service—but he was alive today. Why? A mystery.

The words of a familiar hymn sang themselves to Evelyn.

> *God moves in a mysterious way*
> *His wonders to perform.*
> *He plants His footsteps in the sea*
> *and rides upon the storm.*

How could mortals understand the ways of a God so powerful He created the universe? No, Evelyn must not question Him. She simply had to believe God was in charge of all circumstances, no matter what happened.

Evelyn reached for the well-worn Bible on her nightstand and opened it to Isaiah 55, today's chapter in her one-year reading plan. Verse nine struck her.

> *For as the heavens are higher than the earth, so are my ways higher*
> *than your ways, and my thoughts than your thoughts.*

Mental calisthenics about why George died and Bill lived were fruitless. Some things would never be understood until she joined George in heaven.

Evelyn rose, exchanged her pajamas for a sleeveless calico dress, and joined her family for breakfast. She hoped Jamie hadn't finished off the Rice Krispies. She had a taste for them.

By nine o'clock, Helen buzzed between her children like a frenzied bee. She checked and fussed over every detail of their clothing, ignoring both Lily's protests and Jamie's wriggles. She trapped Jamie and anchored him in her lap while she attempted to tie his white Stride Rite high tops.

Evelyn knelt to help. "I thought the matinee wasn't until two o'clock. Why are we leaving so early?"

Helen secured Jamie with an arm around his waist. His whines escalated to wails, and he stiffened his body while rolling his head against his mother's breast. "Bill wants to make a day of it. We'll go shopping at G. Fox downtown and have lunch at Sage-Allen's cafeteria. The grounds open at one o'clock, and the kids want to see the animals in the menagerie. Then we'll need time to stand in line for popcorn and drinks." Helen leaned forward and called into the kitchen, "Bill! We need some help in here."

Lily dangled her glittery red pumps in front of her mother's nose. "Mama, why can't I wear these?"

"They are still a little too big. Besides, you don't want to ruin them, do you? The circus is so dusty." Helen might as well have spoken to the wind.

Lily threw her shoes on the floor, folded her arms across her chest, and stomped. "I want to wear my Dorothy shoes!"

Jamie ignored Lily and kicked violently to prevent Evelyn from tying his shoes. She tugged a bit too hard and broke his right shoelace.

"Now see what you've done, young lady? You've gotten your brother all worked up." Helen grasped Lily's wrist and pulled her close. "If you want to go to the circus, you'd better stop this little performance right now."

Bill rounded the corner and spoke with no hesitation. "What's going on here?" Ignorant people assumed he stuttered because he was dumb. Not true. He sized up the situation and said, "Lily, what's the matter with you?"

In his presence, of course, Jamie sat as still as the statue of Saint Barnabas in the church narthex. Evelyn removed his shoe, knotted the two ends of the lace, and restrung it. She slipped it back on his foot and tucked the knot out of sight under the edge of the leather. She finished tying it while Jamie's wide-set, hazel eyes remained fixed on his father.

"I want to wear my Dorothy shoes to the circus, and Mama won't let me." Lily jutted her jaw and scowled at Helen.

"S–Seems to me the circus is the perfect place to wear pretty shoes." Bill raised an eyebrow at his wife.

Helen's shoulders slumped. She let Jamie escape, and he ran straight for his beloved father. "This family is its own circus," she muttered. "All right, Lily. Your father is on your side, as always. Just don't come crying to me when they are ruined. At least go and put on a thicker pair of socks."

Lily tossed her mother a triumphant smile, snatched up the shoes, and scooted off to her room.

"Honestly, Bill—" The phone on the end table jangled, and Helen scooped up the receiver. "Halstead residence, Helen speaking."

Evelyn smiled but turned away so Helen couldn't see. How could she manage such a polite tone when seconds before she'd been ready to screech at Bill? Helen had one thing right—the circus could hardly be more entertaining than this.

"Yes. She's right here." Helen passed the receiver to Evelyn.

Charlie demanded Evelyn come to work, pronto. Not surprising. She was his most efficient waitress, although he never thanked her. Her heart sank at the thought of disappointing the children. Was it too much to ask to have a little fun? Life had become so wearisome.

After hanging up, Evelyn announced her news and planted a kiss atop Jamie's head. She hugged her brother and drew Helen into a stiff embrace. "Bury the hatchet, you two. Have fun."

Bill, still holding the cool-as-a-cucumber Jamie, wrapped his other arm around his wife and drew her in for a heart-stopping kiss.

As always, Helen melted. Cheeks prettily flushed, she said, "Oh, Bill. Not in front of the children."

Lily descended the staircase, as regal as Marie Antoinette before her courtiers. Not only had she changed her shoes and socks, but she also wore her blue-and-white gingham pinafore. Judy Garland would have been proud. It was a good thing Lily didn't own a wicker basket or a cairn terrier.

Helen disentangled herself from her husband. "Young lady, that's too much."

"What's the harm?" Bill handed Jamie off to his glowering mother, took Lily's hand, and twirled her around. "My b-b-beautiful girl. You'll make those circus ladies jealous."

Evelyn hugged Lily, said goodbye to everyone, and made a hasty exit. Hurricane Helen was about to make landfall.

Chapter Four

He feigned sleep when Russell returned to the car after blowing off some steam, but Hank had lain awake all night. Once the boy fell into deep slumber, nothing short of a blitzkrieg would wake him. At break of dawn, Hank dressed in his civvies for a visit to Charlie's Diner and admitted to himself that it wasn't for the food. But first he needed to find Eddie. The boss might not listen, but Russell's eerie warning twisted Hank's gut into knots like he'd heard air-raid sirens.

Hank searched the small tent the bigwigs used for meals. No luck. He trotted to Eddie's fancy railcar but hesitated. Would Eddie extend a welcome or a rebuke? It depended on his mercurial mood.

Before Hank knocked, the door burst open. Eddie checked the clock. "Webb. What do you want?"

"I—" How could he put something so strange into words? Hank didn't know where to begin.

Eddie hopped down the steps. "Hurry up, man. I need to eat and get to work. Aylesworth left with the advance team for Springfield, so I need to supervise the canvas men as well as my own."

Hank stood tall and thrust out his chin. "It's Russell Segal. He's a mental case, and you need to get rid of him."

The statement rooted Eddie's restless feet in place. "Is this about what happened yesterday?"

"Yes and no, sir." Hank prepared to elaborate, but Eddie cut him off.

"I don't have time for this today. I've already decided to fire him, and I'll do it after we tear down. For today, just watch him like a hawk. I'm trusting you to keep him out of trouble."

"Yes, sir." Hank retraced his steps, but he overheard a stream of profanity from Eddie that didn't bode well for Russell. He didn't want the duty of minding the boy, but how could he refuse? His stomach churned. He shouldn't feel guilty for Russell's firing.

Or should he? Russell had shared snippets of his abusive, turbulent home life, but he fell silent if anyone asked probing questions. Whatever the cause, simple observation told the tale. Russell struggled for mental and emotional balance.

Hank's mother—reared in North Carolina—often said, "Every tub sits on its own bottom." A person couldn't be liable for the choices and actions of another man, but he was uniquely and solely responsible for his own deeds. He'd have to keep an eye on Russell and make sure he didn't do anything crazy.

Hank climbed into the railcar and shook Russell awake. "Time to get up."

Russell didn't stir. His Zippo rested on the mattress beside his pillow, and Hank considered confiscating it. But that would only lead to more confrontation. Hank yanked the pillow from under Russell's head.

The boy sputtered to life. "What's that for?"

"I told you to wake up, but you were still sleeping like the dead."

Russell yawned and stretched his arms wide. He stared at Hank like a puppy waiting for a treat. "What's for breakfast?"

"I don't know, but you need to get moving. There's a lot to do. Eddie wants me to keep an eye on you today."

"Why? I don't need a babysitter." Tension rippled the muscles in Russell's clenched jaw.

"I'm just following orders."

"You told him, didn't you?" Russell jumped to his feet and fisted Hank's shirt. "You told him about the Red Man!"

Hank's two-handed shove knocked Russell back into his berth. "Look, I don't want to get into this with you. Stick with me today. That's all." Hank exited the car before Russell could say another word. He waited outside while the car rocked with Russell's efforts to get dressed.

Therefore to him that knoweth to do good, and doeth it not, to him it is sin. His father's favorite verse crept into Hank's thoughts. He'd like to have told Eddie everything. Russell's instability needed to be exposed. To hide it would be a sin. So why did Hank feel like there was a baseball stuck in the back of his throat?

Surely the boy couldn't make trouble during breakfast. Hank had one task on his schedule this morning that he needed to do by himself.

Russell stomped down the stairs and shoved a cap over his disheveled, greasy hair. He followed Hank, radiating an aura of anger. But for once, he didn't run his mouth. They joined the line of other roustabouts waiting for breakfast. Hank walked beside Russell but didn't get his own plate.

When Russell sat at an empty table and started gobbling his breakfast, Hank said, "Meet me at the animal chutes at ten."

His mouth full, Russell grunted agreement.

"Ten o'clock and not a minute later."

"I heard you. I'm not deaf." A bit of food flew from Russell's mouth with the last consonant. Chimpanzees had better table manners.

Hank turned and strode for the exit.

"Where're you going?" Russell's question followed him, but Hank didn't pause or answer on his way to the diner. Alone.

Perhaps a drink of Evelyn's loveliness would help him swallow his unease.

———— ◆I◆ ————

"What'll ya have?" Darla was a cute dish for sure, but Hank only had eyes for one waitress, and she wasn't there.

"Eggs, two sausages, and pancakes."

"Maple syrup or blueberry?"

"Maple. And a cup of black coffee, please."

Darla hollered toward the kitchen, "Adam and Eve on a log and a stack of Vermont! Draw one in the dark!" Diner lingo had a charm all its own, but nothing would warm Hank's heart like seeing Evelyn.

After Hank's third cup of coffee, Darla chided him. "It's been forty-five minutes, mister. No campers. I need to turn this table."

The diner bustled with life, and people waited in line. Courtesy demanded he vacate his spot, but he hated to do it without a glimpse of his new favorite sight—a petite beauty with stormy-gray eyes and a very unladylike belly laugh.

A busboy began clearing his dishes. Hank stood and donned his hat. He tossed two quarters on the table, and the boy pocketed the money lickety-split. Hank said, "That's for the waitress, not you."

"I know, sir. Darla's busy, and she can't get over here to pick it up. I'll save it for her." Wet dishcloth in hand, the gangly youth swiped the Formica top with a dishrag, placed the salt and pepper shakers in their stainless-steel holder next to the napkins, and trundled off to the kitchen.

Maybe Darla knew Evelyn's phone number, but how would Hank explain why he wanted it? Without makeup, she'd never recognize him as Fraidy Freddie. He wanted Evelyn to see him—really see him. He craved it as much as a thirsty man in the desert wanted a Coke.

But Darla flitted from table to table like a hummingbird to red flowers. She'd never stop to answer such a personal question. Besides, it seemed too creepy. Charlie probably had policies in place to protect waitresses from stalkers.

Egad. Was Hank one of them? He paid the middle-aged woman who ran the cash register and threaded his way through a queue of hungry people. The overhead bell jangled when he tugged the front door open, and he ran headlong into a small woman with her head down.

"Oh! I'm so sorry!"

The melodious voice belonged to none other than the woman Hank sought. What luck! "No harm done." Hank should step aside, but he didn't want to.

"Pardon me. I have to get to work." Evelyn turned sideways and tried to slip between Hank's brawny frame and the door.

"Wait, Evelyn—"

"Do I know you?" Evelyn sized him up quickly. "I don't think so. Just because you can read my name tag, it doesn't mean we are friends. Let me pass. I need to get to work."

Hank didn't have time to explain he was Fraidy Freddie. He complied, and Evelyn quick-stepped to the kitchen. She emerged scant seconds later, tying her white apron around her slim waist. Snatching up her pen and order pad, she wound her way through the tables and engaged customers in the booth Hank and his friends had occupied last night.

"Excuse me." A portly gentleman used his girth to bump Hank out of the doorway. "Are you coming or going?"

Hank offered a philosopher's answer to the simple question. "Honestly, sir, I don't know." He sidled out the door and strode down the sidewalk. When Evelyn glanced at him out the window, he tipped his hat. She turned back to her customers without smiling.

Hank's father often quoted the book of James in his sermons, saying,

> *Ye know not what shall be on the morrow. For what is your life? It is even a vapour, that appeareth for a little time, and then vanisheth away.*

Hank couldn't predict what would happen today with any certainty, let alone tomorrow. He was no better than a vapor.

So he vanished.

———————— •◦• ————————

What law of probability had gone askew and made all the rude customers sit at Evelyn's tables? Surely not everyone in town was impatient, abrupt, and snappish.

Five Ringling roustabouts sat at table six this morning instead of yesterday's genial clowns. One said, "Hey, Ducky. Hike that skirt a bit and show us your landing gear." He eyed Evelyn's legs, expecting her to comply.

Evelyn handled rudeness every day, but she never tolerated vulgarity.

"I'm not on the menu, gentlemen—and I use that term loosely. I'll do you a favor and not mention your request to my boss. Otherwise, you might leave here bruised as well as hungry. Shall I call him over?"

Charlie had a sixth sense for brewing trouble, and even without needing to look, Evelyn felt the burn of his fiery glare aimed at the mischief-makers. The sight of the enormous man holding a meat cleaver reformed even the boldest flirts. The men straightened up and mumbled their orders.

"Flop two and let the sun shine. Whiskey down. Send Noah's boy to Pittsburgh and put him in the alley!" Darla's shout carried over the din of clinking dishes. Conversation stopped as perplexed commoners stared her way. Few would guess Darla's customer had just ordered scrambled eggs, rye toast, and a side of fried ham. Evelyn's best friend thrived on the attention, and Charlie tolerated it because it was good for business. People flocked to the diner like eager patrons to the Strand Theatre. If she'd not been a waitress, Darla could have been a B-movie queen.

With all attention firmly on her coworker, Evelyn wound her way through the tables toward the kitchen. She tore off the ticket with the roustabouts' orders and fastened it to the circular clipboard, spinning it so Charlie could get started.

"Drop two and let the sun shine. Two zeppelins and a checkerboard, skip the cow paste!" Darla's customer looked confused, but Charlie wasn't. He plated two sausages, cracked two eggs on the griddle, and poured batter into the waffle iron. Charlie—widely respected as the fastest cook in the business—managed a busy kitchen without a helper and never flubbed an order. Most people admired his skill, but in truth, Charlie was simply a bog-pocket. Minimal labor costs translated to maximum profits.

Evelyn grabbed a fresh pot of coffee to top off empty cups, but before she was out of earshot, Charlie growled, "Just a minute."

Evelyn steeled herself.

The waffle maker dinged. Charlie flipped the golden confection on a red-rimmed Walker China plate and drizzled it with maple syrup. "No wonder them men were gawking at your legs. I seen that runner too. You know the dress code."

Really. Charlie wanted to chastise her for a hole in her stocking when she'd come to work on a day he promised she could take off? She hadn't had time or money to replace them last night. Evelyn suppressed an angry retort. Arguing with Charlie never led to anything good. *A soft answer turneth away wrath.* Good advice from the Good Book. "I'm sorry, Charlie. This is my last pair of stockings. I either had to wear them or come to work with bare legs."

"That's no excuse. My sister has the same problem, and she uses Max Factor makeup and eyebrow pencil for the seams."

Helen had done that very thing to attend church the previous Sunday, and by the time she arrived home, her calves had looked like she suffered a skin disease. In a competition between makeup and July humidity, the weather won every time.

Evelyn played her ace. Mustering all the sweetness she had left, Evelyn put down the coffee and said, "Well, rules are rules. I'll go shopping right now and remedy the problem. With the war on, it's hard to find hosiery in stock, but I'll try." She strode toward the exit, untying her apron as she went.

"Stop!" Charlie broke the yolk of one of the sunny-side-up eggs when he plated it next to the waffle. "See what you made me do?" Charlie brandished his spatula like a deadly weapon. "You know that's not what I meant. Careful, or this will be the last day you work for me."

Evelyn picked up the carafe and resumed her rounds, but when she turned her back, Charlie muttered, "Dames."

The overbearing blowhard. Evelyn worked long hours for low pay, and for what? A measly salary and war-deflated tips? The idea of this being her last day at the diner suddenly dazzled like a diamond. What if Evelyn went back to school? To pursue the dream she'd had since childhood? Evelyn had always loved children, and teaching Sunday school at South Congregational Church was the highlight of her week. What if she were a teacher instead of a waitress?

Evelyn's imagination transformed the din of the overcrowded diner to happy children in a school cafeteria. Payday had been last Friday, and she'd given most of her money to Bill and Helen to contribute to the mortgage. She couldn't make a decision without discussing it with them, but would it be possible? It might.

Tucking that pleasant thought into her weary heart infused Evelyn with genuine joy. An authentic, broad smile garnered one unexpected blessing.

Tips went up.

Chapter Five

Russell was late. Of course. The rising temperature under the big top fueled Hank's temper into a simmer. Where was the boy, and why had Hank agreed to watch him? He would rather supervise Spartacus than the egotistical, uncooperative teenager.

Hank and his team set up the animal chutes and tested every junction. All secure. He was about to leave his capable men to their task when an unduly cheerful voice called a greeting from the bleachers above.

"I'm here." Russell clambered through a section of chairs about five rows above the ground. When he jumped, he knocked off a chair, which landed on the chute and rang it like a bell. "Wow," Russell said, dusting sawdust from his hands, "they really ought to fasten those things down."

The falling chair had narrowly missed Hank, who heated past his boiling point. He grabbed Russell, shoved him against the iron bars of the chute, and pressed his forearm across the boy's throat. "You're a menace and a fool!"

A couple of Hank's men pulled him off, but no one restrained Russell. His punch landed squarely in Hank's gut, doubling him over. His men released him immediately, and Hank launched himself at Russell, tackled him to the ground, and wrestled him onto his back. He sat on top of Russell, prepared to beat the idiot senseless, when Eddie came on the scene and uttered an epithet not suitable for polite company.

"Break it up." Eddie grabbed Hank's collar and yanked, but Hank's bulk stopped the smaller man from hauling him to his feet. Hank got up and stood as immovable as a wizened oak in a virgin forest. The boss man pointed at Russell, saying, "If you know what's good for you, you'll stay put until I tell you to get up."

"He jumped me!" Russell's defense was drowned out by the protests of Hank's crew, who all spoke at once.

"Quiet!" Eddie's command took immediate effect. He turned to Hank and poked him in the chest. "What are you doing? I said watch the nitwit, not beat him to a pulp."

Hank bit his tongue. His actions spoke for themselves.

"In less than three hours, eight thousand people will fill this tent." Ashes from Eddie's cigar dropped into the sawdust, and he stomped on the spot where a curl of smoke rose. "We aren't ready, and I don't have time to be a referee."

"But Mr. Vermeer—" Russell whined like a two-year-old.

"Shut up, Segal. You're nothing but trouble. I never should have hired you in the first place."

"Whatever Hank told you is a lie." Russell got up and advanced on Eddie.

A mistake. Eddie not only stood his ground, he stepped forward. "What do you think he said?"

Russell fell unnaturally silent.

"I thought you'd clam up." Eddie took a deep draught of his cigar and puffed out white smoke. "Hank's not the boss. I am. After the matinee, you and me are going to have a talk. You'll be lucky if you still have a job."

"But—"

"No buts, boy. Get to work. If I see you loafing, you'll be fired on the spot."

Russell didn't move.

A wave of red rose up Eddie's neck and crested in his cheeks. It crashed onshore. "Do you need another slap? Get moving!"

Russell spurted curses like blood from a severed artery. He got in Hank's face and said, "I'll get even. Just you wait."

Hank released a sigh as Russell stalked to the exit and left. It would have been better for everyone if Eddie had simply fired Russell on the spot.

"You all have jobs," Eddie said to the men. "Do them."

The show over, the men muttered as they resumed their work. Chutes still needed to be deployed at the southwest exit for May's act.

"Webb. A minute." Eddie chomped his cigar and folded his arms across his chest.

Hank wouldn't explain himself. Nor could he, really. He wasn't prone to violence, but Russell brought out the worst in him.

"I don't trust that jerk any farther than I can throw him. I gave you an assignment this morning, and I want you to keep at it. If you or any of your men spot Segal doing anything suspicious, I want to know right away."

"Yes, sir."

Eddie headed for ring one, and Hank hurried to catch up to his men. He informed them of Eddie's order, and each one pledged to watch out for Russell.

But how much could eight pairs of eyes do to spot one immature, deranged boy among a horde of thousands? The hair on the nape of Hank's neck stood on end because he knew the answer.

Not much. Not much at all.

———◦◦◦———

Evelyn's early-morning energy flagged. Lunch was no less busy than breakfast. If anything, the line of people waiting to be served had grown longer. Excessive noise inside the diner drowned out almost all conversation, so Darla had ceased calling out orders. Instead, she carried them to the window with steps as weary as Evelyn's.

The bell over the door jangled incessantly as customers came and went. The hands on the clock above the Coca-Cola advertising sign crawled toward noon. Three servicewomen clad in khaki uniforms were taking "the pause that refreshes." Evelyn could use one of those about now. Good luck getting Charlie to agree to it.

"Aunt Evie!" A familiar voice penetrated Evelyn's drudgery. Lily and the family waved cheerfully from inside the door. Evelyn, weighed down under a tray carrying six plates toward the corner booth, could only smile in response.

"Aunt Evie, we want to sit at your table!" All eyes turned toward Lily, but the girl never blushed. She preened.

Evelyn delivered food to a group of snooty patrons, including a state senator's wife, Mrs. Gillette. She'd had no compunctions playing the "I'm a very important person" card the minute she sat down. The woman wasn't Bess Truman, for goodness' sake.

"Miss." When Evelyn didn't respond right away, the odious woman snapped her fingers. "Are you listening to me?"

Evelyn had been taught not to hate anyone, but intense dislike was permissible, right? She forced her mouth to smile. "Yes, ma'am."

"I ordered this sandwich on toasted bread." Mrs. Gillette peeled the slice of Charlie's famous homemade sourdough bread off the top of her tuna salad sandwich and dangled it like a fishing worm from a hook. "Does this look toasted to you?"

"I'm sorry. I'll ask for a replacement right away." Evelyn sneaked a glance toward her family, where Jamie squirmed in Bill's arms, pointing at Evelyn and wailing like a police siren. To a toddler, hugs delayed were hugs denied.

"How long will that take?" Mrs. Gillette pushed her plate away. "My party received VIP tickets for the circus matinee, and we will already be late because of this infernal crowd."

"I'll put a rush on your order."

"You'd better." Mrs. Gillette smoothed her Lana Turner curls even though every hair was glued down by pomade. The style looked ridiculous on a woman old enough to be the starlet's mother. "My husband is a state senator, and he could make health inspectors shut this place down."

Not likely. Charlie kept a spotless diner. Evelyn dared anyone to find a speck of dirt. Nevertheless, fleeing a battlefield when there was no hope of victory was an honorable retreat. "Yes, ma'am. I'll have it to you right away."

Evelyn slithered through the crowded aisles to the kitchen and hoped Charlie was too distracted by profits to be grumpy. She passed close enough to Jamie that he ratcheted up his screams, but she couldn't take a detour to quiet him. She leaned in through the kitchen window and hollered above the din, "Tuna salad on *toasted* sourdough, and give it wings."

Charlie gestured toward Jamie with his spatula. "Shut that kid up." He put bread into the toaster and jammed down the lever.

Evelyn left her tray on the shelf below the window and scooted over to her family. The minute she relieved Bill of his tiny burden, Jamie rested his head against her shoulder and tried to tug a tawny curl from beneath her hair net.

"I'm sorry, S-s-sis." Bill tried to take Jamie back, but the child clung even tighter. "This was a bad idea."

"We wanted to surprise you, Evie." Helen reclaimed Jamie after a little struggle, but his cries had softened to whimpers. Still, he reached for Evelyn, and her heart wept. "The cafeteria was swamped, and since you were working—"

"It's such a nice thought. But you see how crazy things are here. I'm afraid if you wait for a table in my section, you'll be late for the show."

Charlie rang the service bell. "Order up!"

"We'll make do with food from the midway." Bill pecked a kiss on Evelyn's cheek, and asked, "How about a hot dog, Lily?"

Lily's favorite words. She squealed and tugged on her father's hand. Bill tucked her under his arm and cleared a path through the crowd with his broad shoulders. Helen followed, offering Evelyn a little wave goodbye. Jamie started crying again and still reached for her. Evelyn's vision blurred with tears, but she watched their progress until they disappeared around the corner.

"I said, order up. Get a move on, Evelyn." Charlie spun the order wheel and started preparing food on the next ticket.

"You should be glad I'm not going with them." Evelyn snatched up Mrs. Gillette's sandwich and plonked the plate on her tray. "You promised me the day off."

"Promises and pie crusts are made to be broken." Charlie flipped three burgers, pressed them on the hot grill with his spatula, and topped them with cheese.

They sizzled, but so did Evelyn's temper. Charlie might have a repertoire of pithy sayings he trotted out on occasion, but he should be grateful Evelyn also remembered proverbs her mother had taught her. *A fool's wrath is presently known: but a prudent man covereth shame.*

Evelyn was no fool. She'd not make her wrath known today.

But she made no promises about tomorrow.

———————•ı•———————

"Take your men and check the setup under the stands. Find any crooked jacks and straighten them up. Then get in position. The matinee starts in an hour." Eddie barely stopped walking as he gave Hank his marching orders.

This aberration from the crew's procedures caused creepy-crawlies on the back of Hank's neck. Leonard Aylesworth—the man usually in charge of the canvas and seats—had gone to Springfield, Massachusetts, with the advance team. "Seat men" returned dropped items to patrons in the seats above and put out small fires caused by people who flicked cigarette butts through the convenient openings. Everyone's routines were a little out of whack, and only eight seat men were on duty—not enough in Hank's estimation.

Hank's propmen, although a little aimless because of their ignorance, did their best. They straightened up a few jacks, but like Hank, they really didn't know what else to do.

"Hey, boss."

Hank trotted toward the man who called him.

"How do I put this out?"

A smoldering cigarette lay in the sawdust, creating a ghostly wisp of smoke. The stands were empty right now, but employees also had the bad habit of tossing still-burning butts aside with no regard for safety. Hank's lips formed a hard white line. Why couldn't smokers be more careful?

Hank searched for a fire extinguisher, but there wasn't one. Where were they? He grabbed a nearby bucket of water and doused the spot. Handing the vessel back to his man, Hank said, "Go refill this at the water truck and put it back where it was." He should tell Eddie the fire extinguishers weren't in place. With seat men in short supply, they would need more than a few buckets of water.

"There you are." Blinko pushed a man aside and grasped Hank's elbow. "Come on. You're late."

"Late for what?"

"You haven't clowned in this much heat yet, have you?" Blinko blinked.

A drop of perspiration fell from Hank's nose. "No, but I'll make it."

"Yeah. But your makeup won't if we don't add an extra layer of powder. We don't have much time, so get a move on."

Hank turned supervisory duties over to Clyde, his most experienced man, and hurried toward the performer's tent with Blinko. He looked for Eddie along the way to mention the fire extinguishers but never saw him. As soon as he ducked into the tent, a gaggle of clowns in character hustled him toward the dressing area, clucking, honking, and creating their usual hubbub. Every thought of finding Eddie fled Hank's mind, chased away by layers of grease paint, powder, and padding.

<hr>

Under the bleachers lay an empty wooden bucket, tossed aside by a prop-man who'd hurried away for an alleged crisis involving the animal chute. Nearby, two more cigarette butts glowed in the sawdust.

But most troubling of all, the sidewall of the tent near the men's room sported a charred spot which slowly grew larger, spreading like a herd of black beasts consuming a wheat field. Excited patrons—mostly women and children—took their seats, oblivious to the danger lurking beneath them, which wafted into the stifling air on wisps of gray smoke. When it burst into open flame, it would dance like a bally girl clad in orange sequins.

Spartacus wasn't the only monster attending the circus that day.

Chapter Six

⌒

The grandstands filled with bright-eyed children, frazzled mothers, and the occasional husband and father. Able-bodied men were hard to spot, most of them having gone overseas to fight the Nazis and Japanese. The circus atmosphere formed a bubble—an alternate universe in which war, death, and suffering were held at bay by the music of the calliope, the aroma of roasted peanuts, and a glittering rainbow of sequined costumes.

Hank's cravings for circus fare fled long ago. He never ate popcorn anymore, and in his more anxious moments, the smell sickened him. He often longed for the quiet, secluded spot he'd loved as a boy, lazing away sweltering July afternoons fishing beside the Deep Kill River, the only sound the buzzing of insects and bubbling of water on its happy path to the Hudson. But his former life in Speigletown was a chimera, alive only in Hank's sentimental dreams. Lost to him now, and perhaps forever.

Children's shrieks, blaring brass instruments, and the trumpeting of elephants jolted Hank from his daydream. The show had started a couple of minutes late, and the brief opening parade was nearly finished. Tall iron railings separated the crowd from the eight-foot-wide hippodrome, an oval track, to be sure no one interfered with the procession.

Hank's job was the safety of circus patrons, especially latecomers in a hurry who needed to navigate the narrow step apparatus that helped them climb over and across the animal chute. Ladies often teetered on the four-foot-wide wooden steps in their ridiculous high heels, and Hank's quick action had saved many a hapless woman from an ignominious tumble into the sawdust.

Despite his disappointment that morning at the diner, Hank kept a keen lookout for Evelyn. He hadn't spotted her. Not a surprise, given the size of the crowd. But a clown could hope, couldn't he? She'd been at work that morning, so perhaps she planned to slip in at the last minute. It would be just Hank's luck if she had a seat at the opposite end of the tent.

Merle Evans' band was almost finished with the "Colossus of Columbia March," the musicians following the baton in his left hand as he deftly played his cornet with his right. Since Hank's station was in the northeast section near the band, the concussions of the booming bass drum thudded against his back.

One last family scuttled in, led by a precocious girl dressed in costume as Dorothy from *The Wizard of Oz*. She carried a stuffed Toto dog Hank had seen for sale on the midway. People stared and pointed, but the child accepted the attention with the poise of a seasoned performer. A wide-eyed toddler boy sucked his thumb as he rode atop the strapping shoulders of a sturdy man who'd barely broken a sweat.

"Dorothy" took Hank's hand, completely unafraid, as if it was her due. She marched up the steps in time with the music, crossed the platform, and descended without missing a beat. The mother crossed next, and the father boosted his boy across the stepladder into her arms before vaulting over himself. They took their seats about ten rows up into the grandstands, having paid extra for the privilege of not sitting in the bleachers. A seat remained empty near them, a rare sight as people scrambled for tickets after yesterday's cancelled matinee.

"Ladies and gentlemen, boys and girls," crooned the ringmaster, "welcome to the greatest show on earth!" Fred Bradna excelled at whipping the crowd into a frenzy, his mellow bass voice amplified to a perfect volume. It carried over the music of the band, which had decreased its volume in a delicate interplay of masterful accompaniment.

The crowd rose to their feet with deafening applause and cheers. Dorothy's face shined with joy. She squeezed her Toto and jumped in place, knocking her chair askew. She'd have fallen into the row in front of her if not for the steadying hand of her father. Hank deplored the system that left the chairs unfastened to the floor or each other, but he was a propman, not a seat man.

The band switched to the "Bravura March," Hank's musical cue to take his position beside the chute. Although most guests watched the bally girls dressed in lion costumes being "tamed" by a pompous clown, some children watched Hank with expectant faces. Including the Dorothy look-alike. Hank would give her a good show.

He peered down the chute, checking for obstructions, but let his elbows and knees quiver like jelly. Dorothy tugged her father's sleeve and pointed at Hank, and the man tore his attention away from the leggy ladies. Impressive. Not many males would avert their eyes from such a visual treat. He beckoned the father to come protect him, falling to his knees and begging, much to the girl's glee.

The towering, handsome man grinned but shook his head. Hank clasped his hands and took tiny steps on his kneecaps, moaning his distress. Dorothy gave her dad a shove, but he stood immovable as a tree trunk—and almost as big. If Hank didn't cease his routine, he'd place a bet little "Dorothy" would soon persuade her father to descend the steps.

Hank removed his beret and genuflected, raising an appeal to heaven, when the crack of a real whip indicated the tide had turned in the lion farce. The so-called "tamer" became the prey as the women roared and chased him, waving their sinuous tails. Hank leaped to his feet, ran in aimless circles, and finally took his designated position beside the animal chute to do his real job. He performed one last safety check before the lions would be released.

The other lions passed down the chute without incident, but Spartacus did not disappoint. Hank's distraction with Dorothy and her family caused him to make a costly error. He stood a few inches too close to the chute. The vicious beast's razor-sharp talon caught his billowy right sleeve just above his wrist and raked the skin beneath. Hank flinched and jumped back, hoping the patrons were none the wiser.

"Boss. You're bleeding." A newbie crewman whose name Hank couldn't remember pointed to the slashed fabric.

Sure enough, a bloodstain blossomed along with the sting from a three-inch gash. He'd need to visit the troupe's doctor and change into his backup costume before appearing in the firehouse skit. Stupid Spartacus. The murderous brute ought to be put down before he turned on Walsh or injured a handler. Blood and gore in the circus were supposed to be only a threat. The red blotch on his mostly white costume was all too real.

Walsh had started his act when Clyde approached Hank, his shirt plastered to his ebony chest. He tried to speak but leaned over with both hands on his knees, struggling to catch his breath.

Hank clapped Clyde's shoulder. A good man, normally steady as a rock. Only bad business would get him so riled. "Take a minute, Clyde. Breathe. Nothing's on fire."

"Not yet, Mr. Webb, but I'm worried." Clyde straightened and looked Hank in the eye. "I was watchin' out for Russell—" He pushed out the rest between heaving gasps for air. "—like you told us to."

With all the bustle preparing for the matinee, Hank had hardly given a second thought to Russell. The boy should have been attending to his duties, especially after Eddie blew his fuse.

"Did you spot him?"

"Yes, sir."

"Recently?"

"A few minutes ago, I seen him in the midway chatting up one of the dance girls."

Hank pulled Clyde to a hidden spot under the bleachers. "Where was he headed?"

"I don't know." Clyde tugged at one of his suspenders, and it snapped against his chest. "You know how he is. He's such a doll dizzy. He was flirting."

"He was told in no uncertain terms to pay attention to his job as a seat man. He should be under the bleachers, not in the midway." Hank could try to find him, but his garish costume would draw too much attention from patrons. He asked, "Do you know where Mr. Vermeer is?"

"I suppose he's in his office wagon. That's where he usually is during the show."

Hank grabbed Clyde's elbow and pulled aside the canvas to hustle him out of the tent. "Go to Mr. Vermeer right away, and tell him what you just told me. And hurry."

Why had Hank ever thought Russell would follow orders? Nothing in the kid was wired for obedience. Russell Segal, angry and carrying a grudge, wandered the circus grounds with his beloved Zippo lighter. If he listened to the Red Man and followed his urges, the firebug could be more dangerous than Spartacus on the loose.

Hurry, Clyde.

Once the matinee started, the crowd at Charlie's Diner thinned. After Evelyn served her last remaining customers their dessert and coffee, she joined Darla at the small table near the kitchen where they were allowed a ten-minute break. They could only sip ice water, not tea or lemonade, but any drink provided a respite from today's stifling heat.

"I've had it." Darla crunched an ice cube between her teeth.

"Me too," Evelyn said, "and I mean it. I've really had it." She leaned close to Darla's ear and whispered, "I'm quitting."

"What?"

Evelyn shushed her friend and glanced toward the kitchen. Charlie was outside on his smoke break. "Quiet. I don't want Charlie to know until after the shift is over. He shouldn't have an audience when he has his meltdown."

Darla plucked another ice cube from her drink and dropped it down the front of her blouse. "Well, it's about time. I didn't think you had the moxie."

"I just made up my mind today."

"I don't know why you were surprised Charlie called you in. He's all about the dough." Darla took another long draught of her drink. "And I don't mean pastry."

"Did you see Bill and the family come in?" Evelyn mopped her brow with an embroidered handkerchief she kept pinned to her apron.

"Yes." Darla scooted her chair closer and patted Evelyn's hand. "And I saw you cry when they left."

Tears welled again in Evelyn's eyes, and her lip trembled. "That was it for me. The last straw. I wanted to leave with them no matter what Charlie said. My brother's family is my whole world since George died. They need me, and I need them. If Charlie won't hire more help, that's not my problem. There are more important things in life than earning money. He can find someone else."

"Bravo." Darla chinked her glass against Evelyn's. "You've always been too good for this place."

"But I hate to leave you."

"Don't you dare back down because of me." Darla checked the kitchen over her shoulder. Still empty. "You just visit regular-like, sit at my table, and leave me fat tips."

Evelyn smiled, although money might be tight for a while. "I will. I'll need to find a temporary job, hopefully one with regular hours and a kindhearted boss. I'm going to night school to be a teacher."

"Perfect. You'll be terrific."

The kitchen screen door slammed, and Charlie took his place back at the grill. A bead of sweat dripped from his nose and sizzled on the hot surface. Charlie muttered an oath and squirted it with disinfectant. The next burger might have a unique flavor.

No orders were on the spinner, but the bell over the door tinkled when two men in suits entered the diner.

"You gonna sit there all day, Darla? Show them men to a table and get 'em some water." Charlie didn't bother to look at Darla, who had already risen to attend the customers before he said anything. He always barked commands like General Patton and expected people to jump to do his bidding.

Evelyn checked the clock. Two forty-seven. The mental picture of Lily and Jamie enjoying the animals, the Flying Wallendas, and the clowns erased the deep valley that had formed on Evelyn's forehead. Maybe they had even spotted Fraidy Freddie. How she'd have liked to see the good-looking clown perform.

Hearing a commotion outside, the suited men scooted back their chairs and went to the window. The wail of a siren preceded the appearance of fire engine No. 2, and its tires screeched as it turned the corner from Main Street onto Cleveland.

Darla and Evelyn joined the diner's last few customers in staring at the sky above McGovern's Granite Works, where a plume of gray smoke roiled, growing faster than a spring thundercloud.

Darla pressed against Evelyn's shoulder and asked, "Isn't that where the circus is?"

It was.

Chapter Seven

John Walsh put the animals through their paces with unquestioned competence. He never seemed fearful—a marvel to Hank. He snapped his whip and shouted commands, and the lions performed according to their training. They jumped through fiery hoops, rolled in the sawdust like logs, and danced in very un-catlike pirouettes. In ring one, at the opposite end of the tent, May Kovar did much the same with her menagerie of black jaguars, Bengal tigers, and a vast assortment of exotic cats of every size.

Merle Evans choreographed the entire circus with his musical cues. Performers and roustabouts always jumped into action at the familiar transitions. Noise from the crowd waxed and waned, but the band could always be heard above it.

The "Battle Royal March"—Walsh and Kovar's music—was suddenly cut off before its planned ending, and the band played Sousa's "Stars and Stripes Forever." It took a moment for the meaning to register, but soon every circus employee rallied to the band's signal for an emergency. Hank and every man on his crew rushed to the front of the stands. One roustabout straddled the barrier that separated patrons from the hippodrome.

"There. Is that smoke?" An usher pointed toward the southwest bleachers beside the main entrance. Sure enough, a gray cloud hovered beneath the big top, and a ball of flames rose up the tent's sidewall like the dawning sun.

At first, guests in that section made their way down the steps in an orderly fashion, but it was too far for Hank to see if Evelyn was among them. The piccolo player trilled his solo while many patrons calmly watched the circus personnel try to extinguish the flames with a few buckets of water like their efforts were simply part of the show.

May already had her cats herded and moving through the southwest chute to safety. The Flying Wallendas—who were in place atop the trapeze platforms thirty feet above the circus floor—obeyed their patriarch's signal, descending their ladders as quickly as spiders crawling down a drainpipe.

"They're not going to stop it," the usher said as the flames grew. "We've got to get these people out of here." He climbed over the stepladder and urged guests to leave via the performer's exit beside the bandstand since the northeast aisle was still blocked by the animal chute. An orderly exodus could be managed. The deadliest enemy at this moment wasn't the fire, still too far away to be a threat. But panic could kill.

Hank broke character. He approached a pregnant woman seated on the front row, took her by the elbow, and said, "Ma'am, please exit the tent."

The woman jerked her arm from Hank's grasp. "I will not. I paid good money for these seats."

Oblivious. And foolish. Hank lied. "They will be right here waiting for your return, ma'am. I'll not let anyone else sit there."

The woman's companion pointed to the growing chaos at the opposite end of the tent. "Let's go, Angie. Look."

Hank checked the progress of the fire and tensed. The fireball had doubled in size in the scant minute since he'd last checked. Hank kept his voice calm while urging patrons to leave. Soon, a steady stream of mostly unruffled people followed directions, climbing over the ladder and proceeding at a steady pace toward safety.

Look-alike Dorothy and her family made their way down the grand-stand steps, but a group of panicked men knocked the mother and son down. Hank ached to assist them, but too many people were in between.

The ever-growing crowd jammed against the chute like logs against an ice dam. Also penning them in place was the barrier to the hippodrome. Unless Hank broke the dam, people would be trapped.

A crescendo of screams erupted from the vicinity of the fire, loud enough to be heard over the band music. A small gap between the sidewall and the big top had been left open for ventilation on the scorching-hot day. The breeze fueled the fire, which leaped across the opening with the ease of May's big cats, catching the big top on fire and emitting a fearsome roar of its own.

Hank had manned the crew that waterproofed the big top before the 1944 season. The tent sidewalls easily withstood even driving rain, but the top canvas was another matter. They had used brooms to brush on a mixture of paraffin wax and gasoline—a time-tested method employed for more than a century. The gasoline was supposed to have evaporated over time, but had it? Hank cringed, and his mouth went dry. The tent might combust faster than a Texas canyon full of dry tumbleweeds.

Some patrons still sat in their chairs, either oblivious to the danger or paralyzed by indecision. With every second meaning possible life or death, Hank abandoned all attempts not to spook them. "Everybody out! Now!"

Near the ladder, the crowd surged forward, crushing people—mostly women and children—against the bars. Hank and his team needed to retract the chute or people would die. He rallied his men and rushed to make the attempt.

The chute was constructed in sections that telescoped inside each other. Once in place, they could easily be moved so patrons could pass through on their way to the seats. Walsh, fearful the animals could escape, had insisted that each section be secured to the next by knotted ropes. As a temporary fix, the roustabouts constructed a crossing for patrons with steps up, a sturdy platform, and steps down the other side. This makeshift stepladder was the only means of exit for hundreds of people.

In the crush, they were already too late. They'd never untie the ropes in time. There was also another problem: Walsh had already herded most of his lions down the chute, but one had balked.

Spartacus.

"If you go out that door, don't bother comin' back." Charlie brandished his spatula at Evelyn like a bayonet.

She cast aside her apron, and it fluttered to the floor. "I was never coming back anyway." Evelyn grabbed her purse from under the counter and eased the strap over her head. "I'm through, Charlie. I've had enough of long hours, terrible pay, and a grumpy cook. I quit." It wasn't the way Evelyn had planned to handle her exit from the diner, but she needed to get to the circus grounds. Now.

"You owe me two weeks' notice, girlie."

Darla whirled and fired her words at Charlie like bullets from a submachine gun. "She's no *girlie*. She's a classy lady. Too classy for this joint. If you try to stop her, I'll quit too."

Charlie broke his own rule about no profanity in front of diners. Then he said, "Go on then. Get out. But don't expect another cent from me."

Did he think Evelyn cared about her last paycheck when Bill and the children might be in danger? Evelyn bit back her retort and hoped God noticed. She needed His favor so He would answer her prayers to protect her loved ones.

"Let me know—" The rest of Darla's sentence was cut off when the diner's door thumped shut.

Evelyn joined the growing number of people racing toward the circus grounds. They were only two blocks away, but Evelyn's legs couldn't move fast enough. She regretted the decision to wear her pumps instead of her low-heeled Mary Janes. The closer she got, the thicker the smoke.

When she rounded the corner on Barbour Street, she abruptly halted, standing stock-still. One hand raised itself and covered her mouth. Flames fully engulfed the big top. Oily black smoke curled into the sky while orange tendrils of fire danced like mad witches around a cauldron.

Some people screamed and ran, but others milled in the midway like lost sheep. They pointed and watched the spectacle with faces devoid of emotion. From inside the tent, a medley of ghastly screams accompanied by band music sent jagged shards of glass down Evelyn's spine. She shivered despite the heat and trudged step by step toward the horror, drawn like a moth to the flames.

———————————

Spartacus snarled and swiped ferociously at the legs of children that dangled through the bars of the animal chute. Desperate parents, driven beyond sanity, had urged the children to cross the chute without benefit of the ladders and platform. Hank grabbed a cattle prod tossed aside by one of his crewmen who had fled—the coward—and jolted Spartacus on his hind end. The lion turned and focused all his wrath on Hank. *Good.*

On the opposite side from the grandstands, Hank had a clear pathway to safety. But he'd never take it while people fought for their lives. Flames spread through the big top as quickly as Hank feared. In a matter of minutes, the whole canvas, including that directly overhead, was on fire. Big globs of flaming, melted paraffin landed on everyone, catching their clothing and hair on fire. Hank had extinguished one that fell on his arm, and although he must be burned, he felt no pain.

Spartacus crouched in the sawdust, sniffed the air, and roared. He darted back toward ring three, but Walsh blocked his way. With a furious snap of the whip, he shouted, "Back!" The animal turned and loped in the right direction. Walsh commanded Hank, "When he reaches you, hit him again."

Even amidst the hysteria, Hank timed the jolt just right. He had to. One father had already carried out his bloodied son. Spartacus jerked when the prod touched his hindquarters, but he spotted the opening to his wagon and sprinted out. Clyde Miller had returned to his post and shoved the board through the bars. One less murderous beast to worry about.

The other beast had no tamer. It roared and crackled, unhindered by any attempt to stop its rampage.

———————————

"Tails!" An elephant handler shouted the command, and a line of elephants grasped each other tail-to-trunk. Prodded along by bull men with metal hooks, the lumbering animals passed Evelyn closely enough she could have touched their leathery hides. One of the handlers said, "I hope they don't panic. They'll trample anyone who gets in their way."

The animals flapped their ears, and a few made squeaky noises. Evelyn watched the spectacle, a surreal moment she would remember forever. A parade of elephants in front of a circus tent being consumed by flames.

"Please, ma'am, step aside." Next in the nightmarish scene was Ringling's most famous clown. Emmett Kelly, in his distinctive costume as Weary Willy, wore big shoes, baggy pants, and an oversized white frown. He rushed toward the tent with one hand shading his face and a bucket of water in his right hand. For all the good it would do, he might as well have spit on the fire.

A cluster of clowns worked feverishly to rescue people who had climbed to the top of the bleachers, even though it put them closer to the flames. What desperation would motivate that choice? Having cut the sidewalls into sections, the clowns rolled them into makeshift chutes and urged people, mostly women and children, to slide down from the thirty-foot height. Several "catchers" stood at the bottom to cushion landings. After the harrowing descent, adults snatched the children and ran for safety.

One clown carried a writhing, screaming boy—no more than two years old—away from the conflagration. He crooned soothing words, but the child fought him every step of the way. Evelyn's heart leaped with the hope it might be Jamie, but it wasn't. She looked closer at the clown's face and understood why the boy could not be comforted. The clown's smiling makeup had melted in the heat of the fire, rearranging his features into a grotesque, greasepainted grimace. Red makeup dripped on the boy's soot-smudged white shirt, and he looked like the victim of a stabbing instead of a fire.

Evelyn had no clue where Bill's seats were. She tried to remember the numbers on the tickets, but her brain wouldn't cooperate. She jogged around the tent, searching the faces of those who had escaped but recognizing no one.

"Get back!" A man wearing jodhpurs, riding boots, and a white silk shirt grabbed Evelyn and shoved her away from the tent. "She's going down!" At his warning, the milling crowd stampeded, and a mother and little girl lost their footing, tumbling to the ground. Evelyn tried to help them up but managed only to grasp the child's hand before the force of people behind her carried her like flotsam on an ocean wave. If Evelyn resisted, she'd also fall under the panicked exodus of terror-stricken people.

The same man who had shouted the warning shoved Evelyn forward with both hands on her back. "I'll help the mother," he said. "You get the girl!" He stooped to reach for the wailing woman who was being trampled, but he received a push from a man dressed in a business suit. The Good Samaritan fell and rolled on top of the woman, certain to become a victim himself.

The mob pushed ahead, and Evelyn's grip on the little girl's hand loosened. She needed to pick her up, but in the stampede, she couldn't manage it. "Hold on, honey," she yelled. "Don't let go."

"Mama!" The child cried out, actively resisting Evelyn's handhold. "I won't leave my mama!" With one last violent tug, she escaped, turned, and forced her way toward her fallen mother against the stream of humanity. Her golden blond pigtails—festooned with long, red ribbons—bobbed in the gusts of superheated air billowing from the tent. Then she was gone.

Evelyn tried to follow, but another high-handed man spun her around and forced her to follow the crowd. With her back to the tent, her ears were assaulted with an unearthly howl. Carried aloft on wings of fiery demons, the screams of victims created a macabre symphony of death.

Then the big top collapsed, a whoosh of scorched air followed by eerie quiet.

The silence of the dead.

Chapter Eight

After Hank secured Spartacus, he dashed back to the ladder. Anarchy. A few able-bodied souls attempted to climb over the chute now that the lions were gone. But if they were too slow, someone pulled them off and attempted the feat themselves.

Fistfights broke out among some of the men. People in the grandstands tripped on the loose chairs scattered in disarray, blocking aisles and presenting a significant obstacle to anyone trying to flee.

Merle Evans and the band continued to play. They had switched to a march in a minor key better suited for the unfolding tragedy. Why would the musicians stay in the bandstand while smoke swirled and melted gobs of paraffin plunged from the sky like Nazi firebombs? During a crisis, circus folk liked to say "the show must go on," but the band members' devotion might turn them into human candles.

Everyone else focused on self-preservation except parents with children, who shoved their darlings over the chute even if following them was impossible. Little Dorothy's father climbed atop the platform as unabashed King of the Hill, a Goliath of strength and determination to help those who couldn't help themselves.

His wife, jostled and jarred by people behind her, wrestled with both children. The beautiful girl dressed as Dorothy clung to her mother and screeched in terror, but the determined woman held her toddler boy aloft. She screamed, "Bill! Take Jamie!"

Bill plucked him from her arms like a ripe tomato. He kissed Jamie's tear-stained cheek, broke the chokehold the boy had on his neck, and flung him into Hank's waiting arms. Hank passed the boy off to Clyde and turned to catch the next airborne package—Dorothy.

Hank caught the winsome girl, who fell silent, gazing up at his clown face in apparent wonder. Her captivating personality had enchanted Hank before the show, but now his heart blazed with the joy of saving her. If only he had a moment to savor the sweetness of the girl in his arms.

But the surprisingly strong child sprang out of her reverie. She wrestled herself out of Hank's embrace, knelt beside the chute, and wrapped her arms around the bars. "I'm not leaving till Mama and Papa do!"

"Lily, get out of here!" Bill's deep baritone resonated above the mayhem.

"No! Not until you and Mama come." The girl's stubbornness could get her killed.

Bill paused his rescue efforts and focused on Hank, heedless to people clawing at his trouser legs. "Make her leave. Please."

Hank grappled with the girl—*Lily*, not Dorothy—but her superhuman strength matched her level of panic. He grasped her gingham pinafore by the shoulder strap and yanked, but it ripped. The child wouldn't budge. She'd have to wait. Other people needed Hank's help.

A man in a flashy business suit hollered at Bill, "Me and my family next." He attempted to scramble up the ladder, his wife and daughter on his heels, but he was met by a mountain of immovable flesh. Over six feet tall and more than two hundred pounds, Bill picked the self-important man up and tossed him aside like a rag doll, saying, "Women and children f-f-first, you cad." He helped the man's family, but the oaf's second attempt to cross was met with Bill's meaty fist.

Bill continued grabbing women and children by any available means—collars, belts, or outstretched hands—and pitching them over the chute, where they scrambled to their feet and ran for their lives.

But Bill's wife wasn't among them. "Helen!" Bill stayed in perpetual motion, but he called several times with no answer.

Hank checked on Lily, whose attention was riveted on her mother. Helen lay deathly still near the bottom of a growing heap of bodies stacked against the bars like cordwood. The fallen people had created a human staircase, with others climbing over them in an attempt to escape. Anyone who stumbled simply served as another step.

"Where's Helen?"

Bill's desperate cry chilled Hank to the bone despite the suffocating heat. He pointed to Bill's wife. When the big man spotted her, there was no clear path to help her. He howled like a dying animal. If he didn't find a way—and soon—she'd suffocate.

Not only were people being trampled to death under the weight of fear-crazed maniacs, there was also no smoke-free air to breathe. Hank reached inside the neck of his costume and pulled his sweat-drenched undershirt up over his nose. It helped some, but he coughed incessantly. He had to keep wiping his eyes to see through the blur of tears—some caused by smoke, but some by the unbelievable tragedy unfolding before him in living Technicolor.

The blaze reached its zenith, consuming the hemp ropes that stabilized the tent poles. When they failed, the top would come down. The poles danced a mambo, twisting and swaying like the Cuban bally girls.

"Time to go!" Hank called out to Bill and pointed to the poles, expecting him to leap down, grab his daughter, and bolt for the exit. But he jumped off the platform into the carnage on the opposite side of the chute. He flung people aside and tried to reach his wife. Hank wouldn't leave if Bill didn't, but time was running out.

One by one, the tent pole lashings burned to cinders. Two quarter poles tumbled into the grandstands, crushing people trying to flee, and the center poles wouldn't be far behind. When they collapsed, a blazing blanket of certain death would engulf anyone still inside.

The musicians finally stopped playing and scrambled out of the bandstand. A few moments later, their music resumed at the measure where they had paused. At least they were no longer under the tent.

Bill reached Helen, tugged her to his chest, and tried to stand. He struggled several times, but coughing fits wracked his body. Finally, he pitched forward and fell with his wife underneath him.

"Papa!" Lily's scream jolted Hank as if he'd been hit with the cattle prod. The girl released her vise grip on the chute bars and stepped up on the siderail to cross back to her parents. Hank plucked her off and sprinted for the exit.

The creaks and groans of the center poles culminated with a final, deafening crack. Hank cleared the tent with no time to spare.

An eruption of air hotter than a blast furnace knocked Hank to the ground. He tried to avoid landing on top of the child but failed, his bulk slamming her frail body into the dirt. Hank rolled off as quickly as he could, but the girl didn't move. He must have bashed the breath out of her.

Hank patted her cheek. "Lily? Wake up." When she didn't respond, Hank pulled himself to his knees and crawled. Shielding Lily as best he could, he dragged her farther away from the fire. The heat prickled his skin, his back and legs so hot his costume might ignite any minute. He managed to creep only a few extra feet from his original landing spot before his legs gave out.

He turned Lily on her back and tried to find a pulse, but his heat-swollen fingers couldn't feel anything. One of Lily's ruby slippers was missing, as was her stuffed Toto. Was she breathing? Hank couldn't tell. He yelled for help, but so did everyone else in earshot. Greasy, thick smoke rolled over him like San Francisco fog, eclipsing everything from Hank's sight except Lily's ghostly face, which wore a peaceful expression.

Hank clutched the girl to his chest and wept until the sickening sights, sounds, and smells faded under an acrid cloak of blackness.

———◆◆◆———

"Ma'am." A man's voice roused Evelyn. He shook her shoulder and said, "It's not safe here. You need to get up and move. Come on, I'll help."

Evelyn turned over and rested on her back. Strong hands slipped under her arms, boosting her to sit upright. Her stockings hung in melted shreds from her pinkened calves, her knees bled from deep scratches, and she had scuffed her pumps beyond repair. What would Charlie say about that? Giggles erupted, and although she tried, Evelyn couldn't stop. Hysteria? Probably.

"Up now. On your feet. You can do it."

Her helper's voice calmed her, and Evelyn reined in her emotions. She focused on bending her knees and getting her feet under her, but she'd never have made it to a standing position without assistance. She turned to thank the kind man and stood face-to-face with one of the clowns she'd met yesterday.

"I'm Blinko." The clown steadied Evelyn when she swayed. "You're the waitress from Charlie's Diner, right?"

Blinko looked much different than the clown she had met the day before. His red-sequined hat with the pom-pom was missing, as well as the white stretchy cap that covered his real hair. Brown hair. One of his fake green eyelashes had been torn off, but the other jumped like a cheerleader when he blinked. And he was barefoot. Evelyn studied his pinkish-white toes and lost her balance, tipping headfirst into Blinko's broad chest, her face resting against his oversized, ruffled collar. The silk cooled her hot cheeks.

Blinko peeled her away, but Evelyn held on, clamping her hands around his waist. Her anguish gushed like a fire hydrant and spurted tears from her eyes, leaving a smudge of mascara on Blinko's collar. It didn't really matter. It simply blended in with smears of ash already staining the costume.

"There now, honey." Blinko tapped her back in a comforting rhythm. "It's a terrible day for all of us, but we're alive. Let's think about that and be thankful."

Right there. That was the heart of the matter. Evelyn was alive, but was Bill? Helen? And—*oh, God*—what about the children? How could Evelyn ever be thankful if they were dead?

Evelyn pushed against Blinko, turning her horrified gaze to the still-burning tent. "I have to find them."

"Who, honey?"

"My family. My brother, his wife, and two children."

"Where were you seated? I'm sure they are around here somewhere." Blinko pointed at the clusters of people who milled about, most of them calling out for loved ones.

"I don't know. I got called in to work and couldn't come. I have no idea where they were."

"Look. I wish I could drop everything and help you, but I'm assigned to survey this area to help—" Blinko's voice cracked. "—help the living get to safer ground."

Dozens of people littered the midway like discarded hot dogs. Some moved, some didn't. Some had charred skin—their clothing burned off—and others, although they lay perfectly still, appeared as if the fire hadn't touched them.

Evelyn swallowed hard, but it set off a round of coughing before she could speak. She croaked, "I understand. I can search on my own."

Blinko scrubbed a hand down his face. "See if you can find Fraidy Freddie. He was smitten yesterday by a vivacious, gray-eyed waitress, and I'm sure he will help you if he can." Blinko offered a wan smile. "If you find him, tell him Blinko sent you." The clown moved to the next victim, a matronly woman, and covered her exposed legs with what remained of her skirt. He checked for a pulse but apparently found none. He covered his chest with one hand and closed his eyes.

"Blinko?" Evelyn's word made him look her way. "May God be with you."

"And also with you." The clown moved on with weary steps, one of dozens of circus employees, policemen, and average Joes performing the same grim task.

Was God with her? Faith chimed, *Lo, I am with you always, even unto the end of the world.* But doubt quoted Jesus in His darkest hour. *My God, my God, why hast thou forsaken me?*

Whatever was done, was done. Evelyn couldn't change the outcome. No matter the cause of the fire, God had not ceded His power to the whims of a human being. He had already chosen the divine destiny of hundreds of people today.

Evelyn's pastor often preached that only God holds the keys to life and death. After George perished in Bataan, it had comforted Evelyn to acknowledge her husband wouldn't have died unless God, in His providence, permitted it.

But what destiny had He chosen for the rest of her family today? Evelyn surveyed the carnage of the fire and acknowledged she might again have to walk through the Valley of the Shadow of Death. Would her faith survive the trek?

Chapter Nine

A blanket of black smoke smothered Hank. Far above, a blue patch of sky winked behind gray clouds. A rope ladder dangled beside him, and he summoned all his strength to sit up, slide his foot into the first rung, and climb.

About halfway up, Hank's foot slipped. He dangled over the abyss, kept from falling only by gripping the ropes. But he was weakening.

From above, a voice called, "Mr. Webb! Wake up."

Hank *was* awake. Or was he? And he wasn't Mr. Webb. His given name was Henry Frederick Webster—son of a minister and grandson of a legend. Destined to take up the family business behind a pulpit in the Methodist Church. He couldn't do that unless he kept climbing, but he was so tired.

Hank's cheeks stung like someone slapped him.

"Hank. Don't you just lay there. Wake up."

A naughty response formed, but Hank didn't voice it. Why couldn't the bothersome man see he wasn't asleep? He scaled the ladder faster than ever, and other sounds poured into the well. Wails. Moans. Weeping women.

Water dripped from above, soaking Hank through and through. He shook his head like a dog on the porch after a freak cloudburst. At last, he reached the top and thrust out his arm to get a handhold.

A large hand took hold of Hank's and crushed his knuckles. Pain dispelled the hallucination. He lay flat on his back, and bright sunlight blinded him. When he blinked, a familiar face came into focus.

"Welcome back to the land of the livin', Mr. Webb. I feared you were gone." A black face hovered above Hank, wreathed in a generous smile that emphasized the laugh lines around his eyes.

What was his name? Mack? No—Clyde. Clyde Miller. Reality broke over Hank like a powerful ocean wave, knocking him flat and spinning him in the sand. He came up for air. The circus. "Stars and Stripes Forever." Bill—King of the Hill. Roaring orange flames consuming everything in sight.

Lily! Hank sat up and turned side to side, frantic to know the fate of the little girl. But she wasn't in sight.

"Clyde. Did you see a little girl with me?"

"A child? No, sir."

"About eight years old, wearing a blue gingham pinafore and one glittery red slipper. She must have lost the other one."

"I think you got up too fast, Mr. Webb. This isn't Oz, and there's no Dorothy here."

"A girl, Clyde! Her name is Lily." Hank tried to stand, but Clyde restrained him.

"Hank." Clyde's grip tightened. "There's no girl here that looks that-away. Take a minute and let your mind clear." The compassion in Clyde's deep-set, brown eyes softened the firm set of his jaw.

Hank took a few deep breaths and surveyed the scene. Someone had dragged him farther from the burning tent than where he and Lily had fallen. A Hartford fireman sprayed water on the flames, but the stream was too weak after traveling so far from the city hydrants. Where was the circus fire rig and its crew?

The massive scope of the disaster engulfed Hank much like the blaze that had swallowed the big top. Once it caught fire, fifty fire trucks wouldn't have done any good.

Not far away, the lion chute was still in place, blocking the exit, but the wagons had all been moved. Had the circus lost any animals? Or crewmen? He grabbed Clyde's shirt with both hands. "My men. Are all accounted for?"

Clyde nodded. "We all made it out. The only one we worried about was you."

Hank lost the strength in his hands and released his grip.

Clyde rolled up his left sleeve. His forearm was covered in small blisters, and he grimaced. "You about died in there."

"So did you."

"I couldn't leave all them people." Clyde looked toward the exit where they'd both escaped, now a tangle of molten metal, burning canvas, and—

Bodies. A group of rescuers covered their mouths and noses with bandannas, T-shirts, or neckties. They used strips of cloth to shield their hands from the hot metal and lifted debris until they found charred remains. They pulled corpses—people who had been full of life an hour ago—out of the tent, laid them in even rows, and covered them with white sheets.

Both men silently watched the grim task until Clyde murmured, "I never seen nothin' like that big man, did you?"

Bill. A hero. He saved dozens of people but lost his own life for love of his wife. What would compel him to such an act? She had likely been dead already. Hank's throat spasmed when he inhaled, and a coughing fit ensued. When he could, he rasped, "No. I've never seen so much courage."

"And love." Clyde wiped his eyes. "I don't know if you saw, but he went after his wife."

"I saw." In troubled times, Hank always heard Bible verses in his head spoken in his father's voice. *Greater love hath no man than this: that a man lay down his life for his friends.*

"She's alive!"

A shout of victory rose from the recovery team, and two men bent to help a woman to her feet. Every inch of her was blackened, and her only recognizable human feature was the whites of her eyes. A man in a lab coat checked her from head to toe while the men hovered around her like she was Betty Grable.

"Well, I'll be," said the doc. "There's not a burn on her anywhere. All she's got is a hole in her stocking."

The men cheered at his words, but the woman fainted. A worker caught her, and she was loaded on a stretcher and wheeled to a waiting ambulance. The unceasing wails of sirens from assorted emergency vehicles could be heard now that the band had finally stopped playing.

If one person had been pulled out alive, maybe Bill and Helen—

"Webb. There you are." Eddie Vermeer stepped over an unidentifiable piece of melted metal and strode toward Hank with more than his usual determination. No one could deny this man was in charge, even in the middle of a disaster. "Did you keep an eye on Russell?"

At the question, Hank's irritation gave him strength to stand up. "How could I when you assigned him to be a seat man?"

"Careful. I don't like that tone." Eddie chomped on his ever-present cigar.

What decent man would smoke at the scene of a fatal fire? A proud one, that's who. Hank wanted to punch his boss right in the kisser. He didn't want this job anymore. How could he ever be a clown again? The scenes of today's horror would simply replay in his mind like a newsreel. "You switched Russell, and he wasn't on my crew. I couldn't do my job and at the same time track down that good-for-nothing—"

Clyde stepped in. "Mr. Vermeer, I was on my way to see you to report spotting Russell in the midway."

Eddie's eyes widened. "When?"

"A few minutes before the fire started." Clyde's report wouldn't get Hank off the hook, but at least it showed his men hadn't been completely derelict.

Eddie swore a blue streak and kicked the metal wreckage, which didn't move under his assault. That had to hurt. "If that loon started this fire and they can prove it, we'll be up to our eyeballs in lawsuits." Eddie turned to Clyde and said, "Keep quiet about this. That goes for you too, Webb."

Clyde raised his chin. "I won't be dishonest if someone asks me."

"I'm not asking you to lie." Eddie reduced his voice's volume. "They are already saying the fire was likely started by a cigarette, not arson. Let's let them continue that train of thought."

Clyde nodded and headed toward the chute.

"Leave it." Eddie's words stopped Clyde in his tracks. "There's bodies yet to be removed, and everything needs to stay right where it is until the investigation is over."

"I wasn't gonna touch the chute, Mr. Vermeer." Clyde put on his newsboy cap and jammed it tight on his head. "I'm gonna help get those poor people out of there."

Hank's chest tightened.

Poor people like Bill and Helen.

———•◦•———

Evelyn stumbled through the wreckage and ashes, getting as close to the smoldering debris as she could. Sometimes too close for safety's sake. She'd circled the entire tent twice, searching among the survivors. But her family had not appeared, nor had anyone she asked seen them.

Hordes of people—young and old, male and female—were engaged in the same task. Occasionally, a cry of joy would be heard at a happy reunion, and each one made Evelyn's stomach roil. Would she be granted such a gift?

Most searchers called out names, and so did Evelyn although her smoke-damaged throat only permitted faint and raspy cries. She might walk right by Bill and he wouldn't hear her. It would be like him to help comb the wreckage for survivors. Once in a while she'd spot a man with Bill's build—she couldn't identify by hair color because all the men's hair looked ashy gray—but it was never him.

The plight of the children grieved Evelyn the most. Many simply sat and wept. Sometimes a helpful adult scooped them up, but the magnitude of the tragedy overwhelmed rescuers. Anguished cries of the children for mothers and fathers shot a piercing arrow through Evelyn's heart, but she couldn't cave in to help. She was on a mission, and she wouldn't stop hunting until she spotted one of the dear faces she loved.

Partway through her search, she came across the body of a child which had been draped with a white sheet. Poking out from the edges were a blond pigtail and a long, dirt-stained red ribbon. Her efforts to save the child had been in vain. Not far away, the Good Samaritan sat on the ground beside the child's weeping mother. Both of them had been spared the scythe of the Grim Reaper, but they lost the treasure they'd been trying to save.

Evelyn walked quickly by, not wanting them to recognize her. She rounded the edge of the tent out of their view, knelt, and retched. If only she'd been stronger. If only she'd asked someone for help. If only. . . But there were too many sentiments that began with "if only" to sort through now. Besides, all were meaningless.

Evelyn rose to her feet again and straightened herself as best she could. In the chaos, no one paid attention to appearances anyway. Ready to begin a third trip around the tent, Evelyn stopped cold when she spied a man standing beside a burned-out Coca-Cola wagon, about fifty yards away. Dressed in a clown costume, it couldn't be Bill, but he shared Bill's height and heft. He turned enough to reveal his face. *Fraidy Freddie.* Raindrops splattered in the parched, hot desert of Evelyn's soul. He would help. He simply had to.

Evelyn headed his direction, and her pace increased. Freddie was a magnet and she was iron filings. Freddie didn't see her coming, so when she slammed into him, she nearly knocked him down. Strong arms wrapped around her, steadying them both, and Evelyn reveled in their comfort.

"Whoa, miss." Freddie's hand patted against Evelyn's back like he was trying to burp a baby. "What's this about?"

Freddie's voice, smooth as a malted milkshake, sounded very much like Bill's. Deep. Soothing. Evelyn tilted her face upward like a flower seeking the sun.

"Hey, I know you." Freddie placed his forefinger under Evelyn's chin. "Evelyn. I'm so glad you made it out."

"Charlie called me in to work, so I didn't attend the show." A sour taste rose to Evelyn's mouth, and she swallowed. Hard. "I'm looking for my brother and his family. They were here, and I can't find them."

"That's not surprising." Freddie didn't release her, and Evelyn didn't mind. "Don't think the worst. Chances are good they got out okay. The police are working to reunite families. Let's ask someone where we should look."

We? Evelyn sagged into Freddie's arms and let her forehead rest against his chest. His embrace tightened.

A well-dressed, portly woman cleared her throat and gave them a prudish stare as she passed by. Evelyn really should let Freddie go, but she didn't want to. Although he was little more than a stranger, her instincts said he was a good man.

A wiry man with skin like sable ran toward them. "Look what I found, Mr. Webb." His voice carried an ounce of excitement and a pinch of hope. "I know you were looking for the little girl." He held out his treasure for inspection.

A glittery red shoe. Sized for a child. Only one, and covered with coal-black grime. Evelyn reached for the shoe with a tentative hand like she might touch magic, but was it an omen of good or evil? "May I see it?"

She looked inside. Children's size one. It had to be Lily's. Lily had been so proud to graduate from what she called "baby shoes." Evelyn clutched the treasure to her breast as tears came again, but this time not without hope. "This shoe belongs to my niece. Where did you find it?"

Hank and the shoe finder jerked their heads like she'd slapped them. Why would this news be so shocking?

The roustabout took off his cap and fingered the brim. "Miss, I'm sorry to say—"

Hank interrupted. "Show us where you found it, and we'll look ourselves."

The man pointed to the tent exit where a cluster of rescuers worked feverishly. "Over there."

A clue. At last Evelyn had a starting point for her search. Lily and the family might be among the spectators milling about. A quick scan of the small groups didn't reveal a much-loved face, so Evelyn made her way toward the workmen. Perhaps they had seen them.

Freddie grabbed her arm. "No. Wait."

Evelyn tried to yank her arm away, but Freddie's fingers were steel bands. With eyes as soft as a doe, he said, "Let's let them finish first."

On closer look, Evelyn identified their horrific task. Bodies. Dozens lay scattered on the ground, each covered with a sheet. Her hand rose to her throat. Evelyn screamed, but no sound escaped. Freddie shared his strength with her when she swayed.

Dear God, no. Her family had to be alive. The Almighty was both powerful and loving, so no other outcome was possible.

> *He plants his footsteps in the sea*
> *And rides upon the storm.*

The words of Cowper's hymn. Again. Jesus had planted His footsteps in the sea and invited Peter to join Him. But Peter sank until Jesus took hold of him and gently rebuked him. *O thou of little faith, wherefore didst thou doubt?*

Gusty winds and waves of doubt battered Evelyn. She sank beneath the assault but reached her spiritual hand for the Master's.

Time to ride with Jesus upon the storm.

Chapter Ten

Hank could get used to holding this woman in his arms, but he didn't linger. He had no right to enjoy her embrace, nor to feel worthy of her trust. If she knew his past, particularly the news he withheld about her family, she'd not hug him. She'd slap his face. "I promised I'd help, Evelyn, and I will. No one should have to go through a trauma like this alone."

"Will your boss let you?"

"Our highest duty is the safety of our guests, and in light of all that has happened, I think it will be allowed." Hank put a little more daylight between them. Time to start with one piece of truth. "By the way, let's dispense with Freddie." He stuck out his hand. "You can call me Hank."

"Thank you—" Evelyn's eyelashes dipped, and one corner of her mouth turned upward. But the expression quickly vanished. "Hank."

The sound of his real name on her lips calmed Hank to his bones. Evelyn placed a dainty hand in his, and even the simple pressure of her handshake on his heat-damaged flesh made Hank wince.

Evelyn's eyes widened. "Oh. I'm so sorry, did I hurt you?" She raised the ruffled cuff of his blackened costume and emitted a mouse-like squeak. "You're burned! And look at that gash. You need to see a doctor right away."

Most of Hank's burns were only first-degree, no worse than sunburns he'd had as a boy, although there was a blister on the back of his right hand. He'd see the circus doctor after he helped Evelyn. Pins and needles danced on both hands and forearms, interspersed with an occasional jolt of searing pain.

"It can wait. They don't hurt too bad." Hank's white lie pricked his conscience but not as much as the whopper he was about to tell. "I don't know what happened to your brother and his wife, but let's see if we can find the children first in case they got separated."

Bill and Helen certainly were among the bodies under the sheets, but Hank couldn't bring himself to tell Evelyn yet. If she found the children—no, *when* she found the children—she would have enough courage to hear the truth of what happened to her brother and his wife. Jamie should be found hale and whole, and if his prayers had been answered, so would Lily. "I've been told families are being reunited at the Brown School. Do you know where that is?"

"Yes. It's downtown."

"Can we walk, or do we need to take a cab?"

"I don't know if I can walk that far, so maybe we should get a ride." Evelyn straightened her skirt and frowned at the condition of her stockings. She removed her shoes, yanked the shredded nylons from her legs—shapely legs, although Hank shouldn't notice—and tossed them aside. "Maybe Bill and Helen are already there. They might even be home by now. I came in such a hurry I didn't check there first. If we don't find them at the school, I'll look at home." She slipped her bare feet back in her ruined pumps and said, "But I have one condition for accepting your help."

"What's that?"

Evelyn straightened her posture and set her jaw. "When we find them, you'll go straight to the hospital and get your hands treated."

"Fair enough." Hank offered his elbow to Evelyn, who would need steadying as they walked the debris-strewn yard.

Evelyn rested her hand lightly on his arm. Then she jerked it away. "Wait. Do the burns go all the way up your arm?"

"No, it's mostly my hands." Hands that had held, for the briefest moment, her young nephew and adorable niece. The burns on Hanks hands didn't hurt as much as the failure that scorched his soul. He should have made Bill leave the tent before he got killed. Helen likely was already dead. What got into the man to make him abandon Evelyn and the children to die alongside his wife?

When they reached Barbour Street, Hank hailed a cab, but it already had passengers. After several other unsuccessful attempts, a green Dodge sedan pulled over. Hank opened the rear door for Evelyn before climbing in after her. He instructed the driver, "Brown School."

Evelyn sucked in a breath and touched her lips with soot-stained fingers. "Oh no. I don't have any money."

Hank didn't either. A wallet only got in his way while he clowned. He'd left it in his steamer trunk on the circus train, padlocked to keep Russell from rifling through it. Another failure to add to his rising tally.

"That's all right, Miss." The elderly driver looked up in the rearview mirror to make eye contact. "I'm not able to dig through the rubble, but I can volunteer to drive folks around. It's not much, but it's something I can do. You have my sympathies."

Evelyn crumpled, and Hank slipped his arm around her. She leaned into him slightly, and Hank relished the closeness. Ambulance sirens wailed, and the driver kept pulling aside to let them pass. At this rate, they'd never make it to the school.

Please God, let Jamie and Lily be there. Hank had no right to ask God for help given the state of his soul. His prayers likely rose no higher than the Dodge's headliner. Lots of people offered "foxhole prayers," when they desperately needed an answer from God. But surely God gave preference to those who already had a solid relationship with Him.

Maybe Hank should have a talk with God to clear up a few things before the next crisis hit.

———————•◦•———————

When the car pulled up to the Brown School, Evelyn offered a quick thanks to the driver and hopped out almost before the car had stopped rolling. She trotted up the steps to the entrance, but Hank passed her at a full run. He yanked the heavy glass door open and followed her through.

Not a child in sight. Why did she think Lily and Jamie would be waiting for her and waving a welcome? Her feet suddenly felt like they were encased in concrete.

A well-built desk blocked the hallway, manned by Red Cross and American Legion volunteers. Hank grabbed Evelyn's hand and tried to bypass the check-in point, but he was stopped cold by a resolute legionnaire wearing a blue serge military-style coat with matching trousers. A medal dangled on the middle-aged man's breast pocket beneath a bar that read, SERGEANT-AT-ARMS. Not someone to be trifled with.

"Sorry, sir," the officer said. "No one passes without registering."

Hank tensed and opened his mouth, but Evelyn spoke first. "Thank you. We don't want special treatment." She tugged Hank's sleeve and returned to the end of the long line of people waiting to register. Arguments broke out as tempers flared, fueled by pure terror. Evelyn's stomach churned, and the palpable anguish of the searchers caused her tears to flow again. The wait would be interminable, but necessary.

Hank spoke like a child hushed by a librarian. "You didn't ask me. I *do* want special treatment. Jamie and Lily might be back there right now. Alone."

"That's true for every child here." Evelyn appreciated Hank's passion, but why did he care so much? Wait. "But how did you know their names?"

A flush crept up Hank's neck. "You must have told me."

Trauma did unspeakable things to a person's memory. Perhaps she had told him and didn't remember.

A man and wife tried to rush by, but Hank blocked his way. "Get in line, buddy. We're all as anxious as you."

The stranger perused him from head to toe. Hank did present an odd sight. His makeup was smeared beyond recognition, and his costume was shredded in several places. And was that blood? Hank resembled a character more suited to a Hitchcock movie than the circus.

The man drew himself up to his full height and stood toe to toe with Hank. "Who are you to tell me what to do? It's your fault my Annie is missing. How could the circus let this happen?"

"Milt, calm down." The wife's plea fell on deaf ears.

"No." Milt called Hank a rude name, and soon others in line joined the confrontation, slinging ugly words. Hank's presence might start a riot.

The sergeant-at-arms strode into the fray. When Milt threw a punch, the legionnaire caught his arm and twisted it behind his back. The man struggled, but he could not free himself.

"That's enough of that." The legionnaire's statement boomed down the hallway like the report of cannon fire. "We'll have order here. Any violence, and I'll throw you out. Got it?"

Milt slumped, and the legionnaire released him. His wife stroked his upper arm through his filthy suit. "I'm sorry," he said, "I'm out of my mind with worry."

"We all are." Hank extended his fire-damaged hand and did not flinch although Milt's sturdy handclasp must have hurt like the dickens. "No harm done. I hope you find her."

The sergeant returned to his post, and the former combatant wiped perspiration from his cheek. Or was it a tear? The couple took their place in line three people behind Hank and Evelyn. Time slowed to a crawl, and only by leaning on Hank's strength was Evelyn able to remain standing.

When the couple in front of them scurried past the sergeant-at-arms and down the hallway, Evelyn approached the table and leaned on it, supporting herself with both hands.

The woman behind the desk, also dressed in a legionnaire jacket and skirt, pushed a stray curl off her forehead and pushed up her wire-rimmed glasses. She turned a page on her ledger and asked, "Name?"

"My name?"

The woman huffed out a breath and said in a staccato tone, "Of course, *your* name. You're obviously not Elizabeth Taylor."

"Steady, Marian." The sergeant laid a hand on the woman's shoulder. He turned to Evelyn and said, "I'm sorry, ma'am. It's already been a long day, and everyone is on edge."

Marian's pale complexion pinkened. "Forgive me," she said, taking a hankie from her pocket and dabbing her eyes. "I didn't mean to be rude."

Evelyn wouldn't want Marian's job. Dealing with so many hysterical parents would try anyone's patience. "I'm sure you didn't, and I'm sorry for misunderstanding. I'm Evelyn Benson, and I'm looking for Lily and Jamie Halstead."

The woman jotted names in the columns and asked, "So you're not their mother?"

"No, I'm their aunt, but I'm hoping their mother and father might already have collected them. Do you have any record of that?"

Marian flipped pages, and Evelyn's stomach lurched. She welcomed the comfort of Hank's hand, which rested gently on her back. So many names—each one who might face disaster. What made her hope God had spared her family when so many others were also in peril? But she clung to that hope like the last life preserver in the wide, wild sea.

"No, I'm sorry, I don't see them. Are the children old enough to tell us their names?"

"Lily could. She's eight. Jamie's just a toddler."

"She's not listed, but it doesn't mean she's not here. Maybe they haven't arrived yet. Let's record all their information, along with how to contact you, and we'll let you look out back. If they arrive later, we'll get in touch."

Hank's foot tapped on the terrazzo floor, but he couldn't be more impatient than Evelyn. She rushed through the description of the children.

The only time Marian looked up was when she described Lily's getup. "Ma'am. Do you need a drink of water?"

Hank's fuse burned out. "She's not a lunatic. The girl dressed like Dorothy. Have you seen her or not?"

Evelyn grabbed Hank's hand and squeezed until he grunted.

He relaxed. A little. "I'm sorry. We're just worried."

Evelyn's lips curved upward. Pain was a powerful correctional device. Leaning closer to Marian, she asked, "Is that all you need?

"Yes." Marian beckoned a woman in a Red Cross uniform. "This is Mrs. Witt. She'll escort you to see the children."

Finally. Nervous energy buzzed all over her skin like a bee seeking honey. Evelyn hoped to find the children, but if she did, what did it mean about Bill and Helen? Cowper's hymn about God's mysterious ways urged,

Ye fearful saints, fresh courage take . . .

Evelyn certainly classified as a "fearful saint" at this moment. She had always trusted God until George died. His death had burst her bubble of naive faith, and what was left? Evelyn had presumed her faith in God would preclude the terrible things that happened to others from happening to her. Yes, God gave blessings, but hadn't hardship also come from His hand? If bad things could happen to Christians as well as pagans, what did that say about God?

Mrs. Witt stopped in front of a closed door and said, "This is the room where we keep the littlest ones. You said your nephew was two, correct?" At Evelyn's nod, she continued. "If he's here, this is where he'll be." She swung open the door.

Evelyn stepped through with a whispered prayer. *Take fresh courage.*

Chapter Eleven

Some slept, some screamed, and some sat in stony silence. Evelyn scanned the sweet little faces, grimy with soot and tracked with tears, looking for the one dearest to her. Jamie wasn't among those who were awake. Perhaps he slept on one of the makeshift pallets lined up against the wall and guarded by a teenaged girl who mopped perspiration from her flushed forehead.

"Let's look at the sleeping ones." Hank guided her toward the diminutive forms, but how did he know Jamie wasn't among the children who were awake? He must have guessed from Evelyn's reaction.

The weary caretaker put a finger to her lips. "I just got some of them to sleep. Are you looking for a boy or a girl?"

Evelyn lowered her voice. "A boy. He's two."

"Do you know what he was wearing?"

"A denim short set with brown and blue sailboats on it." Evelyn licked her parched lips. "And he wore Stride Rite shoes with a broken lace—"

"I'm sorry, miss. I don't think he's here, but you can look." The girl tiptoed toward the sleeping children and paused. "All the boys are along this wall."

Evelyn approached each tiny body and shivered. They slept, but their stillness spooked her. One by one she stooped to peek at the little faces. One boy was obviously larger than the others, but a corner of the blanket obscured his face. She peeked under it. Not Jamie.

Hank helped Evelyn to a nearby children's chair. She plopped into it and rested her head on her knees.

The teenager dangled a tissue under Evelyn's nose. "I'm sorry. He might be in the next classroom. If he was big for his age . . ." Her words trailed off.

True. Jamie took after Bill, and he could easily be mistaken for being older than two. Evelyn accepted the tissue, dabbed her eyes, and sent a quick prayer heavenward. Her strength returned. She stood, thanked the girl, and strode for the door with Hank on her heels.

Mrs. Witt ushered them to the next classroom, but it yielded the same result.

Evelyn turned to the woman, whose brown eyes oozed compassion, and asked, "Is there anywhere else he could be?"

"I'm sorry, Mrs. Benson. These two classrooms have the littlest ones. The third room has older children, and some have been allowed outside to play. Didn't you say you also were looking for a little girl?"

Lily. Maybe Jamie had been taken to the hospital, or maybe he was with Bill and Helen, wherever they were. But Lily might be here, alone and distraught. "Yes. Let's check on the playground. She wouldn't like being cooped up inside."

The matron opened the exterior door, and the incongruous sound of happy children thrummed in the humid air. Children rode the swings like Wallendas on miniature trapezes, girls with their braids and skirts whipping in the breeze. One stood on the seat, pumping herself high before an attendant rebuked her. She sat, her disappointment very evident, but it wasn't Lily.

Other children swarmed the teeter-totters and slides like little ants, making it hard to isolate their faces. Evelyn sought a glimpse of a blue gingham pinafore but didn't spot one. She pulled out the lone ruby slipper she had tucked into her pocketbook and wished she was the Wizard of Oz. She'd conjure Lily from thin air.

Hank reached for the shoe. "May I?"

Evelyn relinquished the talisman to him.

Approaching a worker, Hank asked, "Did you see a little girl wearing the mate to this?" He proffered the slipper like a prince looking for Cinderella.

"No," the woman answered. "But children keep arriving. Perhaps you could stop by later."

Hank returned the shoe to Evelyn and wrapped his arm around her. "Let's check the last classroom. Maybe she couldn't play outside without her shoes."

She and Hank searched inside to no avail. Surely the family was all tucked in their cozy bungalow on Capen Street, gathered around the dinette while Helen prepared dinner. What an adventure they'd had! There would be stories galore, especially from Lily, the drama queen.

Evelyn's burden lifted. Slightly. "I need to check at home, Hank. They are probably all there waiting for me to finish my shift and join them for dinner." Evelyn extended her hand but then drew it back. It might be a while before handshakes were comfortable again for Hank. "I appreciate your help today. I'm sure you have better things to do than follow me around."

"It's no bother." Hank's eyes sparkled as blue as the summer sky. Kindness shone from them, but was there something else? "Do we need another ride, or shall I walk you home?"

"No, really. It's only a mile from here, and I can make it on my own."

"Nonsense. Do you think I could sleep tonight not knowing they are safe? Let's go." Hank took a few steps in the wrong direction before he halted. "Wait. Where is Capen Street?"

Evelyn stuck out her thumb and pointed over her right shoulder. "Thataway."

"I'll get there with a good guide." Hank paused beside Evelyn and again held out his elbow. "Now, no more arguments. I'm going with you, and that's that." He guided her slowly at first but matched Evelyn's pace when she quickened it.

They passed Clay Arsenal's brownstone apartment buildings, and after a few blocks, Hank's strength became much more than a convenience.

Evelyn's steps grew less steady block by block, and she leaned hard on Hank. Her blouse stuck to her damp skin, and she might have to locate a bench for a brief rest. Uncertainty encroached on her hopes, and Evelyn chased it away with Cowper's words of encouragement.

The clouds ye so much dread
Are big with mercy and shall break
In blessings on your head.

When Evelyn counted her blessings from this horrible day, one would be named Hank.

Hank sank deeper into remorse with every step toward Evelyn's house. If the sidewalk was made of metal, Hank's shoes were magnets.

An awning shaded the street in front of the Hartford Eclectic Dispensary, and a wrought iron bench offered a much-needed rest. "Let's take a break," Hank said to Evelyn. "You sit here, and I'll get us a cold drink."

Evelyn plunked down on the bench. "Okay. But only for a minute, and only because I'm exhausted. I need to get home."

Hank slapped at his pockets, and his cheeks turned beet red. "Sorry. I forgot I'm broke. If you'll lend me a few coins, I'll pay you back."

"I don't have any. Remember?"

Heat rose to Hank's cheeks, and not from the weather. He rushed inside, bullied the proprietor into giving him two cups of ice water, and hustled back to Evelyn. He sat, but the bench was so small he couldn't avoid touching her. She trembled, and he slipped his arm across the back, resting it on the bench instead of her shoulders. "I know this has been a tough day. I hope I've been helpful."

"You have. I'd hate to do this all alone. But it's kind of strange since we've barely met."

"It doesn't feel that way to me."

"Me either. I feel like I've known you for ages. It's nice to have a new friend."

Hank took a sip of the ice-cold drink and sighed. Friend? To his surprise, the description didn't please him. He might want the relationship to be more, but he needed to lead with his head, not his heart. Besides, he'd wreck their budding relationship when he told her the truth. Best to get it over with. "Evelyn, friends don't keep secrets from each other."

Evelyn uncrossed her legs and sat forward on the bench, turning to face him. "What secret?"

"I saw Lily at the circus."

At his words, Evelyn's eyes widened. "You did? Why didn't you tell me?"

"Because I got knocked out, and I don't know what happened to her."

"Tell me everything."

He couldn't. "Everything" would be too devastating all at once. His protective streak toward this beautiful, brave woman was a mile wide. "I saw a girl dressed like Dorothy near the exit of the tent, right before the roof collapsed. It must have been Lily." There. That was true. "I helped her out, but we got knocked down by a blast of hot air."

"Was she okay?" Evelyn swallowed several times and blinked her gorgeous gray eyes.

"She was in front of me, so I landed on her. It knocked her out, but I think she was alive."

"You *think*? Don't you know?"

Hank stood and paced. "I didn't want to fall on her. It just happened. It was crazy, Evelyn. Everyone running, pushing, and screaming—"

Evelyn stood and rested her delicate hand lightly on his forearm. "I'm not blaming you. You're an absolute hero for rescuing her. I'm simply trying to understand why you don't know if she was alive or not."

Hank's heartbeat pounded in his ears. He'd give anything to know that answer himself. A pale, lovely little face popped into his thoughts, and he hung his head. "When I woke up, she was gone. I'd been moved, so someone must have moved her too. I wish I'd been awake."

Evelyn grasped his hand. "At least we know she made it out of the tent. Did you see Jamie? Or Bill and Helen?"

Hank couldn't reveal all he knew. If he had to fudge, dissemble, or outright lie, so be it. She might hate him later, but he had Evelyn's best interests at heart. "It was pandemonium. People were in a frenzy, clawing at each other—"

"I'm sorry. It must have been awful. Besides, you've never met them. I don't know why I even asked." Evelyn tossed her empty cup and straw into a nearby trash can. "Now that we know Lily got separated from the family, it makes sense they won't be at home. They will be looking for her too. If they weren't at the school, they must be at the hospital. And they probably have Jamie. The house is only a few blocks away. Let's get there, clean up a little, and call a cab." Without waiting for Hank's agreement, she whirled and flitted toward her destination like a homing pigeon.

Any normal female would have screeched at Hank like a banshee. But Evelyn was no ordinary woman. Hank's admiration soared at her fortitude and no-nonsense attitude. He chugged his last few swigs, chucked his cup in the trash can beside Evelyn's, and trotted to catch up to her.

But Hank's guilt jogged just as fast. He wouldn't outrun it now—or perhaps, ever.

Home. Evelyn opened the wrought iron gate and took the sidewalk that curved toward the front door. She opened her purse and got her keys. Their musical tinkle usually cheered her, but not today. The jangle jarred her nerves.

She swung the door open to ominous silence, as if she had entered a funeral home at midnight. A verse popped to mind.

> *Why art thou cast down, O my soul?*
> *And why art thou disquieted in me?*
> *Hope thou in God: for I shall yet praise him*
> *for the help of his countenance.*

Leading Sunday school children to memorize scripture meant Evelyn had to know it herself. The words of Psalm 42 nourished the hope that had blossomed when Hank told her about Lily.

They all must be alive. Maybe Lily had broken a bone. Perhaps they wanted Jamie checked out. Bill was a strapping man—if anyone could get his family out of a burning tent, it would be him. Still, she'd give a month's wages to hear laughter and thumps from upstairs.

Hank followed her across the threshold and stopped a few feet inside.

Evelyn put her purse and keys on the console table and said, "I'll go up and change. You wait here, and I'll see if I can find something of Bill's for you to wear."

Hank's complexion blanched until it almost matched the smudges of his white grease paint. He shifted his weight to the other foot. "No, it's all right. I'd hate to impose."

"It's no imposition. Bill would be happy to help anyone who helped Lily." Evelyn scurried up the stairs and changed her dress in a flash. She also donned a pair of white ankle socks and her Mary Janes. Practicality over fashion today. Stopping at the bathroom, she took a swipe at her scraped knees with a wet washcloth and slapped Band-Aids on the abrasions that were still bleeding.

She scooted to Bill and Helen's room and headed straight for the closet. Pulling out a pair of trousers and a chambray shirt, she hustled back to Hank. Every minute that lapsed between now and her reunion with the family seemed an eternity.

When she offered the clothing to Hank, he said, "Thank you, but I can't—"

"Yes, you can. And you will. Hurry up." Evelyn pointed to the downstairs half bath. "You can change in there. There's a washcloth on the towel rack, and you can use it to get off the rest of your makeup."

Hank didn't move.

Evelyn stepped close and prodded his chest with her index finger. "Hank—"

Oh, for goodness' sake. She wanted to call him by all three names like an authoritative mom, but Evelyn didn't know his last name. "Fraidy Freddie, you get in there and change your clothes. No arguments. Time is wasting." She pushed the clothing against his chest.

Hank plowed one hand through his hair but took the garments. She might as well have offered him a slimy snake for all the enthusiasm he showed. He slipped into the bathroom and latched the door.

Why would he be so reluctant?

Chapter Twelve

Evelyn slipped into the kitchen and grabbed two bananas. Lunchtime had passed long ago, and no telling when they'd have a chance to eat supper. A glance at the kitchen sink made all her limbs feel heavy. The cut-glass tumblers stained with dried lemonade awaited their owner's return, prized talismans of the joys of everyday life. Evelyn prayed Helen would be able to return to wash them herself. She took the small hallway back to the living room, her thoughts a bottomless, black chasm.

Hank opened the door at exactly the wrong moment—as she passed. It thumped her head and squished the bananas against her chest.

"Are you all right?" Hank backed up and steadied her with one hand. "I didn't hear you coming."

Evelyn nodded and surveyed Hank from face to feet. She'd never seen him without his makeup. Fathomless sea-blue eyes sat atop high cheekbones, balanced by a straight nose with narrow nostrils. His full lips and square jaw were adorned with a five o'clock shadow which contributed a roguish air.

The sight of him in Bill's clothing should not have lifted her heart as it did. The shirt fit him well through the shoulders but bagged around his midsection. Hank had tucked the tails neatly into the trousers buttoned at his waist, but he was slimmer than Bill.

Hank scrunched the excess fabric in his fist. "Sorry, but I'll need a belt if I'm to stay decent."

Evelyn's lips lifted at the corners along with her spirits. When she completed her inspection all the way to the floor, her laughter erupted like Mount Vesuvius. Hank looked every bit a gentleman from the ankles up, but he still wore his oversized clown shoes. Crafted to look like red and white wingtips, the heels were normal-sized, but the toe boxes could conceal a small rodent.

Hank's laugh lines crinkled. "What? You don't approve of my sartorial choices?"

"Sartorial? That's a big word for a clown."

"Clown by day, scholar by night." Hank waggled his eyebrows and quoted Groucho Marx. "Outside of a dog, a book is a man's best friend. Inside of a dog it's too dark to read."

For a shimmering instant, Evelyn's troubles took flight, replaced by the joy of Hank's company. But they quickly came home to roost like buzzards on fence posts. She put the slightly mashed bananas on the end table. "Here. You might want a snack while I go get a pair of Bill's shoes. Even if they don't fit, they will be better than what you're wearing."

Evelyn scuttled upstairs, grabbed a belt, a pair of loafers—and socks, just to be sure—and returned to Hank.

Hank slipped on the shoes, which were also a little too big. He donned the extra pair of socks over his own and tried again. After a few tentative steps, he said, "Compared to my clown shoes, these fit just right." His pleasant smile faded. "Should we call a ride?"

Evelyn dialed the cab company. Had it only been this morning that Charlie's call changed the course of her day? And perhaps saved her life? She gave her address to the dispatcher, listened to her instructions, and hung up. "It might take a while for a cab to get here. As you can imagine, they are overwhelmed."

"Do you have a car? I could drive."

"Bill and Helen share their car with me when I need one, but they took it today to the circus, and I don't know . . ." Evelyn's tears flowed again. Would they become her food day and night like the psalmist? They seemingly sprang from an inexhaustible well.

"There, now." Hank tucked her under his arm and gave a gentle squeeze. "Don't worry. We'll find their car, and for now, a cab will be fine."

Since her next payday wasn't until tomorrow, Evelyn purloined enough money from the mad money jar in the kitchen, enough to pay for fare. When they were reunited with Bill, she hoped he would still have enough money in his wallet for dinner. She and Hank walked through the front door, and Evelyn locked it behind her. They sat on the wooden porch bench Bill had crafted from scrap wood and waited.

And waited some more. Evelyn's nerves frayed nearly to the breaking point, and Hank seemed to understand she couldn't chitchat. Rather than being awkward, her connection to Hank soothed the silence. She'd never known a more intuitive man, including Bill.

Had she only known Hank twenty-four hours? And she didn't really know him—he was a mere acquaintance. Evelyn needed to get her guard up. A circus man's life was transitory, and soon Hank and his troupe would decamp on carbon steel rails to the next town. A wise woman would keep that in mind.

Her mind might be wise, but Evelyn's heart was foolish.

Bill's shirt, Bill's trousers—a little threadbare in the knees—and Bill's loafers. Hank was swathed head to toe in the clothing of a dead man. A faint aroma of Old Spice clung to the short-sleeved Dickies work shirt, and there was a neat crease on the wide-leg trousers. The clothing showed faint signs of wear but also revealed the loving care of two women devoted to Bill's well-being. One was with him in heaven, but one didn't know yet he'd left earth.

Every time Hank tried to let the words flow, they were blocked behind the lump in his throat like the waters of Lake Mead behind Hoover Dam. He needed to open a floodgate, and soon.

The cab arrived, picked them up, and stopped when multiple cars blocked any further progress. The driver took off his cap and swabbed his brow with a handkerchief already soggy with perspiration. "Sorry, folks," he said, "Municipal Hospital is still a quarter mile away, but this is as close as I can get. It's a madhouse."

"We'll walk from here." Evelyn paid the fare and thanked the cabbie before heading at a brisk pace toward the hospital. If she'd been a needle, she threaded the maze of people as if she were in the hands of an expert seamstress, darting through openings too small for Hank.

"Wait up." When Evelyn didn't slow down, Hank called louder. "Evelyn, please. I have to tell you something."

"What?" Evelyn's words wafted over her shoulder, but she kept moving.

Hank jostled an unfortunate man aside and leaped for Evelyn, grabbing her arm in a grip none too gentle. "I need you to stop and listen to me. Now."

Evelyn jerked her arm loose, none of her sweet nature in evidence at the moment. "If you can't keep up, I'll go on alone. Someone I love is in there injured, or God forbid, dying."

That might be true, but Hank didn't want to entertain the possibility. The situation was worse than Evelyn knew, and no caring human being would let her walk through the doors without a warning of what she'd discover. Hank wrapped a burly arm around her and shuttled her off the sidewalk into a spot of trampled grass. Evelyn resisted, but Hank would not yield.

Had Hank thought her as meek as a kitten? This Evelyn was a bobcat. Slapping and kicking, Evelyn soon formed fists and pounded his chest. People stared, but no one intervened. Evelyn wasn't the only woman—or man, for that matter—who'd lost her composure today, and her behavior didn't seem as outrageous as it would have in normal times.

Hank let Evelyn exhaust her strength, which waned in less than a minute. She collapsed against him and sobbed while Hank embraced her with all the familiarity of a beloved husband, not a mere friend. So distraught was the crowd that no one stared. Soon, Evelyn gripped a handful of Bill's shirt and inhaled the scent, which acted as a calming elixir.

"You smell like Bill."

Evelyn's words struck Hank with physical force. He swayed but stayed on his feet. He was about to shatter this woman with a few simple sentences, but he'd fall to pieces alongside her. Tendrils of emotion had lashed him to Evelyn—tender, but strong. Where she went, Hank was sure to follow.

In a miracle akin to the parting of the Red Sea, an empty bench appeared under a nearby tree. He hustled Evelyn there and sat her down before kneeling beside her on one knee. Clasping her hand inside both of his, Hank forced himself to look directly into her beautiful eyes the color of silver mist on a moonlit lake. The moment for full truth had arrived. He cleared his throat and said, "Evelyn, I saw the whole family at the circus. Not just Lily."

Evelyn's eyes widened, but she said nothing. However, her fingernails dug into the flesh above Hank's thumb.

Time to open the floodgate. "Bill and the family arrived right before the show started. With Lily along, they were hard to miss."

A tiny portion of the corner of Evelyn's mouth lifted. "I'm sure they were."

"They sat in the grandstands near my station, and Lily was positively enchanting. I fell in love with her a little, I think. Who wouldn't?"

"Anyone who had to put up with so much drama every day." Evelyn's visage softened. "But I do love her. So much."

Hank drooped his head. Why couldn't he have convinced Bill to leave? If he'd been able to manage the crowd better, all of Evelyn's family might have escaped alive. Lost in a morass of guilt and regret, something irreparable broke in Hank's heart. He'd never be the same from this day on. Hank leaned his head into Evelyn's lap.

Evelyn stroked his hair until Hank calmed. All sounds faded, even the wailing sirens and women. She slipped a slender, ice-cold finger under his chin and lifted Hank's gaze again to hers. "You know what happened to them, don't you?"

"Your brother was the bravest man I've ever seen."

Evelyn stiffened. "Was?" Her hand crept to her throat.

"Bill climbed to the top of the stepladder over the animal chute and lifted—no, tossed—dozens of people to safety." In his mind's eye, Hank saw Bill again. Stalwart, unflappable, and as strong as a lumberjack. "He threw Jamie to me, and I put him in the arms of a man I trusted to get him out."

"And Helen?" Evelyn grabbed the collar of Bill's shirt with both fists.

"She was trapped against the bars and trampled. The last I saw her, she was buried three deep by people on top of her."

Not letting go of the chambray, Evelyn's fists pounded a slow rhythm against Hank's breast, each blow increasing in intensity. "Bill?"

"He threw Lily across, and she refused to leave the tent."

Hank welcomed every thump, but suddenly Evelyn stilled. "He wouldn't leave Helen." Evelyn clutched the honey brown hair at the sides of her head, and it tumbled loose from the bobby pins. "He'd never leave her." Her arms fell limply to her lap, and one wispy curl fell across her cheek as the light left her eyes. "Oh, dear God. Bill's dead."

Hank leaped to his feet to steady Evelyn as her eyes rolled back into her head. He eased her to the ground and straightened her skirt to protect her modesty.

"Help!" Hank's cry went unheeded.

So he cried out in prayer to the only one who could possibly answer.

Dappled sunlight filtered through the leafy branches that obscured the sky. Evelyn blinked a few times and attempted to get her bearings. Sounds returned, and the bustle of activity around her came into focus. The hospital.

Bill. And Helen, both dead. But how could this be? Evelyn strained to sit up, but a giant, gentle hand pushed against her shoulder. "There you are. You left me for a minute or two."

Hank. He leaned into her field of vision, but Evelyn did not welcome the sight. Even though she craved the comfort he offered, she pushed his hand away and sat up. He withdrew somewhat, but she would not be swayed by chivalry. She stood without accepting his help and stepped closer to Hank than a polite person would. "You lied to me."

"I didn't lie . . ." Hank blinked twice and swallowed. "Not exactly. I never said Bill and Helen were alive."

"A lie of omission. You should have told me right away they were dead." And he should have, right? Even though it would make no difference, Evelyn had every right to know. But the rock in the pit of her stomach told the truth—the news would have been devastating no matter when it was delivered.

"I thought it would be better to wait until we know what happened to the children." Hank's gaze flitted away. "But I couldn't let you go in without knowing."

"Who are you to make decisions like that for me?"

"I thought I was a friend."

"I thought so too, but now I'm reconsidering." A wave of dizziness crashed on Evelyn's shore, and Hank steadied her again. This time, she permitted it. With Bill and Helen no longer alive, the chain to Evelyn's anchor was broken. She'd be adrift, unmoored. No parents or grandparents. No husband. A strong yearning for George swirled like a vortex, threatening to suck her underwater so deep she'd never surface. After all the tragedy in her life, why would God allow Evelyn's two remaining shipmates to be lost at sea?

But no. There were two little mates to be found. Perhaps Lily and Jamie had followed their parents to safe harbor in heaven. But perhaps they were lost and alone, with only Aunt Evie to rescue them. She must not sink in grief. She had to batten the hatches and sail on, heedless to the tempest.

Hank stood and extended a hand, and Evelyn accepted it. "Do you still want me to come with you?"

Hank's eyes—not the gray of a storm but the blue of fair skies—radiated hope. And strength. Something Evelyn needed as much as a sailor needed a compass. She shrugged. "What do they say? Any port in a storm."

Hank put a hand on the small of Evelyn's back and guided her toward the entrance. Evelyn's steps felt wooden, and for all the world the ground swelled and ebbed like she stood topside on a schooner in Long Island Sound.

Time to find her sea legs.

Chapter Thirteen

Agitated people lined up five deep at the information desk, which was manned by one pitiful, frazzled volunteer. She sputtered at every question and flipped through the pages of a yellow notepad, but she failed to answer even one inquiry in the moments Hank watched. Getting in line served no purpose.

Before Hank suggested a different course of action to Evelyn, a stout nurse in a crisp but blood-stained uniform marched down the hallway like Napoleon to Waterloo. Maybe she'd be more effective. She surely looked made of sterner stuff than the volunteer, but madness fomented in the crucible of the unknown had poisoned almost everyone.

"All right, listen up!" The nurse's voice had the resonance of a Marine drill instructor. Throaty and full, it commanded attention. "Make a line. Single file. We are doing our best to take care of the injured and assist families, but this chaos isn't helping." When no one obeyed her command, she bellowed, "Get in line or get out!"

In the scramble for the best position, Hank's bulk gave him an immediate advantage. Only about ten people were ahead of them, but kindhearted Evelyn waved an elderly man to stand in front of her. His yarmulke askew, he eyed her like she was an angel. Perhaps she was.

With a gentle pat on his forearm, Evelyn asked, "Who are you looking for?"

"My w—" The man choked back a sob and centered his headpiece on the crown of his head. He pushed up his round, wire glasses, cleared his throat, and tried again to speak. "Rosie Lasoff. My wife. I've searched everywhere, but I can't find her."

Many of the dead who couldn't escape had been women and children. In the mad rush for exits, foul, heartless men had shoved aside the weakest, those most needy and deserving of assistance. This day had proven that not all men were heroes.

But then there was Bill.

"I'm Mrs. Benson, and I'm looking for my family as well. Don't you have anyone to search with you?" Evelyn brushed some lint from the shoulder of the man's threadbare shirt.

It jarred Hank again to hear Evelyn speak her married title. Hard to think of her as a missus, but such was the fate of many a young woman in wartime.

"My daughter is on her way, but she lives in New Haven. I hope by the time she gets here I'll have found her mother." The gentleman wiped away a tear. "We've been married fifty-five years. My fondest wish is to make it to fifty-six."

Evelyn kept up a constant stream of conversation with the man until they approached the desk. Speaking to the volunteer, she said, "This is Mr. Lasoff. He's looking for his wife, Rosie. She's in her seventies, slender in build, and she was wearing a blue frock."

The nurse stood like a guard dog over the volunteer who searched her tablet. She muttered to herself until she found the name. "Yes. Mrs. Lasoff. She's been admitted for a broken ankle, but otherwise she's fine. She's in Ward B. Down that hallway to the end, then turn left."

Mr. Lasoff slumped into Evelyn's embrace and wept openly. "Thank you, dear Mrs. Benson. I'll never forget your kindness."

Evelyn summoned an orderly, and the young buck smiled at her in a way Hank found licentious. He emitted a warning grunt before he could stop it. Evelyn looked at him strangely, but the orderly got the message. He trundled Mr. Lasoff down the hall to his happy reunion.

The sight caused the ache in Hank's throat to throb. They simply had to find the children, and they must be well. Hank couldn't tolerate the thought of any other outcome. Evelyn watched Mr. Lasoff's departure, and she exhaled a deep breath.

"Next!" The hospital matron shouted at Evelyn although she was easily in hearing distance. Evelyn's future would be fraught with trouble. Couldn't she savor just a moment of contentment?

Hank glowered at the nurse. Unintimidated, she stared right back.

The little volunteer asked, "Name, please?"

"I'm searching for a boy and a girl, Jamie and Lily Halstead. Jamie is two years old, wearing a matching nautical short set, but he's big for his age—" Evelyn faltered.

Hank finished the descriptions. "His sister, Lily, is eight, and she was dressed in a Dorothy costume."

The nurse asked, "Have you checked the school?"

Evelyn found her voice again. "Yes. They weren't there."

"And the morgue?"

The nurse's question made Hank stiffen. "Are there two children here matching these descriptions or not?"

Evelyn's small hand found her way into his. "Please, ma'am," she addressed the insensitive bully, "if they are here, I'm the only one—" Evelyn took a hard swallow.

A rustle of papers on the yellow tablet indicated at least one of the two women cared about Evelyn's distress. The volunteer scrutinized the list for a moment, raised doleful eyes to Evelyn, and said, "I'm sorry. There's no evidence they're here."

Fingers fueled with the strength of a grieving woman gripped Hank's to the point of pain, a reminder Hank welcomed. It relieved his guilt to suffer for his failure.

The brusque nurse softened somewhat, saying, "If you'd like to search for your son and daughter, you're welcome to visit the children's ward."

"Oh, they're not—"

Hank stopped Evelyn's admission with a squeeze of his fingers. Hers loosened, and he stopped himself before crushing her hand. "Thank you, ma'am. Can you point us that direction?"

The nurse complied, and when Hank refused a guide, he and Evelyn walked in the indicated direction.

"Why did you cut me off?" Spitfire Evelyn had returned.

"It's better they assume you're the children's mother. Then there is no obstacle to you finding and claiming them while they determine your identity."

Some of the starch left Evelyn's spine, and she wiped moisture from her upper lip. "I hadn't thought of that, but you're probably right."

Pushing through a set of double doors, Hank guided Evelyn down a long hallway, past moaning and weeping adults. The sounds of suffering were almost too great to bear. Only the thought of sweet Lily lying alone in a hospital bed kept Hank from shepherding Evelyn out a side door.

The nurse had said the ward would have a sign, and it did. Grim, foreboding cement blocks were painted an indeterminate color somewhere between beige and green. The door's windows contained a metal mesh grate that made them look more like prison doors than those of a hospital.

Evelyn placed a hand on the door to push through, but she hesitated. She drew aside and leaned against the wall. Bending forward at the waist, she gulped lungfuls of heaving breaths.

Hank steadied her. "Hey, now. You'd better sit down somewhere."

She stood again, but her complexion was as green as the Wicked Witch of the West. "No. This will pass. The children need me, and I won't let them down. But before we go in, would you offer a prayer? I need strength."

Hank would rather she'd slapped him. He hadn't prayed out loud since he was a boy of eleven who'd told his father he was too old to say the blessing for meals. Besides, why would God listen to the appeal of such a sinner? Perhaps even someone who was guilty of murder? He'd have to refuse.

"Please."

Evelyn's plea pricked Hank's shame. How could he deny such a simple request when this good woman had no one else to comfort her? How many ways could he be inadequate? He needed to set his reluctance aside and say a prayer, even if it only rose as high as the ceiling. He bowed his head, but no words came. What would his father have prayed?

A scripture Hank had memorized at his mother's knee came to his rescue like a rope dangled to a man clinging to a cliffside. "God is our refuge and strength, a very present help in trouble. Therefore, we will not fear, though the earth be removed, and though the mountains be carried into the midst of the sea."

As soon as the words passed Hank's lips, others flowed. From whence they came, he did not know. "Lord God, we seek Your help. Calm our fears in this time of great distress. Lead us to Lily and Jamie and grant us courage to face whatever we find. Amen."

Hank squashed the thought he was a hypocrite. He still believed in God, though he'd quit having fellowship with Him. God might be judgmental enough to ignore Hank, but He'd surely not abandon Evelyn now. Or Lily and Jamie.

Peace swept Evelyn's features, her brows and mouth relaxing. An ethereal beauty replaced the worry lines. She'd never appeared more like an angel.

"Thank you. I'm ready now." She pushed open the doors and walked through.

What would she find? Hank's hand shook, but he followed.

"How could two children have simply vanished?" Evelyn collapsed again onto the outside bench where Hank had made his horrible confession. He sat apart, apparently distancing himself lest they touch. Evelyn did the same.

Hank's hand gravitated toward hers, but he drew it back. "We'll find them. We need to keep searching and have faith."

Faith? Ha. What good had faith done Evelyn today? It only inflated her hopes like a dirigible filled with hydrogen. When reality punctured the silk, she'd fall back to earth faster than the *Hindenburg*.

"The nurse said we should check the Brown School again. If they weren't badly injured, that's where they would be sent. This is good news, really." Hank stood, tightened his belt, and hailed a cab. "Let's go. They're waiting for us, and they need their aunt."

Evelyn climbed in the cab, which smelled like smoke. Everything in Hartford stunk like an ashtray. Evelyn wiped her nose and blew it, but it didn't help. She clutched her pocketbook and watched familiar scenery go by without noticing its passing until the cab stopped again in front of Brown School. Concrete evidence life was leading her in circles today.

Hank hopped from the car, rounded the rear, and opened Evelyn's door. When she grasped his helping hand, she allowed herself to receive the comfort it offered. What use was it to hang on to foolish resentment over a perceived lie? Although Hank was a near-stranger, he'd helped her when no one else would.

Evelyn paid the cabbie with her mad money, and once again put her hand in the crook of Hank's elbow. The same volunteer manned the desk, but Mrs. Witt wasn't present. No parents stood in line, meaning there must have been many reunions. She checked her watch. Six o'clock. Had she only been searching for four hours? It seemed like four months. Her stomach growled, and Evelyn squelched the protest.

"I remember you, ma'am." The frazzled girl's voice sounded somewhat stronger than earlier. "You can go back without an escort. Only a few children are here, but maybe you'll get lucky. We've put them all together in classroom three."

Luck? Evelyn had always believed in providence, but today's events had shaken that belief to its core. Perhaps fate was truly in charge—a faceless conglomeration of nature and human choices. If God was Master of the Universe, surely His goodness would force His hand to action since He had the power to intervene. A loving God would never allow innocent children to die in such a gruesome way.

When they opened the door, a harried woman stood watch. A quick scan of the dozen or so children revealed no toddlers among them, and no gingham pinafore either. Another waste of time. But if they weren't at the hospital and weren't here, they could only be at the—

"Wait. Take a close look, Evelyn. Is that her?" Hank pointed to a weary waif wrapped in a blanket. Like dark chocolate pools, wide brown eyes were turned their direction, but there was no acknowledgement from the child of knowing them.

Evelyn stepped closer, and joy exploded in her breast. She wasn't wearing her own clothes, and her chestnut hair was no longer in its lovely style, but the girl was definitely Lily. She ran to her niece and scooped her into a fierce embrace. "Lily! I've found you! Everything's all right, darling."

When there was no recognition whatsoever from the girl, Evelyn thought she might be mistaken. The child lay in her arms as limp as a worn-out Raggedy Ann doll. Her vacant eyes didn't focus on Evelyn's face, and her shallow breathing didn't deepen. No sign of her effervescent niece remained. She might as well have been a stranger.

"Lily?" Evelyn's question evoked no response.

Hank knelt beside them and took Lily's hand in his own. "Dorothy? Do you remember me? Fraidy Freddie?"

Lily lurched to awareness and flung herself into Hank's waiting arms. She struck his Adam's apple with her shoulder and tightened both arms around his neck like a noose. Her legs wrapped around his waist, and she flattened against him like a baby monkey with her mother. She rubbed her full face in his shirt and squeezed her eyes shut. Her tears flowed freely, but she said not a word.

The wary attendant approached and surveyed Evelyn from stem to stern. "Is she yours? She don't act like she knows you."

"She's my—"

"Yes. She belongs to us." Hank wrapped his arms around Lily, and he rubbed small circles on her back.

But the "us" was only for show. A waitress and a clown couldn't form a relationship in the throes of disaster. It sounded like the plot of a dime store novel.

"We'll take her home now." Hank's baritone voice held all the authority Bill's would have. "Does she have her shoes?"

A glance downward revealed Lily's little pink toes rolled toward the soles of her feet as she hooked her ankles around Hank's waist. He tried to set her down, but she only clung tighter.

The attendant rubbed a finger under her nose and sniffed. "She arrived about an hour ago, dropped off by a couple who took her in, fed her, and let her have a nap. They said her clothes was ruined, so they gave her some of their daughter's."

Another couple entered, spied their son, and wept for joy as they rushed to his side.

The attendant turned toward the happy family. "I gotta go now. I'm supposed to be sure everyone is legit."

"Come on." The urgency in Hank's voice got Evelyn's feet moving. "Let's get out of here." He reached into his pocket, pulled out Lily's shoe, and showed it to her.

Lily's head tilted, and her eyes softened, but not even the sight of her beloved shoe was enough incentive to make her release her hold on Hank.

Hank turned and strode for the door. "It's been a long day, Dorothy. Let's return to Kansas."

Chapter Fourteen

The doors of home opened with a genial embrace, and Evelyn relished it. When she'd last left, she'd thought Bill and Helen might still be alive. Although her head knew they were dead, her cheeky heart challenged the notion. If she could just pretend, she'd make it through this evening.

Hank still carried Lily, who had not spoken a single word since they found her. Nor would she allow herself to be pried from Hank's arms. He had mumbled something about an unusual connection fueled by shock, but Evelyn couldn't understand it. Why wouldn't Lily come to her? Had her psyche been damaged somehow, and would she ever be herself again?

The loss of Lily's innocent vivaciousness felt like an amputated limb. This morning the child had only been worried about whether she'd be allowed to wear her red shoes, and now they meant nothing to her. Her parents had both been alive, and she had nothing but joy to expect from the events of the day. The speed with which tragedy stripped a person bare was nothing less than terrifying.

Hank gently shut the front door behind him and kept up his stream of conversation with Lily. She only responded to yes or no questions, but at least she reacted. That was something to be thankful for.

"Would you like something to eat?" Hank's considerate question provoked a shake of chestnut brown curls.

"Banana?"

No.

"Toast?"

No. Lily swiped a tear.

"Worms?"

A teeny twitch of her mouth was the first sign Lily was still there. Locked inside a frail, traumatized shell, but there, nonetheless.

Evelyn took weary steps into the kitchen, grabbed Lily's favorite Woody Woodpecker tumbler, and filled it with the last of Helen's lemonade. Evelyn succumbed to the temptation to take a small sip, but she struggled to swallow it. How long would it be before she could tolerate drinking lemonade again?

She returned to the living room and used her best mom voice. "Lily, take a drink. It's time for bed. Let Freddie go."

Evelyn reached out a hand, and Hank attempted yet again to set Lily on her feet. He leaned over, but Lily locked her legs tighter. Hank recoiled from the scream she emitted right into his ear.

"Young lady, that's quite enough. Let go of Freddie and come to bed. *Now.*" The emphasis on the last word always worked for Helen, but evidently it didn't hold the same magic for Evelyn.

"It's okay. Let me carry her up." Hank peeled Lily away until he could look her in the eye. "Would you like that, sweetheart?"

Lily nodded, leaned her head against Hank's shoulder, and stuck her thumb in her mouth. She had given up thumb-sucking years ago, but Evelyn wasn't about to argue tonight. With anything.

"Okay then, let's go." Evelyn led the way up the stairs, with Hank's heavy, even tread following from behind. His weight made the third step creak, just like it always did for Bill. He'd meant to fix it, but . . .

Oh, dear God, would every memory snuff out the breath from Evelyn's lungs? The house had always seemed alive, a recorder built of mortar and brick that had preserved every sound of life and laughter. Now, the echo of emptiness betrayed Evelyn's thoughts and made pretending harder.

Evelyn snapped on the light beside Lily's bed, set down the glass of lemonade, and turned back the baby-pink quilt that bore Helen's even, neat stitches. She fluffed the feather pillow, and when Hank sat on the end of the bed, she fetched a fresh pair of Lily's pajamas from her dresser drawer.

Softening her voice to a low tone, Evelyn said, "We need to change you for bed, darling. Come now, help Aunt Evie." When Lily didn't respond, Evelyn took hold of her bicep and tugged. In a firmer voice, she said, "I'm doing this with or without your help. So choose. Will this be agreeable, or will we have a fight on our hands?"

Lily was so still Evelyn's heart broke. Along with it, her resolve. Lily could sleep in what she wore. This wasn't a hill to die on.

Hank spoke up, and Lily laid a hand on his cheek as his mouth moved. "Dorothy, you're back home. There's no witches, no flying monkeys, and you're the only Munchkin here. Time for bed now, sweetling. You'll sleep better in your pajamas. Will you put them on?"

Silence.

"For Fraidy Freddie?" Hank steepled his fingers and begged.

Lily giggled, the sound sweeter than Bit-O-Honey.

"Hooray! But Freddie shouldn't see a girl change clothes." He covered his eyes and turned his back. "Let Aunt Evie do it. Hurry!"

Lily scrambled off Hank's lap, and in a flash, she was dressed and under the covers. Hank placed a tender kiss on her forehead and said, "Good night, Dorothy."

The wails of a brokenhearted girl made Hank rebound as if he was tethered to a rubber band and Lily held the ends. He knelt on the floor beside her and stroked her hair until she quieted. "Would you like me to stay until you're asleep?"

Hank glanced Evelyn's way, and she nodded agreement. She scooted the tiny chair of Lily's vanity beside the bed. When Hank sat, it groaned under his weight. "Okay then. Here we are."

Earlier that day, Hank had offered such a comforting prayer. "Would you like Hank to say your night-night prayer?"

Hank stiffened at the question, but Lily nodded yes.

Evelyn breathed her own prayer, asking God to send comfort when it seemed she couldn't. Inadequacy coiled in the pit of her stomach like a viper. Soon, it would strike.

Then what would she do?

———————◆◆———————

Pray? Again? Whether he wanted to or not, it seemed Hank was destined today to speak to the Almighty. This time, however, no words came. This child had witnessed unspeakable, gory death, and she'd been parted from her parents forever. What could Hank possibly say to a God who'd sanctioned that?

A melody intruded on his mental rant, accompanied by words he'd not sung since he was a boy in Sunday school. They repeated on a loop until Hank found himself singing without meaning to.

> *Jesus loves me, this I know*
> *For the Bible tells me so.*
> *Little ones to Him belong;*
> *They are weak, but He is strong.*

Evelyn joined in on the chorus with a sweet alto, the harmony perfect with Hank's baritone.

> *Yes, Jesus loves me.*
> *Yes, Jesus loves me.*

By the time they reached the final refrain of the familiar song, Lily mouthed the words although she did not sing.

> *Yes, Jesus loves me.*
> *The Bible tells me so.*

Could life be so simple? Could all the grand philosophies of centuries past be distilled into the words of a children's song? The Bible clearly stated, "God is love." Could His love be strong enough, vast enough to bridge the gap between the circumstances of life and heavenly peace?

Hank tucked in the quilt that swaddled Lily, and her eyelids began to droop. Soon, her breathing came in a soft, even rhythm. Hank watched, mesmerized by her serenity in slumber after such a dreadful day.

If God tucked Hank under a blanket of eternal love, would it smother the flames of his anger and grief?

Maybe. Maybe so.

Darla arrived like a balmy spring breeze after a frigid winter. Comfort, confidence, and concern swirled around her in little eddies of encouragement. Evelyn had never known a truer friend.

"I'll watch over Lily like she was my very own. Don't give a thought to worry." Having stopped by her home to change, Darla had tied her hair up in a kerchief. Her blue seersucker slacks and short-sleeved sweater were immaculate. Everything about the woman was soft, in sharp contrast to her diner persona, proven by the fact she didn't challenge Hank's presence. At least, not yet.

Hank looked at the floor and shifted his weight to his other foot.

"I'm surprised Charlie let you go early." Evelyn still marveled at the modern-day miracle.

"I didn't give him no choice." Darla smirked. "I called his mother and told her Charlie needed her real bad. She came right over. Charlie nearly dropped his spatula when he saw her."

Charlie's mother terrified everyone, including Charlie. Evelyn would like to have taken a seat in the corner booth to watch the entertainment. Given the tragedy of the day, Charlie likely wouldn't close till midnight.

Evelyn already felt like she'd run a marathon, but it was only eight o'clock in the evening. She checked her pocketbook and opened the small change purse that held the rest of her mad money. Hardly enough for a cab ride.

"Now, none of that." Darla pulled out a couple of five-dollar bills and shoved them into Evelyn's purse, snapping shut the latch. Before Evelyn could object, she said, "You can pay me back later."

"Thank you." The words seemed so inadequate for such largesse. Darla merely scraped by on her salary. Only one thing was certain during wartime. Everyone rubbed their pennies together.

"So you're going to the. . ." Even Darla struggled to speak the ugly word *morgue*. ". . .the armory?"

"I have to find out what happened to Jamie, and I've exhausted the other options." Evelyn cranked up her courage and said uglier words. "Bill and Helen are likely dead. Someone will need to identify and claim their bodies."

Darla shuffled backward a couple of steps. When her calves hit the sofa, she plonked down like her legs had lost all strength. "No, baby. They can't be dead."

Evelyn peered at Hank, but he didn't seem inclined to answer. "Hank saw what happened, and he thinks they didn't survive. Anyway, going to the armory is a necessary step." She ran her forearm through the straps of her pocketbook and stood as straight as a schooner's mainmast. "Thank you for staying with Lily. We'll be back as soon as we can."

"I'll stay all night if I need to." Darla stood, her feet slightly apart and her weight evenly balanced. "I'd offer to pray for you, but God and I aren't on speaking terms right now."

The statement finally got Hank's eyes off the floor. He studied Darla, and his right hand went to the nape of his neck.

"Don't say such a thing." Evelyn pushed out the words through pursed lips. Darla never listened to scolding, but this was more important than diners who'd been left too long for water refills.

"Naw. I'm mad at a God who would let such a thing as this happen to a bunch of women and children who weren't doing nothing but trying to have a little fun." Darla crossed her arms. "Either God didn't care, or He was lookin' the other way, or something. If He was as good and powerful as everyone says, He'd a stopped it."

The words bordered on blasphemy, but hadn't Evelyn entertained the same thoughts? She'd not been bold enough to speak them aloud—that was Darla's long suit.

Hank cleared his throat. "We will have plenty of time to sort this out in the days to come, but it's getting late. Let's go, Evelyn."

Darla rediscovered her scrappiness. "That's a mighty friendly address for someone who met her only yesterday. Try Mrs. Benson."

"Hush now. Hank—I mean, Mr. Webb—has been a faithful friend all day. He's helped me when no one else could. We can set aside social conventions for one day, right? Especially today."

"Well—" Darla stepped up to Hank and poked a stubby index finger in his chest. "No funny business, got it?"

Hank didn't back off, not one bit. "Ma'am, there's absolutely nothing funny about anything today. Your friend is very safe with me."

Darla startled Evelyn with a hug. She loved Darla to pieces, but the bristly woman never hugged anyone. Tears threatened a return, but Evelyn banished them. She allowed the rare embrace to last a few extra seconds, then disentangled herself. Darla's eyes shone with impending tears as well, and she'd never forgive herself if they fell.

Evelyn changed the subject. "Just one thing, Darla."

"Yes, dear. Anything for you."

"Please don't wash the glasses in the sink. I'd like to do it myself."

"Are you sure?"

"Never more certain in my life."

The strange request silenced Darla, a rare feat. Evelyn would explain later, but if she started down that road right now, it would only lead to a meltdown.

Hank opened the door like a gentleman. Evelyn passed through, savoring another whiff of Bill's Old Spice. She marched down the sidewalk like she was headed for the guillotine. An apt comparison, because Evelyn felt as if a vital part of her body was about to be amputated.

———————◦•◦———————

Hank and Evelyn joined a long queue of anxious, weeping people facing the most horrific day of their lives. City officials limited how many people could be present in the armory at a time, so everyone made agonizingly slow progress.

Hank used the time to contemplate his reaction to Darla's indictment of God. He couldn't argue with her logic. A good and merciful God would have snuffed out the flames before they climbed the canvas. But wasn't that the job of the seat men? And why weren't the fire extinguishers in place? How much was God responsible for the failures of men?

Throughout the emergency, people had made decisions and acted upon them without God's approval. Those choices weren't God's fault. Where did the providence of God end and the responsibility of man begin? Was God's power limited by the free will of mankind?

And what about his own choices? Hank should have been more forceful with Eddie in reporting Russell as a deranged firebug. And he should have grabbed Bill by the seat of his pants when the tent collapse was imminent, dragging him out of danger even if he didn't want to go. So was Bill's death his own fault? Or Hank's? Or, if he set the fire, Russell's?

Hank's thoughts chased each other like two squirrels up a tree trunk in mating season. Around they went in rapid-fire circles, one leading to another until Hank's head throbbed. He massaged his temple until a gentle hand on his forearm interrupted his internal frenzy.

"Headache?" Evelyn patted his arm twice.

Yes. A bigger headache than this softhearted woman needed to understand. None of today's events were Evelyn's fault. To prevent his turmoil from spilling into words, Hank simply nodded.

Evelyn scrounged through her purse and brought out a bottle of aspirin like it was a blue ribbon pie in the county fair. "There you are! I knew you were in there." Triumphantly, she screwed open the lid, took Hank's hand, and shook two tablets into it. She closed his hand around them. "Now all we need is a glass of water."

No. Not true. There wasn't enough water in the whole universe to make Hank swallow his angst and confusion. He'd need more than a simple glassful. He'd need immersion.

Hank chewed the tablets and swallowed. A nasty taste filled his mouth, but it was no more bitter than the flavor of his soul.

Chapter Fifteen

Hank had never pondered the sound of death. In the burning tent, wails, screams, and angry shouts had combined with the crackle of advancing flames. Inanimate objects like canvas and poles had groaned like living beings, seemingly in anguish. He no longer had to wonder what hell sounded like.

But death sounded different at the State Armory. The hushed conversations of shell-shocked people consumed with dread were punctuated with an occasional shriek of anguish. At the sound, everyone shrank in fear like Londoners during the blitzkrieg. Would the next bomb of grief drop on their heads? The uncertainty was crippling.

A police car topped with a loudspeaker blared the names and locations of people who had been identified among the living. Joyous people jumped out of line and into cabs, but not Evelyn. She appeared more and more dazed, and Hank focused on the announcements in case Jamie's name was called and she missed it.

Hank kept a weather eye out for anyone from the circus who might demand his return to the rail yard. He'd not seen anyone since leaving the grounds with Evelyn, and he hoped it stayed that way. Anyone from the circus who was injured would have been treated by the Ringling doctor, so he felt safe at the hospital. But the possibility of encountering Eddie or an official from the circus was much higher at the armory.

Hartford policemen and Connecticut State Troopers patrolled the streets, chasing away ghoulish spectators. Tragedy brought out the worst in some people, and Hank's right eyelid twitched at the thought anyone would get a twisted thrill from watching Evelyn stand in line to identify her dead brother and his wife.

The Red Cross had set up a table with refreshments, but few people ate or drank anything. After Lily fell asleep, Hank had asked Evelyn if he could fetch her a sandwich, but she politely declined. Hank's stomach growled, but a snowflake would appear in Hades before he'd take a bite if she didn't.

At last, they stepped inside the lobby. In the corner, under a sign labeled VOLUNTEER NURSE SIGN-IN, ladies in crisp, white uniforms also stood in a line. As they received their assignments, they hurried soundlessly away on their white shoes with rubber soles.

A bank of extra phones had been brought in. Their insistent rings skittered up Hank's spine and irritated his already-frayed nerves. An attractive, youngish woman with long brunette curls sat behind a sturdy wooden table, her pen poised to take notes as people registered. Her cheery yellow dress seemed out of place, as if sunshine had pierced the clouds right after a thunderbolt. Although she wore a serious expression, her demeanor was kind and calm. She asked, "May I have your name, please?"

The attendant's question hung in the air for a few seconds too long without an answer from Evelyn. The woman leaned forward and asked again. "I know this is difficult for you, ma'am, and I'm sorry. Would you please tell me your name?"

When Evelyn still didn't answer, Hank wrapped an arm around her waist. She leaned on him without hesitation, and her ghostly complexion spurred him to action. Snapping his fingers, he got the attention of a male volunteer and said, "A chair, please, and make it quick."

Evelyn's expression put the man in overdrive, and when the chair bumped the back of her legs, she collapsed into it. Huge, stormy-gray eyes pleaded to him without words.

"Mrs. Evelyn Benson. She's here to search for her brother and his wife, Mr. and Mrs. William Halstead."

The woman wrote in beautiful, flowing script. "And Mr. Benson, what's your first name?"

Hank's ears burned, a sure sign they were turning red. "I'm not her husband. I'm a—"

Evelyn found her voice and rescued Hank. "He's a dear friend. Hank Webb."

The attendant frowned and looked toward a man wearing the sash of an officer in the Civil Defense. He was deep in conversation with a legionnaire. She leaned forward and whispered, "I'm not supposed to allow anyone in except family members."

Evelyn clutched her middle and began rocking herself. She turned limpid eyes on the attendant. "Please, miss. Don't make me do this alone. I couldn't bear it."

The attendant made her decision and communicated with Hank. "Mister *Benson*," a brief pause indicating her intentions, "please give me descriptions of those you seek for our records, and I'll let you *both* go to the armory."

Surely the Almighty would permit a little white lie under the circumstances. Hank completed the physical description with amazing accuracy, the faces, clothing, and general details flowing from images forever etched in his brain. He reached a hand to Evelyn, and she clung to it like a woman gripping a rock while dangling from the edge of a precipice.

In a few minutes, a nurse and a trooper came to their sides, and they ushered them upstairs into the temporary morgue which had been set up on the drill floor. Evelyn's heels clacked on the highly polished wood. The stench of smoke and burned flesh assaulted Hank's nostrils, and he reached under Bill's shirt to pull his undershirt over his nose. Evelyn took a handkerchief from her pocketbook and did the same.

The trooper, a round-bellied mountain of a man with hair plastered to his head by perspiration, stopped inside the door. How could he endure the smell? He inspected the card the registration attendant had given him, and said, "I'm Sergeant Thomas Amato of the Connecticut State Police. I understand you're seeking a man and his wife. Perhaps we won't have to look very far. I'd like to make this as easy as I can."

The bodies had been organized on cots according to age and gender. The feet of the first man's body stuck out from underneath the blanket shod in expensive, soot-covered wingtips. Too rich for Bill's humble salary.

Hank scanned the long row of corpses, and the horror of Evelyn's task spread through his gut like fast-acting poison. A wave of nausea attacked, and he might cast up his accounts right on the spot. Disregarding the foul smell, he pulled down the shirt, inhaled through his nose, and exhaled through his mouth.

Based on Bill's description, Amato led them to several cots. Scars, birthmarks, and dental work were noted on a card and pinned to the blankets along with envelopes containing jewelry that might aid in identification. None of the bodies had information that exactly matched Bill.

After searching through the effects of the last adult male without success, Evelyn's face brightened. She looked heavenward before turning hopeful eyes on Hank. "Maybe the man you saw wasn't Bill. Or maybe he escaped after you left the tent."

The optimistic thought thudded in Hank's midsection like a punch. Denial was a natural part of grief, but there could be no doubt. The dead hero was Bill.

Amato placed a gentle hand on Evelyn's arm and garnered her attention. "Ma'am, before you get your hopes too high, there is one more possibility." He addressed Hank. "I'm sorry, but it's a grim prospect."

Evelyn wilted like a thirsty bloom in the scorching July sun.

Hank steadied her before she simply crumpled to the floor. "Evelyn, do you need a drink?"

"No. Let's get this over with."

The trooper signaled a volunteer who brought a cool cup of water to Evelyn despite her objection. "Please have a drink. We don't want you to faint."

Evelyn relaxed her clenched jaw and took a sip. Then two. Then she drained the small paper cup. She crumpled it in her hand, turned to

Amato, and said, "Now, show me. No matter how horrible it is, I need to find my brother."

Hank's admiration soared. How strong was this woman? All over the room, people screamed, wept, or fainted. Evelyn's loss would be just as great. She was already a war widow, and now the two most important adult relatives in her life were also dead.

Amato signaled the nurse, who'd been silent, to follow them to a single cot along a side wall. Body parts didn't protrude from the edges of the green wool blanket, thank God, but the mound underneath was a little larger than most. The sergeant reached down, unpinned the manila envelope from the blanket, and poured the contents into his meaty hand: two gold wedding bands, a delicate cross necklace, and a man's watch.

At the sight, Evelyn took two steps backward. She covered her mouth with her hand and buried her face in Hank's shoulder. "Please, Hank, will you see if there's an inscription on the watch?"

The watch's plastic face was scorched and badly warped, but someone had already cleaned off the back. Hank picked it up and scanned the inscription. His eyelids and ears felt hot. "Yes. It's engraved."

"What does it say?" Evelyn's question came from far away, like it traveled down a tunnel to reach him.

"To B.H. from E.B."

Evelyn's knees gave way. Hank pitched the watch to Amato and scooped her into his arms. He carried her to a nearby chair and sat her on his lap as she sobbed.

The nurse stood by, smelling salts in hand. How many times had she done this for other bereaved people today?

After clearing his throat, the sergeant said, "Mrs. Benson, I take it this watch belonged to your brother."

Evelyn couldn't manage words. She simply nodded.

After a few minutes of patient waiting, Amato returned to Bill's body and revised the green casualty tag, making the identification official. He straightened, sighed, and returned to Evelyn. "Ma'am, I'm sorry to ask this, but do you recognize the necklace and woman's ring?"

Evelyn returned to self-awareness. She said so only he could hear,

"Hank. Please put me down. People are staring."

Although he enjoyed cradling her, their closeness was entirely inappropriate under the circumstances. Hank might masquerade as Evelyn's husband, but he didn't hold that enviable role. He placed Evelyn on her feet, vacated the chair, and let her sit again.

After arranging her skirt for modesty, she turned to Amato and said, "They belonged to Helen, his wife. But why would Bill have them?"

"Ma'am, this is the hard part." The sergeant got on one knee beside Evelyn and held her hand. "In time, you may see it as a blessing. This couple has been the subject of lots of chatter among the volunteers. It's clear their love for each other was a powerful force."

Evelyn raised her chin even as tears flowed unattended down her cheeks. "Bill always told Helen the sun would seem dim compared to the brightness of their love. He was such a poet for a man with a stutter." She glanced again toward the cot. "They were found together, weren't they?"

"Not just side by side, ma'am. Their limbs were so intertwined we couldn't separate them, no matter how hard we tried." Amato's voice trembled, and he cleared his throat. "After a while, it seemed wrong to pull them apart. They will need to be buried together. The flames joined their bodies for eternity."

----------◆◆◆----------

Bill—a poet, a romantic, a mountain of strength and dignity despite his speech impediment—dead. Evelyn's head swam, and the sounds in the room faded again as the nurse pushed her head between her knees.

If Hank had told the truth about his demise, Bill *chose* death with Helen instead of life with Evelyn and the children. A thorny vine of resentment grew from the ashes of Evelyn's grief and wound around her breaking heart. Oddly, the fainting spell passed. Evelyn pushed away the smelling salts, sat up, and dried her eyes.

He deserted us. Evelyn attempted to cut off the disturbing conclusion, but it only curled tighter. Bill had chosen not to live without Helen. Now Evelyn would be utterly alone with his two bereaved children to rear.

Lily might never be herself again, and Jamie? *Dear God in heaven, where could he be?*

Amato asked a question, but Evelyn had to ask him to repeat it. A little louder, he asked, "Where would you like the remains sent?"

A cadre of people from various mortuaries hovered around the edges of the hall. Although they were there to help, they still appeared as specters of death. Evelyn couldn't possibly make a decision like that right now. She shuffled through memories of recent funerals at her church but couldn't remember the name of the mortuary who organized them.

The sergeant pulled a scribbled, handwritten list from his pocket and gave it to Evelyn. "I know this is hard, Mrs. Benson, but it's already evening and . . ."

Right. Bodies rotting in the furnace of July. Practicality above all, for goodness' sake. Evelyn scanned the list and a name stood out. She pointed to it.

"Danforth. Very well. Don't worry, I'll take care of it. You can go by tomorrow and make arrangements for the funeral." Amato beckoned two men forward, and they stood by Bill and Helen's cot. "Now, go get a breath of fresh air and a good night of sleep, and tomorrow will be a new day."

Tomorrow? A new day, yes, but the dreaded first day of stepping into the unknown. Suddenly overcome by weariness, Evelyn rose, but her feet disobeyed her command to begin walking. She held out a hand, and Hank's firm, warm grip—which was becoming all too familiar—supported her.

Evelyn was halfway to the exit when she stopped. She turned, seeing the Danforth men carting away the cot with its gruesome but treasured contents, and almost ran into Amato. "Sergeant, I don't think he's here, but my nephew is also missing."

Amato's eyes narrowed. "Why didn't you report it downstairs?"

Hank put his arm fully around Evelyn's waist, and she fought thoughts of it being a pleasant sensation. "We have every reason to believe Jamie is alive. I got him out of the tent and put him in the arms of a man who took him out of danger. He was uninjured."

"Then why put yourself through more agony?" Amato's voice was kind, but his eyes were flinty. "Besides, there's a long line of other people trying to find loved ones."

Evelyn couldn't leave without looking. She just couldn't.

"Please, Sergeant Amato." Hank's voice was like velvet. "Don't ask Evelyn to go to sleep tonight wondering if by some terrible happenstance her nephew is here."

Amato softened and led Evelyn to a row of cots she assessed by looking at the lumps under the blankets. Only two matched Jamie's size. One still wore a grimy, brown leather shoe. Not Jamie.

They moved to stand beside the other body. After nodding to the nurse, who was hovering nearby with her smelling salts, Amato peeked underneath the blanket and his face blanched. "Are you sure you want to do this?"

"No, but I must." Evelyn stood next to the sergeant and nodded.

Amato lifted the blanket.

One brief glimpse, and Evelyn welcomed the blessed blackness.

Chapter Sixteen

Darla may have worn seersucker and cotton, but her manner was as imperious as a Russian czarina swathed in ermine. No sooner had Hank arrived with a barely conscious Evelyn than he'd been scolded, thanked, and hustled out the door. It slammed shut behind him, and Hank stood on the porch trying to collect himself. He'd been chained to Evelyn all day, and now he'd been cut loose like an anchor tangled in seaweed.

The horrifying shock of seeing the boy's body, his face completely burned away, had nearly made Hank pass out. The fire had been thorough in erasing the child's identity. He'd like to scrub the memory from his mind, but no bleach in the world would be potent enough.

Amato was a man among men. Not only did he manage to combine compassion with forthrightness, but he'd also tended Evelyn like she was his own daughter. He sent the nurse away and performed her duties himself. When Evelyn had come to, she'd said she didn't know if the body might be Jamie's. Amato promised to track Jamie down himself when he was no longer needed at the armory.

Didn't Evelyn trust Hank? Confusion and exhaustion walk hand in hand, so he chose not to be insulted by her uncertainty.

WHEN THE FLAMES RAVAGED

It would take a detective to figure out what had happened. Hank had carried Jamie from the tent squalling and alive, and he'd handed him off to Clyde—one of the most reliable men Hank had ever met. Then what? Jamie should have been at the school or the hospital, and there was no explanation for why he wasn't.

It took the entire thirty-minute walk back to the yard, where the train was on a side rail, for Hank to clear his mind. In a strange way, it no longer felt like home. Home was a cozy bungalow on Capen Street, where a sweet treasure of a woman was tucked in and asleep by now, he hoped. Common knowledge said tragedy formed artificially strong bonds between people, but nothing about his relationship with Evelyn felt fake.

He'd made a promise, so he swung by the doctor's car for treatment of his burns. They were only first-degree, except for where the blob of paraffin had burned him. The doctor punctured the blister with a sterilized needle, and in an ironic twist which Hank didn't miss, he slathered on a layer of petroleum jelly. But the stitches to close the latest wound Spartacus inflicted hurt like the dickens. The doctor said very few circus employees were injured and none had been killed. A miracle.

A cursory search for Clyde was unfruitful. He wasn't in his berth. Circus people milled in the yard, huddling around burn barrels and conversing in small groups. Some still wore their ruined costumes. Clyde was likely among them somewhere, but exhaustion made Hank seek his own bed. Even so, sleep would be elusive tonight.

Russell's snoring reached Hank's ears even before he tugged the door open. Not surprising. Psychopaths couldn't feel compassion. Had the crazy boy set the fire?

Hank snapped on the light.

Russell stirred, sat up, and rubbed his eyes. "Hey! I was asleep."

"No kidding."

"Why did you wake me up?" Russell stretched his arms, his bare chest glistening with perspiration. Not a smudge of soot anywhere.

"We need to talk. I want answers, and I want them now." Hank yanked Russell's feet and swung them to the floor. He crouched down until he was nose to nose with the boy. "Did you set the fire?"

Russell grabbed his pillow and clutched it to his chest. "Are you crazy? Why would I do that?"

"Because you're as nutty as a pecan pie. You just don't know it."

More sweat beaded on Russell's upper lip. He wiped his forearm across it. "I don't answer to you."

Hank picked up Russell's shirt and tossed it to him. "Then get dressed. We'll go see Eddie. You can tell him why you were spotted in the midway right before the fire."

"I had to go to the bathroom."

"A likely excuse. The fire started near the men's bathroom. Did you and your Zippo have anything to do with that?"

"No! I used the bathroom, and when I came out, I saw the seat men trying to put out the fire. The buckets of water did nothing, and there were no extinguishers." Russell's eyes glittered. "They didn't have a chance."

"Why do you seem so happy about it?"

"You have to admit fire is a beautiful thing. So many colors. So much power." Russell's glazed expression and his even breathing made him look like the victim of Harry the Hypnotist. He belonged in an asylum.

Hank snapped his fingers, and Russell came back to himself. "Where were you after the fire? Why couldn't anyone find you?"

"Clyde handed me a little kid and told me to take him to the hospital. The police was runnin' around like chickens with their heads cut off. He told me the boy was important, and to get him out of there." Russell thrust out his chest. "So I did."

Jamie had been entrusted to a madman? What on earth had Clyde been thinking? Hank's blood boiled like water in a whistling teakettle. "Where did you take him?"

"I got in a cab." Russell grinned.

"Tell me what you did with the boy before I beat it out of you." Hank formed a fist so Russell would know he wasn't funning.

"Okay, okay. Calm down. Sheesh. You'd think the boy was your son or something."

The statement pierced Hank's soul like a javelin. Oh, how he wished he had a life in which he could enjoy a sweet wife and children. "Out with it. Where did you take him?"

"I told the cabbie to take us to the hospital. He did."

"Municipal Hospital?"

"How should I know? I don't live here. It was a big building with lots of people running around." Russell laid back down in his bed and turned his back to Hank. "Now leave me alone. I was sleeping good."

Hank's barely-there control fractured. He grabbed Russell's arm and pulled until the boy hit the floor. Hard. When he jumped to his feet, flailing and kicking, Hank grabbed a handful of Russell's hair and held him at arm's length. The boy had a fist the size of a small melon, but he was no match for Hank's rage.

Soon enough, Russell tired. "Let go of me."

"Are you ready to finish our conversation?"

"Yes. But I still don't know why one kid is so important to you." Russell sat back on his bed and turned impassive eyes on Hank. "Lots of kids died today."

If Hank had allowed himself to speak, the words would have been ones that always provoked his mother to get the soap.

Russell sighed. "I took the kid to the hospital and gave him to a priest."

"What was his name?"

"I don't know. I didn't ask. He was a priest, just standing there in a long black robe."

Hank sat on his own bed and barely managed to remain upright as exhaustion ran over him like a freight train. "Let me get this straight. You took him to the hospital and gave him to a priest, but you don't know his name."

"Right."

"But he was alive, right?"

"Yep. I couldn't get rid of him quick enough. The kid cried the whole time, screaming for his mama."

How many gut punches could Hank endure in one day? If he didn't get some sleep—and soon—he'd hallucinate again. If Jamie had been at the hospital, where was he now? Without another word, Hank fell into his berth while still wearing Bill's clothing and shoes.

"Hey. What about the light?" Russell always whined like a baby.

"Get it yourself."

When the light was out, so was Hank.

———————◆•◆———————

Russell's full-blown scream interrupted Hank's fitful sleep. The dim light through the window shone on Russell as he thrashed and wrestled his pillow. Hank rose and shook him until the boy's teeth rattled.

Russell grunted and awakened with a jerk. A moon ray lit his face in stark light and shadows like one of the plaster demons in the midway's haunted house. In a creepy, even tone he murmured, "She said it was my fault." Russell rifled through his things, found his rumpled shirt, and put it on.

"Who?"

"The woman."

"What are you talking about?"

"I had another dream. A woman came up out of the flames. She pointed at the fire, and then she stared at me and yelled, 'You are the cause of that.'" Russell put on his pants, fastened his belt, and put his shoes on without socks. "I'm getting out of here."

He flipped on the light, knelt on the floor, and rifled through his things, grabbing the picture he'd drawn of the Red Man and his horse. He also pocketed his lighter. With no further words, he bolted from the car.

Hank was hot on his heels. He sprinted until he caught Russell just as he passed one of the burn barrels containing flames that danced into the night air. No other circus folk were around at this hour. He tried to wrest the drawing—which might actually be evidence of a crime—from Russell's hands, but he only got a small corner. The rest tore away, and Russell pitched it into the fire. It immediately incinerated.

In the instant it took Hank to decide it was unsalvageable, Russell had vanished into the darkness.

Who would believe Hank now? Without a scrap of evidence, all he had was his own word. Besides, if he talked to the police, they'd surely connect him to what had happened in Speigletown. Hank would be more likely to end up in jail than Russell.

A hard knock echoed across the lot. When he turned to his railcar, three beefy police officers stood outside. One pounded on the door again and shouted, "Police. Open up!"

Hank was so tired of running. He wanted more than anything to be a man worthy of Evelyn's affection, to say nothing of the gaping wound his disappearance from home had surely inflicted on his parents. Should he fight or flee?

Neither. Hank walked to the car and asked, "Who are you looking for?"

The man who had knocked said, "Hank Webb. He's wanted for questioning. Do you know where he is?"

"I'm Hank."

The policeman shoved Hank toward the street. "Come with us, and no funny business or I'll get out my cuffs."

Hank gave him no reason to be rough, but he was anyway. One of the officers muttered words Hank couldn't hear except for an epithet connected to the words, "Circus freaks."

Whether or not police identified him as a man wanted for murder in Speigletown, New York, being a circus employee in Hartford, Connecticut, was a bad enough indictment for today.

———————•◦•———————

The organ prelude was nearly finished, and Evelyn allowed herself to enjoy the music for its own sake, not the lyrics she'd memorized long ago. They offered little comfort while she still nourished anger at God.

She was a hypocrite, really. Sitting in God's holy sanctuary with a heart of stone, without the tiniest urge to worship or pray. Words suitable for the Almighty's ears wouldn't be the ones she'd speak if given the chance. She would only spew accusations and questions He wouldn't answer. Still, she'd go through the motions for the sake of appearances.

Her mouth and throat were parched. She'd love a draught of Helen's lemonade, but even the last remnants were gone, washed down the sink when she'd lovingly cleansed the two glasses dirtied the last night she'd seen her sister-in-law. The lipstick on Helen's glass had dried to a red smudge, and after several tries, Evelyn had given up scrubbing it off. It could remain there for eternity as far as she was concerned. She patted the tumbler dry, opened the cupboard, and put it in the back corner, never to be used again.

Bill and Helen's funeral would start in a few minutes. Friends, church members, and strangers packed the pews of the South Congregational Church. After the Sunday morning service, everyone had taken a break for lunch and returned to the church for the series of funerals that would take place that day, Bill and Helen's coming first. More than a thousand people were in attendance.

Except one. She'd not seen Hank since he dropped her off at home the night of the fire. Perhaps she'd imagined the affection she sensed in his every word and gesture that day. Goodness knows he had no more reason to come to her aid. He had a job and a life apart from Evelyn's, and besides, he'd be moving on with the circus when their train pulled out.

Still, Evelyn couldn't help but crane her neck once in a while. She was met by sympathetic expressions from congregants who had no idea she searched for Hank. She'd much rather have sat in one of the side alcoves where she wouldn't receive so much attention. Darla would have come, but with Lily so out of sorts, Evelyn had decided not to bring her niece to the funeral. Darla was the only one she trusted to babysit.

And Jamie? Evelyn's nephew seemed to have vanished into thin air. The morning after the fire, Sergeant Amato had taken her to the only other place Jamie might be—Hartford Hospital across town, where a very small percentage of victims had been treated. It had been a long shot, so it hadn't taken long to learn Jamie was not among them. Their search hadn't turned up any leads.

Hank had promised to help in the search, but so far, he'd not reported to her in the two days it had taken to organize the funeral. The whole city was in crisis. Of what importance was the fate of one little boy when hundreds had been killed or injured?

The organ finished with a final crescendo, the last chord of "It Is Well with My Soul," and the sound echoed from the white plaster ceiling and walls long after the musician lifted his hands off the keys with a flourish.

Reverend Archibald mounted the podium and stood behind the pulpit. He raised his arms, and the congregation stood. Evelyn faced forward although everyone else turned to watch the procession. The Wurlitzer organ blasted a hymn Evelyn loved—"Face to Face"—and the words vaulted over the barrier she had formed against spiritual thoughts.

> *Face to face I shall behold Him,*
> *Far beyond the starry sky;*
> *Face to face in all His glory,*
> *I shall see Him by and by.*

Only days ago, that "by and by" had seemed a far-off dream. But death was a capricious enemy, sometimes striking without notice and sweeping people into eternity. Today, Bill and Helen looked upon the face of Jesus, and a small part of Evelyn wished she could be with them.

Bill and Helen's oversized walnut casket had been donated through a charity hastily formed by community leaders. It was adorned with a beautiful spray of red and white roses, also donated. Evelyn was grateful, since she didn't have two pennies to rub together. When the procession passed Evelyn's pew, a light scent of smoke overpowered the fragrance of the flowers. A powerful wave of heartache swept over her, and she tumbled beneath it. Her knees gave out, and she made a spectacle of herself by collapsing on the pew. She had never felt more alone.

The funeral proceeded as it should. Later, Evelyn marveled that she couldn't remember a word Reverend Archibald had said.

Chapter Seventeen

Hank slipped into the back of the church and stood in the narthex with the other latecomers to the funeral, which had been swarmed by people who had learned of Bill's heroism. The inspiring tale had spread both in the newspapers and by word of mouth.

He did not regret coming, although he had to endure the stares and whispers of folks much more appropriately dressed. His "Sunday best," didn't include a suit and tie. Roustabouts had no need for such finery.

To his chagrin, he had arrived right before the sermon was over. The congregants inside the sanctuary stood for the final hymn, "God Moves in a Mysterious Way." The words of the third stanza scraped against his soul like fingernails on a chalkboard.

> *His purposes will ripen fast,*
> *Unfolding ev'ry hour.*
> *The bud may have a bitter taste,*
> *But sweet will be the flow'r.*

Could God's purposes ripen fast, even hour by hour, in this circumstance? Not enough time had passed to process all that would happen as a result of the fire. Hank's interrogation by the police had lasted four grueling hours. When they had asked him for identification, Hank said he'd lost his wallet in the fire. A lie, yes, but a necessary one.

Investigators never discovered his true name and identity, so they dismissed him with the firm order to return to the rail yard and stay there. He arrived shortly after dawn, only to learn five Ringling officials had been arrested and charged with manslaughter, Eddie among them. That night, some of his friends had ventured to a local bar, where they faced harassment from angry locals who said the circus valued their animals more than patrons. A nasty fistfight broke out.

By the second day after the fire, circus folk were not permitted to leave the yard. Most of his fellow employees seemed content with that edict, since hatred and blame for the circus made the threat of more physical violence very real.

But they didn't have a connection to a sweetheart of a woman who needed a friend. Hank still pretended Evelyn was only a friend, but every day that passed without seeing her caused the ever-present ache in his chest to intensify.

When he learned the date of Bill and Helen's funeral from a newspaper announcement, Hank dressed and slipped past the guards. He walked to the church—since a garrulous cabbie might discover he was with the circus—but the trek took too long, making him late.

After the closing prayer, pallbearers carried the casket down the aisle with Evelyn following. Her hollow cheeks and black circles under her eyes made her look like an underfed orphan. Hank tried to elbow his way past other worshippers, but a stocky usher prevented him from reaching her. He wanted to call out, but he'd already received enough unwanted attention. He'd have to catch up to her later.

The graveside service at Spring Grove Cemetery was blessedly brief. The scorching July sun pounded everyone except Evelyn and a few elderly women who had been granted the privilege of sitting under a small tent.

The minister read from Psalm 103.

As for man, his days are as grass: as a flower of the field, so he flourisheth. For the wind passeth over it, and it is gone; and the place thereof shall know it no more. But the mercy of the LORD is from ever-lasting to everlasting upon them that fear him, and his righteousness unto children's children; to such as keep his covenant, and to those that remember his commandments to do them.

The scripture cast a spotlight brighter than the ones under the big top on Hank's problem with God. The Almighty made promises He didn't keep. If the Lord's love was with Evelyn and her family—very devout believers—why had this tragedy befallen them? Why was Evelyn deprived not only of a husband she loved but now also a brother and sister-in-law? Why should Lily have both mother and father ripped away from her? And why should a beloved toddler be swept away like flotsam in the sea?

Hank shouldered his way, very slowly and hopefully unnoticed, to a spot where he could see Evelyn. Her head was bowed, and she wept into a flowered hankie. She never looked up.

A loving God wouldn't do this to her, and a powerful God would have prevented it. Russell's face and that of the Red Man he drew invaded Hank's thoughts. Good and evil were locked in an everlasting struggle, and humans were mere pawns stuck in the middle. What was the use of serving God if He wouldn't protect you?

The hymn sung at the funeral had promised the bitter bud of God's mysterious ways would turn into a sweet flower, but Hank could only see dried weeds.

After she'd shaken the last hand and received the last hug, Evelyn trudged alone down the path through the cemetery toward her home. The crowd rushed off, likely to attend the next funeral. So many people had died that folks might do nothing else all day.

The backyard of Evelyn's home bordered the cemetery, so she would be able to see the mound of Bill and Helen's graves from her bedroom window. The thought of having them nearby should have comforted her, but how would she tolerate the constant reminder of her loss?

The front gate creaked open when she pushed it. Bill intended to oil it, and he also planned to fix the porch light, which only worked sporadically. This home, which had always been a haven, now felt to Evelyn like a gorilla riding piggyback. How would she maintain it, let alone pay the mortgage? Darla wouldn't bring up the subject, but Evelyn hadn't reported to work since the fire. Charlie hadn't called.

She fastened the gate behind her and slogged toward the porch with heavy steps. When she put her key in the door, the gate creaked again. She turned, ready to shoo away reporters who'd been hounding her for interviews.

Hank. What a welcome sight. He trotted up the sidewalk, and Evelyn opened her arms without a second thought to who might be watching. His embrace felt like heaven.

Evelyn peered up into his handsome face, jaw set in stone, but eyes as soft as the wings of a bluebird. The church matrons who lived across the street might cluck like angry hens tomorrow—but today? Evelyn tucked her shoulder under Hank's arm and accepted the clean but slightly wrinkled handkerchief he offered when her tears dampened his white cotton shirt.

"I'm sorry, Evelyn." Hank patted her back between her shoulder blades. "I tried to come sooner, but police ordered us not to leave the rail yard."

"Won't you get in trouble?"

"Only if they catch me." Hank leaned in, his breath tickling Evelyn's neck. "And I don't intend to get caught."

"Where have you been?"

"I was taken in for questioning, but they released me the next day."

Evelyn's mouth went dry. "But you had nothing to do with it."

Hank's gaze traveled across the street, where a window had opened. Mrs. Finkerman's beady eyes stared their way with too much interest. Her neighbor, Mrs. Riegel, a kindhearted lady by reputation, glanced briefly but pulled her curtain. Darla was a perfectly acceptable chaperone, so she peeled herself away from Hank, finished opening the lock, and pushed the door open. "Please, come in."

Darla entered from the kitchen hallway, wiping her hands dry on a towel. She scowled at Hank but said nothing.

Evelyn headed off the impending challenge by asking, "Where's Lily?"

"She's napping."

Before the fire, Lily had declared herself too old to need naps, but now she preferred her bed to anywhere else.

Darla flipped her towel across her forearm in a move Evelyn had witnessed many times at work when her friend had been agitated. "I had plans for this afternoon, but I'll not leave until *he* does. I'll just busy myself in the kitchen." Darla returned to her work, but the clatter of dishes was louder than necessary.

Hank cleared his throat. No evidence of frustration with Darla marred his attractive features. "Has Lily spoken yet?"

"Not a word." Evelyn wanted to break through to Lily with motherly affection, but how could she? She clutched at her cross necklace, one that matched Helen's. Bill had given them both on Valentine's Day, joking that he had two "best girls." Sweet Helen had not a jealous bone in her body. How could Evelyn ever live up to the memory of a woman like that? Tears threatened again, and she squashed them without mercy.

"It's still too soon to worry." After a quick look at the kitchen—where it sounded like Darla was abusing a pot—Hank pulled her into a side hug and released her. "She'll talk when she's ready, and my guess is she won't stop for a month."

"When did you become such an expert on children?"

"Don't forget, I work with circus animals. Most of them are just as spoiled as any child." Hank paled. "I didn't mean to imply—"

At his discomfort, Evelyn obeyed the urge to offer her first genuine smile of the day. "Don't worry. I know Lily is spoiled. I think she's proud of it." Evelyn would pay a lot of money to hear Lily stomp down the stairs and demand a cookie. Or any type of food. She couldn't exist on the little bits she'd been eating.

The front gate creaked again, the sound creeping through the open porch window like a burglar. Evelyn pulled the sheer curtain aside to peek. Cap in hand, Sergeant Amato stood on the front porch and shifted his weight from foot to foot before he rang the doorbell.

Evelyn dashed to the door with Hank shadowing her. She opened it and said, "Please come in."

Amato shook Hank's hand and offered Evelyn a nod of greeting. "I'm sorry to bring news on the day of the funeral, but it can't wait."

Jamie? Evelyn's stomach did a do-si-do, even without a partner.

The sergeant didn't wait for permission to speak. "I've talked to someone who saw Jamie after the fire."

He was alive! Not the burned body at the morgue. Alive, but perhaps injured. Evelyn snatched her purse. "Take me to him, please. I'll let Darla know, and we'll be on our way."

Hank grasped Evelyn's elbow but with a touch as light as a gossamer thread of a spider's web. "Do you know where he is?"

"No. Not exactly." Amato gestured to the sofa. "Mrs. Benson, please, sit down."

The urge to sprint out the door struck Evelyn like a freight train, but she tottered to the sofa and obeyed. Hank sat beside her and held her hand.

Amato sat in the side chair Helen had reupholstered last month. "Like you, I've searched everywhere I can think of to find your lad. I came up empty until a few hours ago."

Hank leaned forward. "Sergeant, just tell us what you've found."

"Sorry." Amato mopped his forehead with his handkerchief. "Most patients were taken to Municipal, but I also thought to search again at Hartford Hospital."

A chill invaded Evelyn's body despite the heat in the room. They'd already sought Jamie at Hartford Hospital without success. Had they somehow missed him? Was he across town right now in a sickbed, all alone? She jumped to her feet, but she had to sit down again.

"Now, now," Sergeant Amato crooned, "don't let yourself get all worked up."

Hank bristled. "She has every right to be worked up. She's been hunting for Jamie ever since the fire. Have you found him or not?"

"No. But I've spoken to a couple of nurses who remember seeing a little boy dressed in a short suit like you've given in Jamie's description. I suggest we take a photo of him, go over there, and ask questions together." Amato stood and tucked his damp handkerchief back in his pocket.

"Are you up to this?" Hank's gentle tone matched the concern in his eyes.

"Honestly, no." Evelyn's answer elicited a frown from Hank. "But I have to be. Will you come?"

"Just try to stop me." Hank stood, pulled Evelyn to her feet, and said to Amato, "Lead the way."

———————⚬⚬———————

Evelyn clutched Jamie's photo to her bosom. Taken on his second birthday, May 25th, he wore a colorful, pointed hat. A splotch of chocolate frosting adorned his nose, but it only made him more adorable.

The search party of three stopped at the desk, where Amato greeted the two nurses he'd met earlier that day. He flashed the photo to the women and conducted the interview like the professional he was. Evelyn felt no more capable of speaking than Lily.

Both women shook their heads and offered sorrowful platitudes. Evelyn's stomach plummeted into her shoes.

Amato thanked them and gestured for Hank and Evelyn to follow. They leapfrogged through the entire hospital one desk at a time until all the nurses looked alike to Evelyn. She blinked back the fog that encroached on her vision.

When she stumbled, Hank guided Evelyn to a nearby chair, grabbed a magazine, and fanned her face. "Sergeant, I appreciate your help, but it's apparent Mrs. Benson can't do this anymore."

At the words, Evelyn's brain ordered her spine to straighten, and she took a couple of deep breaths. "I won't stop now, Hank. I can't." Speaking the words sapped all her strength.

Amato said nothing.

A young girl wearing a red-and-white striped pinafore hastened around the corner, spied Evelyn, and hurried to her side. "Ma'am," she said, "one of the nurses thought you should look through our lost-and-found items. Maybe you'll find a clue if your nephew has been here."

"Why didn't I think of that?" Amato smiled at Evelyn. "A capital idea." Turning to the candy striper, he said, "Young woman, lead the way."

Hope infused Evelyn's limbs with just enough vigor to follow. They traveled down several long hallways and entered the administrative wing, where their guide opened a door and ushered them into a room that reeked of smoke. Since the smell afflicted nearly every indoor space in Hartford, it had become all too familiar.

The young woman went into a back room and returned with a large cardboard box. She plopped it down with an apology. "With all the ruckus, we haven't had time to sort and organize it yet, but you're welcome to look."

When Evelyn hesitated, Hank dug in. He removed any item that didn't belong to a child and dumped it unceremoniously into a pile on the floor. A pair of black cat-eye glasses with only one wand, a scorched leather wallet, and a woman's handbag with a rhinestone latch landed on a soft pile of outerwear that included shirts, skirts, and summer sweaters. Each item had once belonged to someone, but where were the owners now?

Evelyn shivered despite the stuffy heat of the small room, but she joined in the treasure hunt, pulling out some girls' shoes, but nothing that would fit a toddler boy. Until—

Nestled in a corner near the bottom of the box, Evelyn spotted the sole of a shoe that would be Jamie's size. Hank spied it at the same time and reached for it, but Evelyn gently shoved his hand away. Gripping the item as if it were a fragile *objet d'art*, she turned the shoe over and set it upright in her lap.

A white leather Stride Rite high top. Shaped for the right foot.

With trembling fingers, she reached under the tongue.

And pulled out a knot.

Chapter Eighteen

Jamie is dead. Oh, God, what do I do now? Evelyn fidgeted with the handkerchief Hank had offered, which now bore stains from her watery tears. She'd put it through the laundry later.

Sergeant Amato and Hank peppered the candy striper with questions she couldn't answer. The poor girl burst into tears and summoned her supervisor, a taciturn woman who had no better answers than the girl did.

With so much chaos after the fire, no one knew exactly how the contents of the lost-and-found box had been retrieved. Rescuers had scooped up items from the circus grounds and taken them to the hospitals, hoping they might help with identification of the fire victims. There was no guarantee the shoe's discovery meant Jamie had been physically present at Hartford Memorial.

Evelyn sat alone in the hallway outside the administration offices. With Jamie not among the living patients, there was no other place to look but the morgue, housed in the hospital basement. Her strength sapped, Evelyn accepted Hank and Amato's offer to go without her. She sat clutching Jamie's shoe like a talisman, a precious link to her nephew whether he was alive or—God forbid—dead.

Every breath failed to inflate her lungs, and soon the room spun. A passing nurse perceived Evelyn's distress and offered her a paper bag. She commanded her to breathe into it while she fetched a cup of cool water. Evelyn took small sips until it was empty and refused the nurse's offer to summon a doctor. Why should they stop their critical efforts to save lives to take care of one woman having a breakdown?

After an eternity, Evelyn's breaths evened out. The nurse continued on her way, and Evelyn was once again alone. This sense of being solitary, with no close living relatives except Lily, would be her new life. She'd better get used to it. Evelyn wiped a bead of perspiration from her forehead, but her shuddering hand felt like ice. How could she be hot and cold at the same time?

Amato and Hank came through the double doors, and their expressions spoke for themselves. Hank seated himself beside Evelyn and put a comforting arm across her shoulders.

"Mrs. Benson," Amato said, "the coroner confirmed that all unidentified bodies of the deceased on the day of the fire were taken to the state armory. My best instincts tell me the boy you saw there must have been Jamie. It's been three days since the fire. Only six unclaimed bodies remain, and they needed . . ."

Refrigeration. Truth settled on Evelyn like a smothering blanket, and she covered her nose and mouth again with the paper bag.

She had to plan another funeral.

———◆◈◆———

"No." Hank squeezed Evelyn close and sought her gaze. "I know I got him out of the fire."

Hank didn't admit the full measure of his fear. What if Russell lied about bringing Jamie to the hospital? Made up the whole bit about the priest, and everything? The lunatic would say anything, do anything to save his own skin. Would he have set Jamie down and let him run back into the tent? If so, Hank's guilt would crush him. Jamie had to be alive.

"Then where is he?" Amato's gentle question tightened Hank's chest.

To Evelyn, Amato said, "I'm sorry, Mrs. Benson, but we've exhausted every other possibility. The city will bury all the bodies of unidentified victims tomorrow. If there is any chance of you claiming Jamie's remains, we need to do it immediately."

Evelyn stood on wobbly legs and turned to Hank. "I want to believe you—I do. But memories can be mistaken. Facts don't lie. I can't let Jamie be buried by strangers." She asked Amato, "Take me there, please." They turned their backs and started down the hallway.

Hank's heart walked away with them, including any hope of a future with her. "Wait. I'm coming with you."

Evelyn halted. When she turned around, she raised her chin and spoke in an even, low tone. "No. Jamie is gone, and I need to accept his death. You keep offering hope that he's alive but no evidence."

Truth. But the words cut Hank's very soul and made it bleed.

"Go home, Hank. Thank you for all your help, but I need to do this alone." Evelyn took Amato's arm again, passed through the doorway, and disappeared around a corner.

Hank stood in the hallway so long a nurse asked if he needed assistance. He did, but not the kind she could give.

Dr. Weatherford, the medical examiner, removed his thick, horn-rimmed glasses and rubbed his red eyes. "I'm sorry, but I don't have an explanation."

Amato's brusque manner softened. "I know you must be exhausted."

"You have no idea." Dr. Weatherford's raspy voice betrayed his stress and lack of sleep. He wiped the lenses of his glasses, donned them, and reexamined the paperwork Evelyn had filled out before entering the morgue. "All the attention, especially on the tragedy of Little Miss 1565, has made this task more difficult. But my team has made every effort to identify all the victims."

Newspapers across the country had published the morgue photo of a little girl, approximately six years old, whose face and curly blond hair had remained almost untouched by the flames. No one had yet stepped forward to claim her body, and the haunting photograph had set off a maelstrom of macabre interest.

Five other bodies besides hers remained unclaimed, including the gruesome skeleton of the boy whose visage in the armory had made Evelyn faint. It simply couldn't be Jamie's. She summoned her inner detective. "You said there was only one boy."

"Correct."

"He was four feet, four inches tall and approximately eleven years old."

"That's right."

Amato interrupted. "You told me Jamie was big for his age."

Why would no one listen? This body was not Jamie's. The paperwork had labeled him Victim 1510, a male, approximately seventy pounds. Evelyn scrutinized the paper further, not wanting to subject herself again to viewing the remains. She zeroed in on the dental examination and waved the papers under Amato's nose. "Read this. It says this boy had only three baby teeth and five fillings. Jamie has never been to the dentist."

Amato fell silent and scratched his grizzled chin. "I'm only trying to help."

"I know, and I appreciate it. But it will give me no peace to accept a body that is not Jamie's." Evelyn laid a gentle hand on the sergeant's forearm. "And out there, somewhere, I have to believe someone else is looking for this child."

The medical examiner cleared his throat. "There is one other option."

Fear tugged Evelyn underwater again. She'd prefer one big wave rather than this trickle of information. It might knock her down, but at least the uncertainty would end.

"The first victim I encountered at Hartford Hospital was an infant, or so I think. It was my impression that the child was crushed by a falling tent pole, burned and trampled beyond recognition. We could not identify the gender because of the condition of the remains."

What a horrible, gruesome ending for any human being, much less a child. Much less Jamie. Evelyn swallowed hard and asked, "Where is the body?"

"It was in the early hours after the fire . . ." Dr. Weatherford's voice trailed off until it was barely audible. "So many dead and dying."

"Where is he?"

The doctor tucked his chin and pulled it back against his neck. He clasped his clipboard to his chest and said, "I had to make a quick decision. We sent it to the crematorium."

How could Weatherford have been so callous as to dispose of Jamie like hospital waste, as if no one loved him? Evelyn made a fist so tight her fingernails cut into the flesh of her thumb. She wept against Amato, thumping his chest with both fists. She wanted to spew angry words but only emitted wails of grief. When her energy was fully spent, Evelyn wriggled out of Amato's arms.

The chilly air of the morgue provoked a bout of shivering. Evelyn longed for Hank's warmth, but she'd dismissed him. It served her right to be cold. The days ahead would be devoid of warmth no matter the weather.

To Weatherford, Evelyn said, "His name was James William Halstead. He was two-and-a-half years old, and he had the sweetest giggle on earth. He wasn't an *it*. He was my nephew." Evelyn retrieved the pocketbook she'd set down on a nearby table and straightened her skirt. "I'm sorry, Dr. Weatherford. As you can see, I'm somewhat overwrought."

"Never mind, Mrs. Benson. Your reaction is much milder than many I've seen." The doctor gave a crisp nod to Amato and said, "Now, if you don't mind, I need to get back to work." He turned slowly, walked into a nearby office, and shut the door.

Sergeant Amato guided Evelyn out of the building into the waning summer light. A pop crackled in the air followed by a bright flash. Photographers. Just what Evelyn needed right now.

Amato growled at them to back away. He jostled a few while escorting Evelyn into a waiting taxi. The flashes continued even after he shut the door, and Amato's angry words to the reporters faded from Evelyn's hearing as the taxi pulled away from the curb.

The driver studied her in the rear-view mirror. "Where to, Miss?"

A good question. Her hunt for Jamie at an end, Evelyn had no idea where to go. Where could she find relief from the crushing pain that threatened to stop her heart? Only one place. "Heaven," she murmured.

The driver took off his cap and tossed it in the seat next to him. "Sorry, I must not have heard you right. What did you say?"

Evelyn might wish to join her family in eternity, save for one detail—a hurting little girl needed her now. She could never leave Lily behind.

"Home." Evelyn recited the address, and the cabbie made a U-turn while honking his horn. He'd be happy to drop off the crazy lady and be rid of her.

Exhaustion trumped grief, and Evelyn's eyelids drooped. She resisted the encroaching darkness. A jazzy tune blared from the radio, the big hit, "I'll Get By as Long as I Have You."

The song provoked mental images in vivid colors unaffected by the gray haze of grief. A few weeks ago, Helen had been alarmed by the arrival of a message from the bank regarding a late mortgage payment. When she showed it to Bill, the popular song had blared from the radio at the perfect moment. Bill swept Helen into his arms for an impromptu dance, and she soon laughed at his antics. He performed an exaggerated dip as he sang along with the lyrics about impending poverty being of no consequence if they were together. It was no joke for their little family, but Bill could always lighten the mood.

Evelyn, an amused observer, couldn't have known Bill and Helen would soon foxtrot together into blissful, carefree eternity. As long as Evelyn had them, she also had believed she could get by. But now?

Anyone's guess.

———————◆◈◆———————

Hank sneaked into the rail yard, flopped on his bed, and stewed. No wonder Evelyn had sent him away. Jamie was officially listed as missing. Not keep-looking-he-might-turn-up-somewhere missing, but we-have-no-earthly-idea-where-he-is missing. Thorough questioning of hospital personnel had been fruitless. Inquiries to local parishes and priests had turned up no one who remembered accepting custody of a child from Russell. Jamie had simply vanished along with Evelyn's star of hope.

Hank faced Russell's empty berth. No one had seen him since the night of the fire. In his haste to flee, Russell had left behind some of his clothing but not his Zippo or his sketchbook. Why couldn't Hank get anyone to believe him? Russell should be a prime suspect in the hunt for an arsonist, but officials were more interested in locking up circus executives.

Admittedly, the evidence was confusing. Some thought a lit cigarette tossed from a patron seated in the bleachers had caught the grass on fire. The seat man in charge of the section had fled the big top as soon as the fire started. He was taken in for questioning, but charges against him had been dropped. Investigators tossed little fish back in the pond while trying to hook bigger ones.

Arguments that a cigarette had started the fire were undermined by a lack of evidence. No one had seen smoke or smoldering grass beneath the bleachers. Virtually every witness had testified they first saw the ball of fire when it was halfway up the sidewall canvas. Near the men's room tent. Where Russell said he'd been going when he was spotted on the midway.

Hank flung his legs over the side of the bed, sat up, and held his head in his hands. Could he have prevented all these deaths if he'd kept a closer eye on Russell? Or if he'd confiscated the lighter when he had the chance? Pain scratched at the back of Hank's throat like a barn cat cornered by a hound dog.

Murder. Again. The words haunted him with more intensity than ever. He hadn't meant to kill the drunken soldier in Speigletown who had accused him of being a coward for not enlisting. The man didn't know Hank was 4F, and Hank had punched him instead of admitting the embarrassing reason why. It wasn't Hank's fault the soldier hit his head on the bar before sprawling on the floor.

The man's friends had cried out for someone to call an ambulance, but not before one grabbed Hank's arm and swung a fist that snapped Hank's head backward when it connected. He'd never forget the accusation. "You killed him!"

Three little words, but they had cost Hank his whole existence, including his peace of mind. Now this. The authorities might never reach the right conclusion about what started the fire, but Hank knew. It was his fault. Murder. By neglect. Almost two hundred times over. He might as well have killed Bill and Helen with his own hands.

What right did he have to imagine himself being a friend to Evelyn, much less anything more intimate? And yet, he could never find the words to tell her the entire, awful truth. She'd hate him for it.

Everyone would be better off if he simply vanished like Russell.

Chapter Nineteen

The next day, July 10th, men held hats over their hearts, women wiped tears, and children peered from behind their mothers' skirts as funerals for the six unidentified victims of the fire were held. Some had dubbed the municipal ceremony "a means of closure for the city." But as she stood among the eerily silent crowd of more than two hundred people waiting for the cortege to arrive, Evelyn didn't seek closure. She sought truth.

Her heart was too tender to stand outside Hartford Hospital as pall-bearers loaded the bodies into hearses. She'd gone directly to Northwood Cemetery, where graves had been dug—three small and three large. One would hold the remains of the boy she'd been pressured to identify as Jamie. She hoped one day his family would be found.

A shred of doubt still lingered, although Evelyn had tried many times to banish it. Logic said it wasn't Jamie, but dread chanted a counterargument. Might she be wrong? Had a mistake been made in the autopsy? If Jamie was being interred today, someone from his family should be present.

The procession finally arrived, led by officers atop motorcycles. City officials followed. Since no one knew the faith of any of the victims, the service included rites from three men: a Catholic priest, a rabbi, and her own pastor, Reverend Archibald of South Congregational Church.

It hadn't rained, but the dank atmosphere fit the mood of the mourners. Three small coffins held the remains of the children, one of whom was Little Miss 1565. Another held the little boy, body 1510. The image of his remains at the armory came to mind, accompanied by bile Evelyn forced herself to swallow. In her distress, she missed her pastor's message altogether.

The rabbi read the burial Kaddish in Hebrew, which was translated phrase by phrase into English. The words scuttled through Evelyn's wilderness like tumbleweeds blown through the Arizona desert.

> *In this holy place or in any other place,*
> *May there come abundant peace.*
> *Grace, lovingkindness and compassion. . .*

Abundant peace? Evelyn might never experience peace again, let alone any semblance of it in abundance.

The rabbi continued,

> *Long life, ample sustenance and salvation*
> *From the Father who is in heaven and earth;*
> *And say, Amen.*

If the heavenly Father promised long life, why were Bill, Helen, and Jamie cut down in their youth? Ample sustenance? Perhaps God hadn't yet read the past due notes from the bank for the mortgage on a little white gingerbread house on Capen Street. Before long, it would wear a sign: FORECLOSED.

Evelyn did not join the resounding "amens" from the crowd of mourners. Another tear joined an earlier one, following a watery path to her chin. From there, her liquid sorrow leaped to the earth like a spurned lover from a cliff, and it merged with the loamy soil. Evelyn joined the crescendo in the music of grief—sobs, sniffles, and moans.

Solidarity among the mourners comforted Evelyn, and she quieted. The priest spoke the words of committal and sprinkled the graves with holy water.

After the closing prayer, the crowd dispersed. Evelyn walked to Matianuck Avenue, where a queue of taxis awaited those who needed transportation. She hazarded a glance back toward the burial site.

Gravediggers, their work not completed before the ceremony, had pushed the coffins aside and jumped into the holes to finish their grim duty. Shovelfuls of dirt were tossed from the graves in a cadence used for centuries. Time would march on. The song of life would continue in its familiar rhythms of work, play, and sleep.

But for Evelyn, the tune had been altered forever.

———————— ◆•◆ ————————

Evelyn walked up the sidewalk to her home with a suffocating emotion rising in her soul like deadly floodwaters. Soon she'd be swept away. Panic accompanied the grief and fear, and she desperately needed to be alone.

Darla yanked the door open and scowled. "There you are. When you were gone so long, I half expected you'd met up with that circus man again. You don't need him skulking around. He needs to go on back to the train with the other degenerates."

Evelyn pushed Darla aside, entered the house, and retrieved her friend's floral tapestry purse. Pressing it under Darla's arm, she said, "That's no longer a concern. Thank you for staying with Lily, but I'm so tired. I'd like to be alone now."

Darla's spine stiffened like a prairie dog that spotted a coyote. She rose to her full height and huffed. "I'm trying to give you good advice. That man can't bamboozle me. Buzzin' bees is always lookin' for honey. I should stay awhile."

Evelyn placed her hand on Darla's forearm and softened her tone. "Please, Dar. I'm grateful for all you've done, but I need some time to myself. I'll see you at the diner tomorrow."

Darla covered Evelyn's hand with her own. "Okay, honey. As long as I know *he's* not coming over—"

"He's not." When Darla raised an eyebrow and opened her mouth, Evelyn pressed on.

"I'm tired, I hurt, and I barely know my name right now. If he came to the door, I wouldn't answer."

"I'm just trying to help."

"The best help you can give right now is to honor my wishes."

"If you say so. The little angel is upstairs, asleep again. She'll be needing supper soon." Darla kissed her cheek, and it was all Evelyn could do not to beg her friend to stay. Her thoughts swam through such murky waters. But Darla simply left.

Evelyn closed both doors and threw the deadbolt. Leaning her back against the door, she let herself slide to the floor. This is what she wanted, right? To be alone? But silence bore down with a crushing weight.

Her sobs won their battle for freedom.

———————◦•◦———————

A timid knock jostled Evelyn to consciousness. How could she have fallen asleep? Surely Lily was awake by now, but there wasn't a sound from above. Guilt pounded like a bass drum in her ears. Could it be Hank after all? She scrambled to her feet, pulled aside the sheer curtain, and peeped through.

Mrs. Riegel. Evelyn's neighbor stood barely five feet tall, and she carried an enormous, blue-speckled roasting pan. She shifted the weight from side to side in an obvious struggle, and a heavenly aroma wafted through the windows on an opportune breeze. Evelyn clutched her stomach. Chicken and dumplings. Everyone raved over the dish at church suppers. She opened both doors, stepped on the porch, and held the screen door open with her hip. Reaching for the roaster, she was careful to handle it with the pot holders emblazoned with red and white roosters.

"Thank you, dearie." Mrs. Riegel fetched an embroidered hankie from her pocket and dabbed her forehead. "I've brought a little dinner. I don't think I could have held it much longer."

Evelyn's ban on visitors needed to be suspended for the sake of courtesy. "Please come in." Perhaps the woman—known for her quiet nature—wouldn't stay too long.

"I don't want to trouble you."

"It's no trouble." A white lie or the truth? "Won't you stay and eat with us?" The long pause without a response grew uncomfortable. A sudden pang of loneliness swelled. Perhaps she'd been too hasty in dismissing Darla. "Please. I'd really appreciate the company."

A small nod was Mrs. Riegel's only reply.

"I'll just get things ready. Please come and sit down." Evelyn stepped aside for her guest to cross the threshold, carrying the roaster to the kitchen and setting it on the burners of the gas stove. She scurried to retrieve Helen's prized Blue Willow dishes from the cupboard to set the table when the sound of sniffles reached her ears.

Evelyn peeked around the corner. Mrs. Riegel sat on the flowered sofa with Lily on her lap. To her knowledge, they had never met. But Lily wept, clinging to the grandmotherly woman like a collie's hair to velvet. Mrs. Riegel rocked her slowly and caressed her sleep-tangled curls, murmuring, "Hush, baby. God is here. He will take care of you."

But will He? Mrs. Riegel's simple statement of faith launched an arrow that hit the bullseye in Evelyn's heart. How could she have faith in a God who abandoned Bill and Helen? Either God wasn't powerful enough to stop what happened to them or He didn't care. Right now, God felt farther away and no more real than Martians.

Evelyn spun on her heel and returned to a very familiar task. Muddy thoughts wouldn't prevent her from setting a spotless, attractive table. She spooned a large helping of chicken and dumplings into a serving bowl and inhaled the comforting aroma. A fruit salad Evelyn had hastily prepared the previous day would have to suffice for a side dish, along with a few precious buttermilk biscuits.

She pulled the yellow Burroughs pitcher from the cupboard before a pang of grief nearly made her drop it. It would never again contain Helen's lemonade. Evelyn tightened her grip. Water would suffice.

Mrs. Riegel was a woman of few words, so dinner was a largely silent affair. Lily had not spoken yet since the fire. Evelyn couldn't summon the energy to carry the conversation, so every clink of silverware on ceramic plates sounded like a jackhammer.

Evelyn refused Mrs. Riegel's offer to clear the table and do dishes. No matter how nice her neighbor was, she'd never spark the easy camaraderie Evelyn had enjoyed with Helen while cleaning up after supper.

After Evelyn had put the leftovers in the refrigerator and rinsed off the dishes, she removed her apron. Helen's flower garden beckoned through the back door, but no escape was possible at the moment. She'd simply have to find a way to prompt Mrs. Riegel to go home.

Evelyn passed under the arch into the living room, and Lily lay curled on the sofa with her head in Mrs. Riegel's lap. The crocheted afghan that usually adorned the back had been tugged down and tucked over Lily despite the heat. She looked as snug as a caterpillar in a cocoon, with hair smoothed by a wrinkled hand.

Mrs. Riegel's eyes were closed as her lips moved in prayer, but she soon stopped. Looking up to Evelyn, she said, "Poor lamb. She's asleep again."

Lily's ebullient nature hadn't returned, and there was no spark of joy in her coffee-brown eyes. Evelyn was losing Lily, and she had no clue how to stop it.

Mrs. Riegel patted the cushion beside her. "Sit here, dearie. As long as I'm Lily's pillow, it seems I'm stuck for a while." She offered a smile with a glint of mischief. "We may as well chat."

Those sentences were the most Mrs. Riegel had offered all evening. Although reluctant to accept the pressure to carry a conversation, Evelyn didn't want to be rude. She took her seat and tried to imagine a suitable topic.

Mrs. Riegel studied Lily's head like it was a work of art. She didn't look up but said, "You may not know this, Mrs. Benson, but I'm also a war widow."

The statement landed in Evelyn's lap like a grenade. She didn't want to discuss her pain, especially not with a near stranger. "I'm sorry for your loss."

"It's been twenty-six years since I lost Alfred in the Great War." Mrs. Riegel's hands stilled, and her fist closed around her hankie. "When he died, I wanted to die too."

Evelyn should say something compassionate, but words couldn't squeeze by the lump in her throat.

"I'm not trying to burden you. I only want you to know I understand your pain."

Grief over George's death had been rendered almost null by losing Bill, Helen, and Jamie, but Evelyn kept that thought under lock and key. She'd never disrespect George by admitting it.

Mrs. Riegel covered Evelyn's hand with her own. A slight tremor marked their handclasp, and Evelyn couldn't tell which of them was the source of the movement. Finally, Evelyn found her voice. "Did you have any children?"

Glancing out the front window toward her apartment across the street, Mrs. Riegel answered. "Yes. One. A little girl who was the light of her daddy's eye."

Memories hurdled over the barrier Evelyn had constructed. Lily riding piggyback around the garden, slapping Bill's arm and screaming, "Giddyup!" Bill kneeling beside Lily's bed for nighttime prayers. Lily sitting in front of Bill so he could brush her chocolatey hair and smooth the flyaways with Suave hair dressing until it glistened. Evelyn suppressed a wail that would certainly alarm Mrs. Riegel.

"I lost Vivienne two years after Alfred died." Mrs. Riegel folded her arms across her stomach. "She was struck by a car while crossing Albany Avenue on her way to school."

Evelyn sucked in a quick breath, stunned by the sameness of their experiences.

She took Evelyn's hand again, drew it into her lap, and looked Evelyn in the eye. "I understand what grief does to a person. I've seen the yawning chasm of fear for the future. I've railed at God for taking my loved ones. I've walked through the Valley of the Shadow of Death."

Could this woman answer Evelyn's most burning question? "Why does God let these terrible things happen? Either He doesn't love us very much, or He's not powerful enough to stop them."

Mrs. Riegel offered a wan smile. "That's a question we all ask in troubled times." She tilted her head toward Evelyn. "I don't have all the answers, and I likely never will, but do you want to know one thought that helps?"

"I do, Mrs. Riegel."

"Call me Bernice and I'll tell you."

"And you can call me Evelyn." She tightened her grip on the old woman's fingers. "Bernice, why didn't God intervene? He could have."

Lily stirred, and Bernice rearranged the tiny, precious bundle to face the back of the sofa. Lily snuggled in like a kitten to its mother's fur.

Bernice returned her attention to Evelyn. "Lots of men went to war. Some lived, and some—like my Alfred—died. I asked my pastor, 'Why didn't God save my husband?' He answered, 'If God saved every person who was ever in danger, what kind of world would this be?'"

The sun of understanding tinged Evelyn's horizon with a hint of dusky rose. "It would be total chaos."

"Yes. God could upend the laws of nature. Sometimes He does, and those are what we call miracles." Bernice leaned closer. "But if they happened every day, they wouldn't be miracles anymore. Sometimes God lets nature take its course."

"But how does He decide who to rescue?"

Bernice shook her head. "That, my dear, is a question I plan to ask when I see Him."

Chapter Twenty

The clinking of dishes and the hum of conversation soothed Evelyn's nerves. Familiar things brought comfort—even dirty dishes, impatient diners, and Charlie's surliness. It was a good thing he pretended to forget she quit, because she could never afford to go back to school under these circumstances.

A letter from the bank had arrived in the mail yesterday, with a kindly worded message. "In light of the present hardships afflicting our community," it began. Hardships? Apocalypse was a more appropriate term—the end of civilization as Hartford once knew it. "Our board has decided to extend a three-month moratorium on collecting past-due mortgages."

Like Bill's. Now Evelyn's, as soon as Bill and Helen's estate was settled. He'd been wise to leave the property to the children with Evelyn as their guardian, but disaster loomed on the horizon like an approaching tidal wave. Even with three months of grace, the house on Capen Street would soon be underwater financially. Evelyn could never keep it with only the income from waitressing.

A second job was out of the question. Evelyn had already taken advantage of free childcare offered by a local church for families affected by the fire. Without their assistance babysitting Lily, Evelyn could not have returned to work. It was a stop-gap arrangement, but she could envision no other option. Lily's heart-wrenching screams whenever she dropped her off made Evelyn want to join in, but she had no choice.

"Bloodhound in the hay and brown bellies, hold the baby sauce!" Darla gave Evelyn a hip check, interrupting her stream of worried thoughts. "Come back to us, sister. Table four needs drink refills."

Sure enough, the three cub reporters sitting at Evelyn's table looked her way with eager expressions, and one tapped the rim of his empty glass. Reporters of all ages had descended on Hartford like locusts set to devour any bit of information without sympathy for victims. These were probably boys with rich daddies who wrangled a deferment from the draft.

They smiled like wolves ready to pounce on a rabbit. Why did everyone think waitresses were fair game for flirting? Evelyn was no hussy. She was a widow, a surrogate mother and father, and a weary veteran in the war to survive. Evelyn set her mouth in a grim line, snatched the aluminum water pitcher, and stalked toward the table.

Before she could douse the boys, Darla wrangled her aside. "Get your head out of the sand, Evie. You need this job, and for now, Charlie needs you. Don't mess this up." Darla pressed her forehead to Evelyn's. "You can do this." She drew back, but her eyes darted back and forth as she sought Evelyn's. "Don't think about yesterday or tomorrow. Just today. Today you wait tables."

Evelyn inhaled a cleansing breath and exhaled slowly through her mouth. Wait tables. One foot in front of the other. She plastered on a smile, went to table four, and poured water in the glasses without spilling a drop.

The bell above the door sounded, its insistent jingle eliciting a trained response from Evelyn like one of Pavlov's dogs. She swiveled her head to see who entered, how many were in their party, and where an empty table might be.

Evelyn almost didn't recognize Hank. His shoulders sagged, and he didn't look for her. He sported a heavy five-o'clock shadow, and wrinkles spoiled the lines of his shirt and trousers. He shuffled to a seat at the end of the long counter and plopped on the red Naugahyde stool.

Darla was assigned to the counter today, but she jerked her chin at Evelyn to serve him. This customer didn't need a serving of sass. He needed a friend.

Charlie loaded a plate with a sauerkraut-covered hot dog and a side of baked beans into the window. He rang the bell and hollered at Darla, "Order up!" A busy Charlie was a happy Charlie. Well—as happy as he could be.

Hank's appearance troubled Evelyn. She hadn't seen him in three days, but she was growing accustomed to his absences. She swallowed hard. The circus was leaving town soon, headed for their home base in Florida. This might be the last time Evelyn would see him, and she wanted it to be pleasant. He'd been more than kind.

Evelyn grabbed a dishrag and wiped small circles in front of Hank. He didn't look up. She bumped it against Hank's elbow and he lifted it but plunked it down again when she moved the rag. She leaned in and said, "Hello, mister. A penny for your thoughts."

"They're not worth that much."

Hank's words rumbled so low Evelyn could barely make out what he said. What had happened to Evelyn's tower of strength, her gallant clown-turned-hero? Even in a town where everyone seemed to be grieving, the invisible burden this man carried seemed staggering.

When Charlie glared out his window, Evelyn grabbed a menu and put it in Hank's hands. With a voice loud enough to carry over the sizzle of the griddle, she said, "What will you have today? The Reuben sandwich is delicious."

One side of Charlie's mouth smiled. Puffing up a gruff man's pride could work wonders.

"I'm not hungry."

Evelyn put her hand over Hank's, and he finally looked up. "Then why are you in a diner?"

"To see you."

The ropes of worry unwound themselves from Evelyn's chest, and she breathed a little easier. "I'm so glad. I was rude to you at the hospital, and I thought you might not forgive me."

Hank's eyes bore into Evelyn's. "You're not the one who needs forgiveness."

What a strange thing to say.

Charlie's spatula clanged an impatient rhythm on the griddle, a sure sign his indulgence wouldn't last long. Evelyn grasped Hank's hand. "My shift is done at four. Meet me, and we'll take a little walk together."

Hank nodded, stuffed his fedora on top of his rumpled hair, and left the diner without looking back.

Evelyn's body returned to work, but her mind worried instead of waitressing.

———————◆◦◆———————

Hank leaned against the brick facade of the diner a few feet away from the door. The bell's ceaseless ringing annoyed him more than a fly at a picnic. If nothing else, a tragedy certainly gave a boost to hotels, newspapers, and eateries. He almost missed Evelyn when she emerged. She looked the other way first, and her features lit when she spotted him. But how long would she be glad to see him?

"Hello, Hank."

Evelyn's voice had the same lilt he'd heard the first day he met her. He'd give anything to listen to that music the rest of his life. But his confession would stop the song forever.

"Let's walk to the park, shall we?" Evelyn's hand strayed to her head, and her eyes widened when she discovered her hairnet. She tugged it off and shoved it into a pocket of her blue pleated skirt. "Sorry about that. I'm so used to how it feels I sometimes forget it's there."

As if Evelyn could ever look anything but perfect. Even in her deep sorrow, goodness rolled off her like waves from the prow of an ocean liner. She slipped her hand to Hank's elbow, and he savored her touch.

Evelyn stepped down the sidewalk in a westerly direction, and Hank's throat tightened. They were headed toward the site of the fire. Hank hadn't been there since that horrible day, and he couldn't bear to see it again. The acrid stench of smoke still lingered when the wind blew a certain direction, and every time it reached Hank, nausea churned his stomach. He stopped.

Evelyn turned her mist-gray eyes on him with a serenity that defied explanation.

"Could we head south instead?"

"Sure. We can reach Keney Park several ways. I'd like to show it to you before you leave town so you have something beautiful to remember Hartford by." She turned left and walked down Main Street. "In fact, we can stop by my house for a moment. I'd like to change out of my work clothes if you don't mind."

Every second with Evelyn stabbed Hank's heart with a shard of ice. He didn't want a date. He wanted to say goodbye. Parting from her would cause him the most pain he'd had since leaving Speigletown, but staying would transfer the pain to Evelyn once she became aware of his part in her family's deaths. He spied an empty park bench in a small green space heavily shaded by maple trees and guided her that direction.

"I don't have a lot of time today. Can we sit here a minute?" Hank pulled out his handkerchief and brushed some pigeon droppings off the seat. When she sat, Hank did as well, careful to put some distance between them, and not merely for the sake of propriety.

Evelyn bit her bottom lip and brushed a hand across the back of her neck. "What's this all about?"

Time to dive in. "You know the circus leaves town in two days."

Evelyn nodded and chewed her lip a little more intently.

"I need to say goodbye."

"I know."

Evelyn's response tugged Hank's heartstrings tighter than a Southern belle's corset. "I don't want to leave, but—"

"Then don't." Evelyn leaned her upper body closer to Hank. "Stay."

Hank withdrew his verbal jackknife and slashed the tether between them. "You won't want me to after I tell you everything."

"What are you talking about?"

"I've not been completely honest with you."

"You lied to me?" Evelyn scooted back until her hips touched the bench's scrolled iron armrest. "What do you mean? You already told me everything that happened during the fire, didn't you?"

"Yes, but I didn't tell you what happened beforehand."

A bird trilled from a branch above their heads, and Evelyn studied it for a moment. Then her shoulders drooped, and she turned limpid eyes on him again. "Please don't draw this out. Just say what you came here to tell me."

Hank almost lost his nerve. Written on her lovely face like a beautiful epitaph were both fear and suspicion. All city sounds faded until he heard only her shallow, quick breaths. "I know how the fire started, and it's my fault. I'm partly responsible for everyone who died, including your family."

Evelyn gasped, and the roses left her cheeks.

"I should have told you sooner, but I couldn't find the words." Hank leaped to his feet and put distance between them. "My roommate was a firebug. The day of the fire I was supposed to watch him, but I got distracted."

Evelyn opened and closed her mouth a few times. She tilted her head to the side and asked, "How does that make it your fault?"

"If I hadn't lost track of him, he'd never have been able to set the fire."

"I thought they said it was an accident, set off by a cigarette."

"They don't know the truth. I do. Russell set the fire as sure as my name is . . ." Hank had never given Evelyn his true name. He wasn't worthy of a woman like her. He was struck by the strongest urge to tell her everything about his life as Henry Webster, but his culpability in the fire was enough to make her send him on his way. Hank couldn't bear her added revulsion once she learned about the fight in a Speigletown bar and that he caused the death of a man who didn't deserve it.

"Wait. You're saying it was arson?"

"Yes, and it wouldn't have happened if I'd stopped Russell."

"Have you told anyone what you suspect?"

"I told everyone, but no one will listen to me."

"Where is he?"

"He ran away the night of the fire."

Evelyn stood and took a tentative step toward him. A little puff of wind carried a hint of her White Shoulders perfume, the same scent worn by his mother. He filled his lungs with it and exhaled slowly.

"Listen to me, Hank Webb, and listen well." In another gesture that reminded him of his mother, she tapped his chest with her left index finger. "No one is responsible for another person's actions. I could have defied Charlie and gone with the family to the circus. Maybe I could have saved Jamie."

The thought of Evelyn singed and dead like Helen made Hank's legs go weak. But she continued to speak, and her words interrupted his trip down horror lane.

"But I didn't. Does that mean I'm responsible for his death?"

Hank shook his head no. But he felt the weight of almost two hundred deaths. It was different.

"Or maybe it's Charlie's fault because he didn't let me go. Or the circus officials' fault because they didn't have enough fire prevention measures in place." Evelyn paused, and when Hank didn't answer, she continued. "Or maybe this is God's fault for not putting out the fire when your roommate lit it. He could have done that, right?"

Evelyn's impeccable logic chipped away at Hank's guilt. It cracked but did not crumble. Now that she mentioned it, where was God in all of this? If Hank had not been so estranged from the Almighty, he might have asked Him.

A gentle hand caressed his forearm, bringing Hank out of his troubled thoughts. Evelyn's countenance held no anger, no judgment. How could she be so forgiving?

"You don't know everything," Hank said. "There are many things in my past I'm not proud of. It's better for everyone, especially you, if I don't stay." When Evelyn averted her gaze, Hank added, "Even if I want to."

Evelyn picked up her pocketbook and held out her hand. Hank took it but didn't pump it up and down. He wrapped her small, trembling hand in his and lifted it to his lips for a kiss. "I'm sorry, Evelyn. I wish I was a better man."

"I'm sorry you're not a man who thinks better of himself." Evelyn withdrew her hand. "Goodbye, Hank. I hope someday you'll see yourself as God does."

Hank watched Evelyn walk away, and with each step she took, the candle of hope in his heart dimmed.

When she turned a corner and disappeared from sight, she left behind only a smoking wick.

Chapter Twenty-One

Pounding on the door awakened Hank. Clyde shouted, "Webb! We're pulling out soon, and Eddie wants your sorry carcass at the electrical car."

A bright shaft of light slipped between the curtains, temporarily blinding Hank. He must have overslept. In the two long days since Evelyn had bid him farewell, he'd managed to stay away from her by sheer willpower. He'd worked side by side with the other roustabouts to load what little equipment remained after the fire, but it wasn't enough to push him to exhaustion. He struggled every night to turn off his brain and get some sleep, but last night had been the worst. The last time he'd looked at the clock it was half past three.

Hank shoved items into his rucksack and exited the train car, ignoring the questioning looks of the people with whom he'd lived for two years. Most paid him no attention, bustling to complete their departure routines. The train would leave in a few minutes for the troupe's home base in Sarasota, but Hank needed to see Eddie Vermeer first.

The cars which normally carried electrical equipment sat mostly empty, a grim reminder of the Ringling Brothers' loss. Everyone focused on the human toll—as well they should—but the circus might never recover.

A lump of ashes from his cigarette fell on Eddie's clipboard. He swept them aside, and they fluttered through the humid air and floated to the ground. Why couldn't smokers be more aware of the hazards of their habit? Although he was convinced of Russell's role in the disaster, if he was wrong, the fire must have been caused by someone so careless as to ignite the dry grass, and Eddie still hadn't learned a lesson.

"Mr. Vermeer. You wanted to see me?"

Eddie looked up, the rings under his eyes dark as soot. More lines than usual crisscrossed his leather-skinned face, and his eyes were as dead as a corpse. Until his eyebrows lowered. "Where have you been, Webb? We pull out in five minutes, and everyone is working to take up your slack."

Hank bore the chastisement, but underneath Eddie's question lay a not-so-well-kept secret. The performers had pulled together, faces turned to the future no matter how grim. But grunt workers were fleeing the circus like ants from a poisoned hill.

A change of subject might prevent a lecture. Hank didn't need one, anyway. "Any news on the investigation?"

"The locals think it was a cigarette." Eddie flicked his still-glowing butt into the grass. The orange glow immediately faded. No flames erupted, only smoke. He ground it out with the heel of his boot. "But see that? It's too humid. Most of us think it was arson."

"Did you tell them about Russell?"

"I'm no fool. I told them everything I know, including the two small fires in Providence and Portland. It was like talking to a brick wall. They put me through the wringer, but they had already made up their minds. They think I was just trying to save my own skin."

The arrest of five circus employees, including Eddie, had shaken everyone. Their livelihoods were all on the line, whether or not they'd been personally charged with a crime.

"But Russell ran away. Doesn't that show he should at least be suspect?"

"They want the heads of circus officials, not a crazy kid." Eddie lit a new cigarette and inhaled a deep draw while dropping his lighter into his pocket. "The first lawsuit has already been filed. We've posted a half a million dollars in bond, but these folks are out for blood. I'll be glad to get out of here."

"Me too." Hank pulled the strap of his rucksack closer to his neck. "But I'm not going to Sarasota."

"What?"

"I'm moving on. It's time for me to get a real life."

Eddie pointed to the train cars as the whistle blew. "You think this isn't real?" Another man ran toward them, but Eddie waved him off. "Quit messing around and get on the train."

"No, sir."

"What about your back pay?"

"Keep it."

His expression went blank, and Eddie shrugged one shoulder. "If you change your mind, come to Florida. You know where we'll be."

Hank stuck out his hand for a goodbye shake, but Eddie left it hanging. The train whistle blew again, and the cars lurched into motion. Eddie jumped onto the steps of the officers' car as it lumbered by, and he never looked back.

Cars passed, loaded with performers and roustabouts, many of them Hank's friends. A few looked Hank's direction, but none smiled or waved. The train chugged out of the yard and gained speed. Finally, the caboose passed around a bend, leaving Hank alone in the yard.

The night before the fire, Hank yearned to be found. Now he just wanted to get lost forever.

———————

No vacancies.

Hank trudged from motel to motel, but the same two words met him at each place. Maybe the inability to find a room was a sign from God he should go back to Speigletown and face his past. But Hank wasn't inclined to listen. He didn't care what he *ought* to do, only what he *wanted* to do. Was Evelyn lost to him forever, or might she extend grace to forgive him? Until he had the answer, he would shut his ears to God.

He loved Evelyn. Why else would he consider setting down roots in

Hartford with no idea whether her love would bloom in return? Besides his magnetic physical attraction to her, he craved Evelyn's kindness, her geniality, and her sense of humor. Surely the fire hadn't burned away those traits. They would return. Her innate goodness and faith would win out in the end over any evil onslaught. She was a once-in-a-lifetime woman. He'd never find her equal.

Fatigue burned Hank's feet. He stood in front of the Hartford YMCA, a gigantic redbrick building with oversized gables. An American flag hung limply from a pole atop the highest turret, an apt reflection of both Hank's spirits and the mood of the city. He trudged up the stairs with little hope of finding a room.

The clerk, a reed-thin youth with round black spectacles, eyed him from behind a huge battleship of a desk. He fired his cannon. "No vacancies, mister. Don't waste your time."

Hank was out of ammo. Without a word, he shuffled toward the exit.

"Unless . . ."

At the word, Hank turned. "Unless what?"

"Are you a religious man?"

Hank didn't consider himself religious anymore, but he'd once been devout. "Yes."

The clerk tapped his pen on the marble desktop. "How would you like to share a room with The Preacher? He's only been here two days, but he's run off three roommates."

"What did he do?"

The clerk pushed his glasses up the bridge of his nose and squinted. "He's annoying, so there's still a bed in his room if you don't mind the sermons."

God must have a sense of humor if the only bed Hank could find would earn him a lecture about his sins. "I'll take it."

The clerk handed Hank a registration form, and he signed his fake name. He'd lied about it so many times it no longer tweaked his conscience.

"I'll need one week of rent in advance, please."

Hank reached in his pocket for his leather Swank bifold—a gift from Dad right before the war started in 1941—pulled out the required sum, and pushed it across the desk.

The clerk's sour expression sweetened. "Thank you, Mister. . ." He squinted at the form. ". . . Webb." He slid a key across the cold, shiny surface. "Don't lose this or there's a two-dollar replacement fee. Your room is on the third floor, number three thirty-three."

Hank mumbled thanks and headed for the stairs.

"Good luck." The clerk's parting words gave Hank pause. He didn't need luck. He needed a flak jacket, or else he might not survive the shrapnel from a preacher's truth bomb.

———————

"Hiya, son. I been waitin' for a new roommate."

The Preacher didn't look anything like Hank's father. A mussed shock of salt-and-pepper hair—a touch too long, since it brushed his collar—and a trim physique were the first of many differences. His shoes needed a shine, and his coat had been patched in several places. With such poor grammar and diction, he'd never been to university, let alone seminary.

Hank deposited his sack on the empty bunk. "Please keep your sermons to yourself and we'll get along fine."

The Preacher rumbled a low chuckle. "I know I have a reputation. I just like to help people, and there's no better help than God's Word." He stood and offered a handshake. "I'm Philip Sullivan, but my friends call me Phil."

"Hank." Offering more than that would overtax Hank's conscience.

"What brings you to town?"

Great. Nosy on top of preachy. "Business."

"I'm here for my sister's funeral. She died in the fire."

Hank's emotional walls tumbled faster than those around Jericho. What could he say?

"I will miss her so much but not as much as her husband and three children. They all survived, but Miriam got trampled. She shielded her baby but gave her life doing it."

Was she among those who were crushed against the chute? Hank belched, and a foul taste accompanied it. "I'm sorry for your loss."

"It is devastating, but our loss is heaven's gain." Phil picked up his well-worn Bible.

Hank didn't want smug religious platitudes. He'd seen hell with his own eyes, and if God was good, He'd never let people go there. Hank headed for the door. He'd settle for coffee, but his gut craved something stronger to quiet the voices in his head.

"Don't leave." Phil laid aside his Bible. "I'm not really a preacher. I'm simply a man who wants to tell others about how God helps us through our troubles."

"If God really wanted to help, He would have kept that fire from ever starting." And kept Russell from ever being born. "Why didn't He?"

"I don't know."

Phil might not be a Bible scholar, but he was honest. Hank plopped in a dark walnut chair with no upholstery, the only furniture besides the bunk beds and nightstands. He gripped the armrests where they had been worn blond by previous use. "I thought preachers knew everything."

"Son, I struggle to understand what I do know, much less what I don't." Phil swung his legs up on the bed and scooted back against the headboard. "I don't know why God let Miriam die." Phil's voice broke. He tugged a wrinkled handkerchief from his breast pocket and wiped his mouth before dabbing his eyes. "She was the best woman I know, and tomorrow I'm giving her eulogy. They postponed the funeral until I could get here from California."

"What are you going to say?"

"I'm not entirely sure, but I will tell one story." Phil balled up his handkerchief and stuffed it back in his pocket. "One day my granddaughter, Irene—the apple of my eye—asked for a drink of my coffee."

Natural storytellers didn't need prompting, so Hank waited silently.

"I told her no, of course." Phil grinned. "She threw a royal hissy fit. Kept crying and asking me, 'why?'"

Hank recalled throwing a temper tantrum or two of his own. His mother was a saint. Literally.

"Well, sir, I knew even if I explained it, Irene wouldn't understand the answer. She's too little."

Hank swallowed. Hard.

"We accept a lot of things about God we don't understand—how He makes the sun rise, how He has always existed, and how eternity works." Phil put a hand between his head and the wall and leaned back, looking toward the ceiling. "These things are mysteries to us because in comparison to Him we're no smarter than children. We aren't able to comprehend the 'why'."

"You're dodging, Phil." Hank crossed over and sat on the foot of Phil's bed. "Give me a straight answer. Why didn't God save those people? He could have, and He didn't."

"We accept blessings from God's hands every day, but when bad things happen, we blame Him." Phil put his feet on the floor and sat beside Hank. "The answer is the same one I gave Irene."

"What is it?"

Phil's eyes teared up again, and he didn't bother to wipe them away. "I took her little face in my hands and said, 'I know you don't understand. You will when you grow up, but for now you just have to trust me.'"

Trust a deity who seemed sometimes not to care whether people lived or died? Whether they were happy or safe? What Phil said made perfect sense, but could Hank stop searching for answers he could never comprehend this side of heaven? He shuddered with the effort to resist God's truth.

Phil slipped an arm around Hank's shoulders. "Son, I don't know anything about you or your circumstances, but I don't have to—God already does. He loves you, and He wants to help you right now. Will you put your trust in Him?"

The Preacher already seemed like a friend, so Hank was perfectly honest. "I did when I was a kid. But I'm a grown-up now."

"So you're just like the rest of us—a grown-up child." Phil picked up his Bible and turned to Mark 9. "Let's pray the prayer of the father with the demon-possessed son." He read,

Jesus said unto him, If thou canst believe, all things are possible to

him that believeth. And straightway the father of the child cried out, and said with tears, Lord, I believe; help thou mine unbelief.

Phil bowed his head, and Hank did too. He didn't know what might happen, but his load of guilt and anger with God would crush him if something didn't change.

Phil prayed, "Lord, Hank believes. Help his unbelief."

When Hank repeated Phil's words in his soul, it severed the ties to his doubt. Faith rose like a phoenix from the ashes. Inexplicable. Undeniable. Freedom whooshed under his spiritual wings, and Hank's rapid ascent took his breath away. The heaviness in his soul lifted, and he experienced an incredible sensation of soaring above his troubles.

Above all, Hank felt *loved.* Unconditional, overwhelming, stuff-of-miracles love. He raised an arm to heaven. "Thank You, God!" Words of thanksgiving spurted through Hank's lips like ketchup from a Heinz 57 bottle. He thanked God for his parents, his upbringing—and yes, even for the past few turbulent years which had led him to this moment. The more Hank praised, the stronger his sense of God's love. At last, he said, "And God, I will trust You for answers too big for me. Help me now to bless Evelyn with all You've shown me."

Phil had been hugging Hank for all he was worth, but he ended it abruptly. "Who's Evelyn?"

A big question, for certain. Would Evelyn become his wife? Or did Hank's change of heart come too late to change hers? "I'm not sure."

Phil rubbed a hand across his forehead above arched, silvery eyebrows. "But I'm finally ready to find out."

Chapter Twenty-Two

A towheaded blond who looked too young to vote summoned Evelyn to ask for his check. The boy—Bobby—was the most flirtatious of the cub reporters, and the one Evelyn had to keep an eye on lest she receive unwelcome touches. "Guess we'll all be going home soon since the circus rowdies left town. No more news here." He reached toward Evelyn's leg and said, "Tell me you'll miss us, doll baby."

Evelyn neatly stepped back and avoided his touch.

Darla swished by, and a cup of hot coffee splashed into Bobby's lap. Her voice laced with sugar, she said, "Oh, I'm sorry." She handed Bobby her tea towel. "I'm so clumsy."

The other reporters guffawed, but Bobby's face reddened. "You'll be sorry you did that."

"Did what?" Darla's eyes were innocent as a doe. "These tables are so close. Accidents are bound to happen."

Charlie chuckled from the kitchen. Even the mercenary, grumpy cook had grown tired of the shenanigans of these rich boys deferred from the draft.

Bobby wouldn't back down. "Do you know who my father is?"

Darla leaned close, and Evelyn strained to hear what she said. "No, and I don't care. You lay a hand on my friend again and there will be bad business, no matter who you are." Scrutinizing every boy at the table, she added, "Take my advice and amscray. All of you." She hitched her chin toward the kitchen. "Charlie don't like campers, especially ones who are fresh with the help. You don't want to see the damage he can do with his steel spatula."

One peek toward the kitchen, and Bobby blanched. Charlie's expression could have frozen a lake of fire.

"Come on, men." Bobby threw just enough money for his lunch on the table and stood to his feet. "We're done anyway." He ogled Evelyn's legs, and his wolf whistle sparked laughter from other diners. "But I have to say, I'll miss those gams."

Charlie disappeared from his window. The reporters hastened their exit. When he appeared at the kitchen door, he beckoned Evelyn, and she went to his side. "Never you mind them. If anyone else gives you trouble, let me know."

Since the fire, Charlie's protective side—hidden under layers of spit and vinegar—had emerged like a grizzly bear after winter hibernation. He'd increased Evelyn's breaks and never said a word when grief drove her to the stockroom to compose herself.

Darla enjoyed no such reprieve. She swooped by the window to pick up a plate of liver and onions for table three, and Charlie grunted. "That cup of coffee is coming out of your pay."

"It was worth every penny." Darla smirked. "Maybe you should pay me for pest control. I don't think they'll be back."

Charlie humpfed and lumbered back to his post. But his eyes gleamed.

"You okay?" Darla asked.

Evelyn nodded and picked up her next order. Chicken salad, potato chips, and fruit ambrosia for the ladies in the corner booth. She still pictured it occupied by a group of raucous clowns, but she could never admit to her best friend how much she would miss Hank. Although Evelyn didn't understand Darla's baseless mistrust, once the woman made up her mind, it was carved in stone like Mount Rushmore.

The angular woman in the booth smoothed her Victory Roll hairdo with a manicured hand sporting a large diamond ring. "They may have left town, but Edward will never let them escape justice. He's not the state police commissioner for nothing. And he saw the whole thing."

Evelyn set down the plates, and the women ignored her. All the better, because she wanted to eavesdrop. She'd hate for innocent people to go to jail. Even circus people. Especially a certain circus clown.

"My husband appreciates all he's doing." The second woman sipped her Coke through a red and white paper straw. "Everybody expects the mayor to work miracles, but William is only one man. He has enough to do without leading the investigation too."

The mayor's wife scrutinized Evelyn, who turned to pour water at the next table. She could still hear the conversation and perhaps learn some inside information about where the investigation headed.

"Who could imagine a cigarette butt could lead to such a tragedy? It's almost unbelievable."

The commissioner's wife had it right. It was arson, not an accident. Evelyn would speak her mind if she thought it would do any good, but who would listen to a waitress? Besides, Hank had already left town. There was no one to defend. Time to get back to her sad, sorry life.

The bell over the door rang, and a bulky patron stepped right into Darla's path on her way back to the kitchen. She bumped into him, and after a deafening clatter, he caught both her and her tray. A tricky feat.

"What are you doin' here? I thought you left town, and good riddance." Darla straightened the dirty dishes on her tray and rescued a coffee cup about to tumble.

A glimpse of the man's face sent Evelyn into a tunnel where no one else existed. *Hank.* He hadn't left. Her heart soared, an unbidden and somewhat unwelcome reaction, but she couldn't help it. A hitch in her breathing left her unable to say anything.

But Hank didn't need rescue. He stepped smartly back and gestured toward the dirty dish station. "Please forgive me, ma'am." Darla stomped by, and he added, "I've missed you too."

"Take a seat at the counter, mister." Charlie pointed to an empty stool with his ever-present spatula. "She gets off at four o'clock, and you can wait for her there." Charlie? A toasted marshmallow—crusty on the outside but with a gooey middle. He'd surely kept that to himself, or perhaps he'd undergone a true change of heart.

"But—" Darla sputtered. "He's—"

"He's none of your business." Charlie's surliness returned. "Just wait tables, Darla. Evelyn don't need a mother hen."

Darla's mood could have frosted the root beer mugs with no help from the freezer. She muttered something and shot Hank a dark look.

His shirt clean and a neat crease pressed into his tweed trousers, Hank looked like a different man. Evelyn stepped behind the bar and handed him a menu. She caught a citrus-sweet whiff of Brylcreem—Bill's favorite. Hank's brown locks were tamed and shiny, except for one curl which went whimsically awry. Evelyn's urge to smooth it back into place came and went quickly.

Hank paid no attention to the menu. "Evelyn, we need to talk. I—"

Charlie cleared his throat.

Hank gave the menu only a cursory glance. To Charlie, Hank called, "What's good today?"

Charlie spoke through teeth clamped on his cigar. "Everything." After a pause, he said, "But I recommend the bossy in a bowl."

Hank gave the menu a good once-over. Evelyn smiled and relieved his confusion. "Beef stew. Charlie's is the best." She regarded her boss with appreciation. Not a mushy soul, he'd never accept her spoken thanks, but later she'd give his grill an extra onceover.

"Perfect," Hank said. "Beef stew, a buttered roll, and a tall cuppa joe." Hank leaned forward and whispered, "But can we talk? Later?"

Evelyn nodded. She went through the motions of waitressing, but the rest of her afternoon lagged like a slug crossing a hot summer sidewalk. Would the sun never go down? She sneaked Hank an extra roll, and Charlie pretended not to notice. Hank ordered apple pie and ice cream, and Evelyn kept his coffee topped off.

At half past three, Darla locked the front door to new patrons. Charlie had returned to a breakfast-and-lunch-only schedule once the crowds had thinned, but those already in the diner could remain until they finished eating. One by one Darla let out the lingerers until only Hank was left. When the clock reached quarter to four, she told him, "You. Time to go."

Evelyn started to appeal to Charlie, but Hank pre-empted her, wiping the last crumbs of pie crust from his lips and smiling at his nemesis. "You may not believe it now, Darla—"

"I never gave you leave to call me by my first name."

"Sorry, ma'am." Hank tossed a five-dollar bill on the counter. More than twice the cost of his food. "But I'm going to win you over."

"When Nazis play 'Boogie Woogie Bugle Boy'."

Hank winked at Darla. "They'd better start warming up." He snapped a salute at Charlie and said to Evelyn, "I'll wait outside." He tucked his wallet in his back pocket and headed for the front door, but Darla stood still as the Statue of Liberty.

Evelyn unlocked it instead. "I'll be there as soon as I can."

Hank found her hand and squeezed it. "Don't rush. I'm not going anywhere."

He wasn't? Now, that news was worthy of a Movietone reel.

Hot air rose from the pavement in undulating waves, yet Hank barely perspired as he leaned against the wall of the diner. The skin at the corner of his eyes crinkled when he spotted Evelyn. "Hello, pretty lady. Can a gentleman walk you home?"

Who was this? Evelyn's Hank was torn apart by regret and false guilt. This man had a spring in his step and a weightless sky-blue gaze. He tucked Evelyn's hand in his elbow and greeted everyone they passed as they took a leisurely stroll to Capen Street.

Uncertainty quelled any comment Evelyn thought to make. Tired of the chitchat, she said, "Out with it. Why didn't you leave town?"

"I'd hoped to wait for a more private place to discuss it, but this will do." Hank took out his spotless starched handkerchief and again cleaned the seat of the very park bench upon which they'd said goodbye and parted mere days ago. Evelyn thought she'd never see him again.

"Ironic to be here. Now. With you." Hank took her hand but released it quickly. "I should ask first. May I?"

Evelyn reached for his hand on her own accord. "I thought you were done with Hartford."

"I was. I fully intended to hop on the train, travel somewhere south, and abandon the troupe before we got to Florida." Hank ran his thumb over the soft spot between Evelyn's thumb and index finger. "But something stopped me."

"What?"

"Not what, but who." Hank sandwiched her hand between his. "You."

Evelyn jerked her hand away. "I didn't stop you. I said goodbye with as much dignity as I could muster." She fiddled with Helen's cross necklace, which she had traded for her own the day of the funeral. "You broke my heart."

"I broke my own heart too." Hank straightened himself against the back of the bench. "And I've been breaking God's heart for a long time." He extended an arm across the back of the bench and touched Evelyn lightly between the shoulder blades. "But no more. I'm a new man, Evelyn, and I want a fresh start."

Evelyn's poor heart couldn't take any more disappointment. Creditors would soon infest the waters around her home like ravenous sharks. Lily had still not spoken one syllable since the fire, and grief weighed her down like a two-ton anchor. She was sinking. "I don't know what to say."

"Don't say anything yet." Hank gave her back two pats and withdrew his arm. "You don't have to make any big life decisions right now. Just let me come by to see you and Lily from time to time and I'll be a happy man. The Good Book says not to worry about tomorrow because today has enough troubles of its own."

A pretty speech. A Bible quotation thrown in, to boot. Every cell in Evelyn's body wanted to cast herself into his strong masculine arms except a few rebels in her bruised heart. Could she let him in? Once broken, trust was hard to rebuild. Evelyn nibbled the inside of her cheek.

Hank crossed one ankle against his opposite knee and jiggled his heel. "If you don't want a romantic relationship, I won't like it, but I'll respect your wishes." Then he stilled and turned pleading eyes on Evelyn. "But please, let me visit Lily. I feel somewhat responsible for her, and I'm worried. Has she spoken yet?"

Evelyn mumbled, "No."

"May I visit her?"

Perhaps this was the answer Evelyn had been seeking. Lily had loved and responded to Bill like no one else in the world. Maybe it would take a man to finally get through to her and help her return to the land of the living. But the thought of anything else with Hank made her pulse rocket. Whether from hope or fear was anyone's guess.

After a long pause, Hank uncrossed his leg, placed one foot beside the other, and stared at his feet. Without looking up, he said. "I'm sorry, Evelyn. I should have known—"

"Yes."

Hank jerked to attention. "Yes? I can visit Lily?"

"Yes, you can visit us both. But not today, okay?"

"Okay. All right, then." Hank stood and offered Evelyn a hand up. "Tomorrow?"

"Meet me after work tomorrow and walk me home." Evelyn slipped the handle of her pocketbook up to her elbow. "But if you know what's good for you, you might choose this time not to wait for me in the diner."

"Why?"

"Charlie is dangerous with his spatula, but Darla can juggle knives."

Hank erupted in musical, soul-soothing laughter. When finished, he said, "I'll keep that in mind. Until tomorrow, then?"

"Yes. Four o'clock."

Hank squeezed her forearm and nodded before taking a step backward. He doffed his hat, turned, and walked the opposite direction, whistling a tune as he crossed the street headed for downtown.

Evelyn watched until he turned a corner. She needed a day's reprieve to prepare Lily for a visit from Fraidy Freddie. Or did she need to prepare herself?

It was a toss-up.

Chapter Twenty-Three

Hank's palms sweated like a beardless boy on his first date. He wiped them on his trousers, passing the floral bouquet from one hand to the other, and pasted on a smile before entering the diner. He hoped his expression looked more like "Hi, how are you" than "I'm a freaky former clown, but I won't hurt you."

He stiff-armed the door, and it swung into the nearly empty room. At three thirty, the busy lunch hour was past, and only a few folks occupied the chrome and Formica tables. His quarry stood directly ahead, hands on hips.

Hank held out the flowers as if they could stop bullets. "These are for you."

Darla grunted. "Evelyn is in the stockroom."

"They're for you. I hope you like daisies." A friendly flower, daisies. Happy. Upbeat. Their white petals framed a sunny center which had always brought a smile to his mother's face. He hoped they would do the same for Darla.

No such luck. Although she wasn't holding a knife, Darla's eyes launched daggers. "Think I'm that easy? Think again, circus man."

Hank jiggled the bouquet and smiled bigger.

"Oh, all right." Darla snatched the flowers and headed for the kitchen. "But I'm only taking them because these poor babies will wilt if they're not put in water."

Hank imagined a bugle calling racehorses to the starting gate. He fell into step behind Darla, close, but not crowding. When Darla turned and pinned him with a glare, he stopped. He didn't want to hear taps.

Hank tossed a question. "Why do you hate me?"

Darla squinted. "I don't hate nobody. Hatin' is a sin." She brushed a daisy against her nose and sniffed. "But I know your type."

"What type?"

"A man who blows into town all fancy-like. Tall, dark, and too good-lookin' for his own good." After a short pause, she added, "Not that I'm sayin' you're handsome."

Hank grinned. Did she blush? She did!

"Oooo. That right there. That's why I don't like you."

Hank languished in the gate. He wanted to hear the starting bell. Off to the race, with the prize being Darla's acceptance. In all seriousness, he said, "I have no idea what you mean, ma'am. Please tell me what I can do to help you know I mean no harm to Evelyn."

"You're just like him."

"Who?"

A shadow darkened Darla's countenance even further. "My husband."

"Maybe we can go on a double date."

Darla snorted. "Not likely. He skedaddled three months after we were married, and I haven't seen or heard from him since."

Ouch. No wonder the woman was leery. Hank used the same tone that would calm a skittish filly. "Then he was a fool. You're smart, capable, and loyal to your friends. A man would be lucky to have you as his wife."

Her stance softened a bit, but Darla rolled her eyes. "Oh, please. That's layin' it on thicker than Charlie's redeye gravy."

Evelyn picked just the right moment to emerge from the stockroom. "No. He's right. I've been saying that to you as long as I've known you." She wrapped an arm around Darla's shoulders and squeezed. Fingering the petals of a daisy, she teased, "Do you have an admirer?"

"Yes. She does." Hank lifted his chin. "Me." He looked straight into Darla's eyes and didn't flinch. "I'm glad Evelyn has such a fierce friend as you. She's growing more important to me every day, and I only want a chance to prove to you my intentions are honorable. I may be crazy, but in time I hope you'll also think of me as a friend."

Darla lowered one eyebrow. "Not likely."

"But not impossible?" Hank breathed a prayer heavenward. It would be hard to court Evelyn if he had to fight Darla every step of the way.

Darla slipped an arm around Evelyn's waist. "This woman has already had her heart broken too many times."

"Agreed."

Evelyn blushed and looked toward the kitchen. Charlie watched but didn't interfere. Hope hung in the air like a savory aroma. Hank hoped Darla wouldn't spray disinfectant.

"You're a rolling stone, circus man."

Did Darla want to duel with proverbs? Hank wasn't the son of a preacher for nothing. "Rolling isn't all it's cracked up to be, Darla. I'm ready for a little moss."

"We'll see." Darla reached for a nearby glass and plunked the daisies into it. She turned toward Hank and crossed her arms. "You hurt this woman or Lily, and you'll find out how skilled I am with a kitchen knife."

"I've already heard." Hank dared a wink. "Maybe you can teach me a thing or two."

Darla barked a laugh and headed for the kitchen.

He asked Evelyn, "Did I win her over?"

"It will take more than charm to change her mind."

"There's more to Hank Webb than charm." And more to Henry Webster too. Hank's stomach roiled.

What would the ladies do when he opened that can of worms?

Comparison was so unfair, but as Hank fell in step next to Evelyn, she couldn't help it. George had been steady, soft-spoken, and shy. At five feet eight inches, he looked Evelyn eye to eye but rarely held her gaze for long. They dated three years before he proposed, and even then, Evelyn had to wait patiently for him to work up the courage to ask. He never made a move without asking Evelyn first, and he seemed happy for her to make most of the important decisions.

Hank couldn't have been more different. More than six feet tall, his presence was powerful and potent. He was a charmer, a smooth talker, and far from shy. Although courteous and considerate, he'd take charge in a New York minute if necessary. More like Bill than George, if Hank settled down, he'd be the Rock of Gibraltar, not a rolling stone.

So why had he joined the circus? And why was he not off fighting the war? He must be 4F, or he'd already have enlisted or been drafted. Bill's experience had taught Evelyn not to make assumptions, but if Hank planned to stay in Hartford, she needed to know more. Especially if he wanted contact with Lily.

When they reached "their" bench, Evelyn stepped off the sidewalk and took a seat.

"Time for another talk?" The corners of Hank's mouth tilted up in an adorable way. "We really ought to find a place a little more out of the way." He sat beside her, his bulk jostling the seat. He didn't put his arm around her, thank goodness.

"I need to clear the air before you see Lily."

"Of course. I expected you to have questions."

"Our relationship is too new. We don't know much about each other, and that was fine when I thought you were leaving town. Now that you're staying, I need a couple of important answers." Evelyn set her pocketbook between them. "And I'm sure you have questions for me."

"I know all I need to know about you already." Hank crossed his legs toward her. "But I know you have to be more cautious."

"Because of Lily." It was cowardly to use Lily as an excuse, but Evelyn needed to keep her galloping emotions in check.

"Right." Hank wasn't fooled for a minute. "I understand. What do you want to know?"

Evelyn opened with a nonthreatening question. "Where did you grow up?"

"Speigletown, New York, right outside of Albany. My father was a preacher."

"So he's gone? I'm so sorry."

Hank jiggled his toe. "No, he's still alive. I should have said he *is* a preacher." He rubbed a hand across his mouth. "I assume he still is. I left town two years ago, and I've not been in touch with him since."

Estranged from his family—not a good sign. Chalk up one in the concerns column. "Why not?"

"I left town under"—Hank crossed his legs the other direction—"difficult circumstances. But now that I've set things right with God, I'm ready to get in touch with my parents again."

"So your mother—"

"Is also living." He cleared his throat. "I've made a lot of mistakes, Evelyn, and you were right about me. I've been running away from God, and in doing so, I ran away from my family too."

A runner. Just like Darla said.

"But I've changed." Hank put both feet on the ground and turned his upper body toward her, resting his arm on the back of the bench but not touching her. "It's going to take some time to work out what it all means, but I'm actively seeking God about the next steps for my life. The first step was to leave the circus, and the next is to settle in Hartford. After that, I plan to go home as soon as possible and clean up the mess I made."

When Evelyn didn't speak again, Hank filled the void. "This isn't anything I'm proud of, and it's hard to be honest with you. I want you to trust me, but all I have to offer right now is the truth. The rest I'll have to earn with time."

Fair enough. Everyone deserved the opportunity to change. If God extended grace to Hank, why should Evelyn withhold it? But she did have one more urgent question. "Why aren't you in the military?"

"I'm 4F." Hank averted his eyes, feigning interest in a family exiting the drug store across the street. "If you don't mind, I'd prefer we know each other a little better before telling you why."

What was he hiding? The reason for Bill's status was readily apparent to anyone who tried to talk to him. If a man stuttered, he was considered too unreliable on the battlefield. But did Hank have health issues? A heart murmur? A chronic illness? Or maybe he'd been convicted of a crime. Heavens. Evelyn snatched up her purse and stood.

"Wait—" Hank stood too, grasped her hand, and blocked her escape. "Please, sit down." He sat and gave Evelyn's hand a little tug. "I'll tell you now, but it's a sad story."

Evelyn took her seat again. "I don't want to force you into anything you're not ready for."

"No, you're right. You deserve to know."

Hank had already hidden his being wanted for murder. He might lose Evelyn altogether with this confession, but she had the look of a hunted doe poised for flight. If he wanted her to trust him and build a relationship, he'd need to find out how big her heart was. And that would make him offer the first of two startling revelations today. But only the first.

"When I was thirteen there was an accident." A chill wind blew through Hank's soul, and he shivered despite the scorching heat. He hated to relive this memory and had pushed it down so ruthlessly he seldom thought of it.

Evelyn scooted closer. "Were you injured?"

"No. Not my body, at least." The black curtain suppressing the memory parted, and Hank glimpsed Frank's ghostly, lifeless face. "A group of us were skating on Old Man Marston's pond without permission. It was March, and my dad warned us the ice wasn't thick enough anymore."

"I'm sorry, Hank. I shouldn't have asked. If it's too painful—" Evelyn touched his arm, the contact soft and soothing.

"No. I've started now. I might as well finish." Hank clasped his hands to keep them from reaching for her. "It cracked, and Frank fell in. He could swim, but his clothes got too heavy and dragged him under. I jumped in after him." He remembered a small white hand sweeping across his sightline but disappearing in the muddy water before he could grab it. "I tried to save him, but he drowned." Hank sucked in a deep, humid breath of life-giving air. Lost in his thoughts, he began to hyperventilate.

"Hey, hey. Slow down." Evelyn had scooted right next to him, and her arm was now around his shoulders. "Easy breaths. In and out."

Hank dared a glimpse at her face. Her gray eyes were as soft as a chinchilla's fur.

"That's awful, but I don't know how this is the reason you're 4F."

"Frank was my little brother." Hank swallowed, and the effort made him cough. "He was my only sibling, and he wouldn't have been there if I hadn't gone." Hank pictured the pain etched in his father's face as he preached Frank's funeral. "His death was my fault."

Evelyn stiffened. "I thought we've been over this. You can't blame yourself for every bad thing that happens."

Right. Hank closed his eyes and asked the Holy Spirit for help. Soon, peace returned. "I'm trying to live in the freedom The Preacher helped me find, but when I was thirteen, I felt I didn't deserve to live."

Evelyn waited for his answer, a sign of her wisdom and compassion. He loved this woman, but would she find the grace to love him back?

Forcing himself to continue, Hank said, "I attempted suicide."

Evelyn didn't flinch. Her grip on his hand tightened, and her gaze never left his.

"I won't go into all the details, but I was under the care of a psychiatrist for nearly a year. When the Army learned about it, they labeled me 4F." Hank took Evelyn's hand in both of his. "I've never been suicidal since, and I was released from psychiatric care long ago. But it wasn't enough for the Army. I tried to enlist, but they turned me down." A fateful decision, one that led to all of Hank's recent troubles. How could you tell soldiers in a bar that you're 4F because the Army thinks you're crazy? Throwing a punch was better than explaining.

Evelyn stood abruptly. "That's enough for today. Come on, Hank. Lily's waiting."

That was it? A huge, soul-baring admission of mental illness, and Evelyn wasn't fazed? "You're okay with this?"

"No. It's a horrible thing to have happened, but which of us can criticize? Certainly not me. I've wondered several times in the last month if I can keep it together." She took a few steps toward her home, and Hank fell in step beside her. "Thank you for trusting me enough to tell me something so personal. And again, I'm sorry I pressured you."

"I'm glad it's out in the open." They walked together in companionable silence, and Hank relaxed. A little bit.

One down, one to go.

Chapter Twenty-Four

Mrs. Riegel patted the long, gray braid wrapped around her head and removed her apron. "Lily wanted to play in her room. I tried to get her to work a puzzle with me, but she refused."

Evelyn had accepted Bernice's offer to care for Lily during the remaining weeks before school started. Both women hoped that the familiar environment of home rather than the church play school would help Lily feel safe enough to begin talking. But so far, she'd remained mute.

Hank cleared his throat.

"Oh! I've forgotten my manners." Evelyn invited Hank—who had politely waited on the porch while holding the door open—to enter. "Please, come in. Bernice, I'd like you to meet Hank Webb."

Hank took off his hat and greeted Bernice. "Nice to meet you, ma'am. Mrs.—"

"Riegel." She put the folded apron on the dining room table. "Evelyn, would you like me to stay? I have a few minutes to spare while you visit with your young man."

Accepting the offer would make Hank's visit more proper. But Evelyn craved the opportunity to spend a little time with Hank privately, especially to allow him to interact with Lily. The two had formed a connection, and she wanted no distractions to spoil the possibility Lily might open up to him. "Thank you, but no. Hank is a dear friend, and I'm perfectly safe." At least physically. No guarantees about her heart.

"Very well. I'm off." Bernice extended her petite hand, calloused by hard work but softly padded by age, and Hank shook it. "Nice to meet you, Mr. Webb." She paused as if she wanted to say something else but headed for the door after casting a concerned glance at Evelyn.

Evelyn followed and whispered, "It's all right. He's an honorable man, and he won't stay long."

Bernice ran an assessing gaze over Hank. "All right, dearie. But if he gets fresh, open the porch window and I'll come right over."

"I will." If ever a guardian angel took flesh, she might look and sound like Mrs. Riegel.

Hank stood in the middle of the living room, hat in hand, and rubbed the back of his neck. When Mrs. Riegel closed the front gate behind her, he offered a sheepish grin. "You sure do have a lot of watchdogs."

"For a man who is supposedly so charming, you do bring out the growlies in my friends."

"It's my strong chin." Hank offered his profile. "Some people say it makes me look like Lon Chaney, Junior."

Evelyn's laughter turned into a snort, and she covered her mouth. When she recovered, she said, "Just don't grow a beard. The last thing Hartford needs is rumors of a wolfman run amok."

Creaks on the stair treads announced Lily's arrival. Evelyn's heart skipped a beat. Her niece was a ghost of herself, all bony angles and blue shadowy veins visible through her pale skin. The circles under her lusterless eyes grew darker by the day. If change didn't come soon, Lily might need the help of a psychiatrist herself.

Hank didn't balk. He strode to the bottom of the stairs and extended his arms. "There's my beautiful Lily. How about a hug for your favorite clown?"

Evelyn didn't miss his use of the possessive pronoun. He spoke as if Lily already belonged to him. Hank had saved her life. If that didn't make him worthy of feeling a special connection to Lily, nothing did.

Lily froze. She stuck her thumb in her mouth—a habit she'd given up long ago—and shook her head.

Hank slapped at his pockets. "Where is it? I know it's in here somewhere." He pulled a red foam ball from his trouser pocket and clamped it on his nose. "Here it is! Do you recognize me now?" He arched his eyebrows and struck a pose.

Lily reached for Hank. She didn't smile, but she didn't need to. Her acceptance of his embrace said everything.

Hank swung her into his arms and twirled her once around. "Lily, you weigh next to nothing. How about a cookie?" Hank peeped over Lily's shoulder to receive permission from Evelyn, although it was too late to rescind his offer.

"Her favorite ice box cookies are in the kitchen." The ones Helen used to make. To entice Lily, Evelyn had included the full amount of sugar, despite the war rationing. But she'd still refused to eat them. Perhaps their connection to Helen was still too troubling.

"Ice box cookies! My favorite too. Especially with cold milk." Hank licked his lips and made a loud smacking noise.

Lily's smile came and went like a chimera. Oh, how Evelyn wished it would stay. Perhaps Hank was just the enticement she needed to draw her out of her shell.

Hank put Lily down in one of the kitchen chairs, but when he sat down, she crawled in his lap. He pulled her against him, and she rested her head against his shoulder. The snapshot of childlike trust in his male strength made Evelyn's throat ache. No matter how many hugs her aunt might offer, Lily craved her father's presence. There was no substitute, but Hank came close.

Evelyn served up cookies and milk and took a seat herself. Lily shook her head and pointed to the living room. Evelyn's heart should have throbbed with the painful rejection, but hope rose instead. If Lily issued orders, perhaps she was about to emerge from the shadowlands of grief.

"That's not very—"

Evelyn cut off Hank's objection. He couldn't know what a good sign this might be. "It's all right, Hank—I mean, Freddie. I prefer the view from the dining room anyway." She took her portion of the snack and withdrew. She sat near enough to hear and see them, but Hank's shoulder blocked Lily's view of her.

Hank took off his clown nose. "I don't want anything in my way. Besides, you know I'm really Hank, right? Freddie is a made-up character I play."

Lily picked up the red ball and squashed it a couple of times. She nodded.

"You can call me Uncle Hank, okay?"

Another nod, but no words.

"All right, then. Let's get busy." Hank sang a little ditty he must have made up. "One cookie, dunk, dunk. In my mouth, ker-plunk." After the last syllable, he shoved the entire cookie in his mouth and spoke over the crumbs. "That's so good, Lily. Try it, and I'll sing."

Lily twirled a lock of her hair but didn't reach for the cookies.

"Okay. But I hate to eat alone." Hank picked up a cookie and dangled it over the glass. "This one's for you. Open up." He immersed the cookie in the milk. "One cookie, dunk, dunk." He lifted it to her lips. "In your mouth—" The cookie wept white droplets on Lily's dress as Hank waited.

Evelyn held her breath.

Lily opened her mouth, and Hank shoved the entire thing in, saying, "Ker-plunk!"

At Hank's victory cry, a tsunami of relief washed over Evelyn.

After a copious amount of chewing, a tiny voice spoke, raspy from disuse. "Another." Three cookies went down the hatch, each accompanied by the song.

Hank called, "Evelyn, what's for supper?" To Lily he said, "After you eat, we'll have some more cookies, okay?"

At Lily's nod of agreement, Evelyn bustled into the kitchen, all business. She scrambled through the fridge for last night's leftovers—meatloaf and mashed potatoes—and dumped them into a skillet to heat before Lily could change her mind.

"Come on, sweetie. Let's set the table for Aunt Evie." Hank set Lily down, but she clung to his leg. Hank chuckled and said, "So that's the way it is. Well, I have two arms. One for you, and one for plates and silverware."

He picked Lily up, and she melted into him like a slice of cheese on one of Charlie's burgers.

Nonplussed, Hank hummed while he set the table as if he always used only one arm. Evelyn spooned some canned applesauce into a bowl, plated the hot meal, and in a jiffy, dinner was ready.

Hank set Lily down again, and at her mulish look, he scolded her just like Bill would have. "None of that, missy. Be nice. Aunt Evie fixed us a delicious meal, and she's welcome to join us."

Evelyn would have skipped ten meals if only Lily would eat, but she still appreciated Hank's defense. Hank didn't know he sat in Bill's chair, and Evelyn wasn't about to tell him. She scooted out her chair and sat, although it was at the opposite end of the table from Hank. Helen's chair remained between them. Empty.

"Let's say grace." He bowed his head, as did Evelyn, but she peeked at Lily. Her expression blank, she stared at Hank as if he had three heads. "Heavenly Father, bless this food to our nourishment and us to Thy service. Amen."

Short and sweet. Although she had no appetite, Evelyn lifted a forkful of potatoes to her mouth. They went down like wallpaper paste and tasted about the same.

Lily pushed hers around on her plate.

Since Hank was nearest, he cut her meatloaf into bite-sized pieces. He forked and gobbled one. "Uncle tax."

Lily scowled.

"What? You don't know about taxes?" Hank smirked, chewing with his lips closed. When his mouth emptied, he added, "Don't worry, live long enough and you will."

When Evelyn chuckled, Hank winked. Contentment anointed Evelyn's head and flowed all the way to her toes. She could grow accustomed to this good man at her table.

Hank tapped his fork on the tabletop. "You'd better take a bite of that meatloaf, young lady. Or else your taxes are going up."

Nothing sparked Lily to action more than competition, and she rose to the challenge. She stabbed and gobbled a bite so fast it stunned Evelyn.

Then a second and a third, before she'd swallowed the first.

"Hey, hey. Slow down." Hank put a hand on Lily's shoulder, and she didn't recoil. "I was just teasing. Don't eat too fast or you'll get a stomachache."

Lily obeyed. She didn't converse, but she listened all through dinner as Hank asked pointed questions about funny things that happened at the diner. Evelyn had no dearth of stories, and she almost didn't notice when Lily took her last bite.

"Good job, honey." Lily turned to Evelyn at the words of praise. "I'm so happy to see you eating."

"Cookies!" Hank's bellow precluded a response from Lily. Deft management of her mood, as if he'd known her forever. Sometimes it was best to let life roll on and not allow Lily's negativity to manifest.

Though she worried somewhat about Lily getting too full, she plated up one cookie for each of them with a glass of milk and set them on the kitchen table. She sat and waited for Hank and Lily, determined not to let herself be chased away again.

Hank entered, carrying Lily as before, but this time he peeled her off and set her in Evelyn's lap. Lily stiffened and stuck out her bottom lip, but Hank ignored it. He sat in his own chair and picked up his cookie. "All together now."

Evelyn picked up hers, and eventually, so did Lily. All three dunked their cookies. Hank crooned, "One cookie, dunk, dunk." He lifted it to his mouth, and Lily copied him. "In my mouth—"

War and Peace could have been written in the long pause that followed. All three cookies dripped milk on their clothing, but Hank and Evelyn waited.

"Ker-plunk!" Lily nearly shouted the word and shoved the cookie in her mouth.

Hank and Evelyn cheered and did the same. Hank play-acted like a dog in ecstasy after swallowing a treat. He howled, hugged his stomach, and threw himself on the floor before rolling to his back and kicking his legs in the air.

Lily giggled, the most beautiful sound Evelyn had heard in a month.

Color rose to her cheeks and her eyes sparkled with delight. The harder she laughed, the wilder Hank's impression. He got to his hands and knees and snuffled Lily's lap like a bloodhound looking for crumbs before sitting up to beg.

Lily held out a hand, and before you could say "Jack Robinson," Evelyn had given her a cookie to offer Hank. He gobbled it greedily, and soon Lily joined him on the floor as his doggy sidekick. Both begged cookies from Evelyn until the last one vanished. She patted their heads, and Lily laid hers in Evelyn's lap.

Hank quieted.

Lily lingered, and soon her scrawny arms encircled Evelyn's waist. Evelyn stroked her hair and crooned sweet nothings. Lily began to weep, and soon she crawled fully into Evelyn's lap, clutching her chest to chest as great, heaving sobs consumed her.

Evelyn dared a look at Hank, who didn't bother to wipe away the tears that traveled down his cheeks and spilled on his shirt.

After a few minutes, Lily calmed. She pulled back her head, wiped her forearm under her nose, and studied Evelyn's face. "Papa's dead."

The two words slammed Evelyn like a sledgehammer. *Oh, God. Help.* "Yes, he is, and I'm sad too."

"He died because he tried to save Mama."

"Yes. He loved her so very much."

Lily's voice turned to the whine of an eight-year-old. "Didn't he love me too?"

Evelyn had asked herself that question many times. Bill had tried to rescue Helen even in the face of certain death. But in doing so, he'd left behind people who needed him alive. It was a gruesome, awful, life-shattering choice, made in the heat—literally—of the moment. Evelyn still struggled to make sense of it, and at times she was furious with Bill. From Hank's report, Helen was likely already dead. What a waste of a good man's life.

Greater love hath no man than this, that a man lay down his life for his friends. One of the children's memory verses Evelyn had taught. To sacrifice one's life for another person was the highest measure of love.

George had done it in his own way, as had thousands of soldiers who went off to war and never came home. Bill had the same capability for heroic sacrifice, although the opportunity to fight in the war was denied him. In his death, Bill had saved dozens of people while losing his own life. He'd never been more like Christ.

But how could she explain this to Lily?

Evelyn took Lily's face in her hands, and the child's quivering tore her heart asunder. "Your Papa loved you, Lily. Never doubt it. He gave you and Jamie to Hank, and he trusted Hank to make sure you lived. You and Jamie came first. Do you understand?"

Lily shivered, but she said, "Yes."

"But he knew you needed your mama. He had to try to save her."

Lily looked aside. "But Mama died."

Evelyn gently turned her head back to gaze directly into her puffy eyes. "He didn't mean for both of them to die. He just ran out of time."

"Why didn't God save him?"

The million-dollar question. She owed Lily all the honesty she could muster, but what could she say?

Hank spoke up. "Lily, we can't understand some things until we are grown-ups."

"But you and Aunt Evie are grown-ups."

"Our bodies are grown up, but compared to God, we're just children like you. We don't understand either."

When did Hank become a sage? Evelyn considered his words, and a seedling of peace sprouted.

"It's okay not to understand. Just like you trust Aunt Evie, we all need to trust God—that He loves us, He is with us, and He will take us someday to live with Him in heaven with your papa and mama."

Lily rested against Evelyn, paradise in her arms. Evelyn rubbed her back, and soon she grew heavy, taking slow, even breaths. However, before she drifted completely into slumber, Lily mumbled a question that uprooted Evelyn's newfound peace.

"But where's Jamie?"

Chapter Twenty-Five

Hank tightened the last bolt on the crankcase and pushed the assembly down the line to the next worker. For the past several months, his role in the production of the Pratt & Whitney R-2800 Double Wasp engine had helped to assuage his guilt over being 4F. Women like Helen had stepped in to help in the war effort, but certain tasks required the strength of a man, sometimes two.

A growing sense of pride staved off morbid thoughts about filling the vacancy left by a man who lost his life in the fire. Every time Hank saw a theater newsreel of P-47 Thunderbolts, Hellcats, or Corsairs dropping two-and-a-half ton payloads on the Nazis, he sat taller. Maybe his hands had touched the engines of the planes that dominated the skies over Europe and Asia.

But working until his muscles screamed and sweat drenched his shirt did nothing to keep Hank from thinking about Lily and Evelyn. It had been three months since Lily asked about Jamie's whereabouts, but the question haunted him like the Ghost of Christmas Past. Yes, he'd prayed many times for God to deliver him from false guilt. But in this case, didn't he bear some responsibility? Bill had entrusted his son to Hank, and Jamie had vanished, perhaps for good.

Two or three nights a week, Hank kept company with his girls. Mrs. Riegel had fought it, but a few invitations to join the fun and play Scrabble after Lily went to bed had done the trick. Her presence made everything more respectable, but truth be known, Hank would have visited anyway. He couldn't have stayed away if he'd been ordered by FDR himself.

His preoccupation with searching for Jamie had turned into a near obsession. But he wasn't alone. Sergeant Amato shared his fixation, and they had decided to leave Evelyn out of the loop until they found something concrete. They met every couple of weeks in secret, and Hank admired Amato's dogged persistence. On his own, Hank might have given up. But Amato? Never. Together they'd find Jamie if they had to hunt until they were in their graves.

He just hoped that wasn't where Jamie was.

After a shower and shave at the Y, where he'd found accommodations comfortable, if cramped, Hank hustled down the sidewalks to the little house on Capen Street. He'd fallen in love with the cozy home, and he helped Evelyn with maintenance. A little machine oil, and the gate no longer creaked. Scraping and new paint for the shutters, and replacing the faulty bulb in the porch light. Replacement of the rotted ropes in the window pulleys in Lily's room. He'd gone over every inch of the place, despite Evelyn's repeated objections, mainly because of Bill. Someone should take care of a hero's loved ones, and Hank wanted to be the man who did.

Hank opened the gate—gratified by its smooth, silent operation—took the right fork in the sidewalk, and hopped on the porch. He knocked in his signature rhythm, and Lily opened it right away.

"Come in. But don't wake Miss Persimmon. She's sleeping." Lily pointed to the orange-haired doll, a gift from Hank for her birthday, which lay face down in the tiny bed Hank had built out of some scrap wood he'd found in Bill's storeroom. The change in the once-mute child was nothing less than a miracle. Although sorrow sometimes colored her features, for the most part she'd returned to her delightful, imperious personality. Hank wouldn't care if she ordered him around forever. But once in a while her constant stream of chatter got on his nerves.

Mrs. Riegel had already arrived, and she smiled at Lily's bossiness. The woman was far too indulgent. They were all so glad to see Lily return to normal they let her get away with murder. Someday they'd need to rein her in. But not today.

"Oh, good. You're here." Evelyn blew into the room like a temperate tropical breeze. She pecked a kiss on Hank's cheek that made him want more. "Dinner is ready."

Everyone sat in their customary places. Once he'd learned he occupied Bill's chair, he'd tried to switch seats, but Evelyn would hear none of it. Mrs. Riegel sat in Helen's chair, and Jamie's high chair had been moved to a corner in the shed. This was the new normal in the Capen Street bungalow, and Hank reveled in every moment.

Evelyn unfolded her linen napkin and draped it in her lap. "Hank, will you offer thanks?"

"My pleasure. Let's bow our heads." Everyone obeyed, but Lily always peeked. Summoning the authoritative tone Hank's father always used, he commanded, "Young lady, close your eyes."

Lily complied, but she wouldn't for long. Irrepressible mischief was part of her charm, and Hank would never do anything to eradicate it. He started his prayer as always, "Heavenly Father—"

A knock at the door startled everyone. Evelyn rose to answer, but Hank said, "No. Please allow me." What ruffian would make a house call at dinnertime? Hank yanked open the door and was greeted by the sight of two men in dark business suits. Cold fingers squeezed his heart. "May I help you?"

The taller man removed his hat. "I'm sorry if we've come at an inopportune moment, but we need to speak to Mrs. Evelyn Benson."

"I'm Mrs. Benson." Evelyn tugged Hank aside and greeted the men. "Please come in and have a seat."

Both men entered and perched on the front edge of the sofa cushions like flighty birds. Policemen? Detectives, perhaps. Evelyn sat in a side chair and Hank stood behind her, resting a hand on her shoulder.

The first man raked a hand through his hair. "I'm Mr. Gooden, and this is Mr. Viller. We're from Hampshire Bank."

"Mrs. Riegel, will you please take Lily to her room?" Evelyn's voice was pitched higher than normal.

Lily clanked her fork on the tabletop. "No. Dinner is hot, and I'm hungry."

"I'm so sorry we've interrupted your meal." Mr. Gooden stood. "We can come back another time."

Evelyn stood and blocked his path to the door. "No. It's fine. Please stay."

Mrs. Riegel dragged Lily toward the stairs, although the child resisted and wailed. German women always found their backbone when they needed to. Hank's mother would have done the same.

When their struggle escalated, Hank started to join the fray.

"No, Hank." Evelyn gripped Lily by the forearm and swirled her around until they stood face to face. "Lily Evelyn Halstead. Go to your room, and right now, or there will be no supper at all for you tonight. Do you understand?"

"But I'm hungry!"

Lily's words, which would have been so welcome a few months ago, now irritated as much as the mating screeches of a barn cat. But Evelyn's glare could have melted steel I-beams. Lily climbed each stair as if marching to her own execution. Mrs. Riegel applied a gentle swat to her backside, and it sped Lily along until the two were out of sight.

"I'm sorry for the commotion." Evelyn gathered her skirt behind her knees and sat again.

Hank stood behind her, poised like an archangel ready for battle.

She asked, "Gentlemen, is this about the mortgage?"

Mr. Gooden cleared his throat. "As you know, the bank has been more than lenient after the unfortunate events of this past summer."

A fire that wiped out hundreds of people was much more than unfortunate—it was a disaster. Hank planted his feet a little wider.

"Yes. And I appreciate the extra time to pay the mortgage. I've been looking into taking a second job—"

Evelyn already worked long shifts at the diner. She would never have the energy for a second job, nor should she leave Lily's care to someone else, even someone as reliable as Bernice. Evelyn was the only family Lily had left.

"That won't be necessary." Mr. Viller stood abruptly. "Richard," he said to his cohort, "It's unkind to drag this out." He turned to Evelyn and said, "What Mr. Gooden is trying to say is it is November. You are several months behind in your mortgage, and the bank has decided to foreclose." He reached into the breast pocket of his jacket and withdrew an envelope, holding it out for Evelyn. "This is notice of our repossession of this property. So as not to create undue hardship, we're giving you until November thirtieth to vacate."

Evelyn stood but swayed. Hank slipped his arm around her waist while Mr. Gooden hustled to the table for a glass of water to hand to her. She thanked him and took a sip.

Hank took over. He'd apologize to Evelyn later. "Gentlemen. What if we can bring her payments up to date?"

Evelyn muttered, "I can't. Not right away."

Hank ignored her and focused on Mr. Viller. "How much does she need to catch up?"

Mr. Viller frowned. "Are you her husband?"

No, but I want to be. Hank's affection had blossomed to full-blown adoration. He wanted to propose marriage, but he'd been waiting for Evelyn to heal from the trauma. Nevertheless, he wouldn't stand idle while she lost her home.

"No." Evelyn's voice was a little stronger. "Hank is merely a good friend, and I can't allow him to assume any of my debt."

"Again, Mrs. Benson, I'm sorry. But Hampshire Bank has shareholders, many whose fortunes and livelihoods have also been impacted by recent events. The bank needs to remain solvent, and we must balance our assets and liabilities." Mr. Viller's pretty speech made it sound like a simple business transaction, but this was deeply personal for Evelyn and Lily.

Evelyn pulled out a hankie from her pocket and clutched it like a lifeline. She didn't cry, but her soft voice shed tears. "May we have more than thirty days? I'm uncertain where we will go."

Mr. Viller set his mouth into a straight line. "Thirty days is the limit set by our board of directors to settle this matter. I suggest you begin packing right away. On December first, any personal possessions remaining in the house or garage become the property of Hampshire Bank." Mr. Viller offered the papers again, and Evelyn accepted them. "All the terms are here. Once again, Mrs. Benson, I'm sorry for your loss."

Mr. Gooden shook Evelyn's hand. "Ugly business, this. If there's anything I can do—"

"Don't offer what you can't give, Richard." Mr. Viller put on his Tyrolean hat and doffed it. Addressing Evelyn, he said, "I'm sorry, but bank personnel are prohibited from intervening in any way in foreclosures. Lawsuits, you know."

Leaden feet anchored Hank to the floor where he stood. It was probably a good thing, because he'd risk a lawsuit himself to give Mr. Viller a good punch in the mouth.

Evelyn ushered the men out the front door. After she shut it, the foreclosure papers fluttered to the floor like a white dove felled by a gunshot. Hank caught Evelyn and cradled her as she sobbed her sorrow. He brushed a kiss to her forehead but couldn't find words. How much was one woman expected to endure? When Hank had a private moment, he planned to give the Almighty a piece of his mind.

But first, he needed to make a telephone call.

———— ◆ ————

"Dearie, I don't know why you won't accept." Bernice chattered while helping to clean out Bill and Helen's closet. The woman was a saint, offering to sleep on her newfangled Estee sofa bed and give Lily and Evelyn her only bedroom. Not only would it impose too much on Bernice, but Evelyn would soon pluck out all her hair if she had to share a bed with her cantankerous niece.

Lily battled Evelyn on every front—meals, attire, homework—all were targets in her ground assault worthy of General Patton. She still grieved the loss of her family, as did Evelyn, but with the limited understanding of a child. Lily was scared, and she had every right to be.

"Please don't think I'm ungrateful. I'd give anything to stay in Hartford. But the prospects of finding a place we can afford on my salary are about as good as Greta Garbo running for president."

"Bubkes." Bernice kept emptying hangers while Evelyn burst into laughter at her use of the new slang term. "That's why you should move in with me. It's a mistake to uproot Lily right now."

Perhaps she was right, but Evelyn was out of options. The day after the foreclosure notice was served, she'd written to her elderly aunt in Georgia and received a lukewarm invitation to move there. Doubtless Clarice had only acted out of obligation to her sister's last living child, but Evelyn would make sure she didn't regret taking them in. "Aunt Clarice lives in a beautiful old farmhouse. I visited there with Bill in the summers, and it was a wonderful environment for children."

"What's the name of that place again?"

"Chickasawhatchee, Georgia."

"Lily won't be able to say it, let alone spell it."

Evelyn tugged open a dresser drawer. Helen's blouses, neatly folded with tissue paper guarding against wrinkles, still smelled like Emeraude perfume. If Evelyn hadn't been forced to move, she might have left them untouched for years. But it was past time to forge ahead. Life in Georgia would be better than life in a city tenement for the poor. "There's an old cemetery there with a statue of an angel sleeping on a pillow. It's charming."

"A baby's grave, no doubt." Bernice tucked Bill's suit into a linen garment bag for donation. She turned to unleash the full power of her ire, her eyes as green as Helen's perfume bottle. "That's a perfect place for a grief-stricken child to play. Alone."

Evelyn felt her walls crumbling, and she scurried to shore them up. "I'll always be grateful to you, Bernice. You've been a true and caring friend in the darkest hour of my life, and I'll never forget it. Please forgive me, but I can't accept your offer. That's my final word."

Bernice tossed an armful of trousers on the bed and rounded the corner for an embrace. Evelyn felt like an Amazon next to the diminutive woman. Bernice was small but mighty, with a heart as big as the Montana sky. Evelyn squeezed gently.

Bernice hugged the stuffing out of her. "I'm the one who should be asking forgiveness. I don't mean to make this any more difficult for you than it already is. We'll put it under the bench, ja?" Bernice didn't often lapse into Pennsylvania Deutsch with the war on, but this was a new phrase.

Evelyn took a stab at the meaning. "We'll forget about it?"

"Yes." Bernice returned to her task. "We'll have this room redd up in no time."

Yes, Bill and Helen's room would soon be cleaned out and put in order, but who would redd up Evelyn's soul?

Chapter Twenty-Six

"I tried, but it's no use." Eddie's voice crackled in the static on the phone line from Sarasota. "They won't pay anyone unless they first have a hearing."

Hank loosened his tie and took a deep breath. "Evelyn might lose her home while she waits. How can you let that happen?"

"My name's not Ringling, boy. This isn't my fault." It didn't take much imagination to picture the veins on Eddie's temples popping out. "Since when did you get to be such a do-gooder?"

"I'm simply trying to help two people whose lives are about to be destroyed."

Eddie grumbled, "Those lawyers mucked it up fast." Compensation would be made to the victims but only after a grueling application process and adjudication by a court-appointed panel. "We paid a large chunk of change before we could leave town, but claims came in so fast they put it all in a receivership."

Good thing he'd called Eddie before getting Evelyn's hopes up. He'd help her apply for compensation, but it would be too late to prevent foreclosure. "Thanks for asking, Eddie. I owe you one."

"You can pay off by coming to Sarasota. I have a new chute man, but

Spartacus likes him. Less of a show that way."

"Not a chance." After a trip to Speigletown, he'd like to follow his girls to Chickasawhatchee. If he wasn't in jail. "My scars are almost healed. Why sign up for more?"

"What'd you ever do to him anyway? He's a pussycat with me."

Spartacus, rigging, sawdust—all in Hank's past. As were cracking ice, psychiatric hospitalization, and bar fights. What would his future hold? And who would be with him in it? "Well, since you're such big buddies, give him a pat on the head from me."

Eddie echoed Hank. "Not a chance. I have to go. Some big stink about a new tent."

He hoped they'd figure out a different way to waterproof it. "See ya. And thanks again." When Hank hung up, he severed not only his connection to Sarasota but also any connection to hope Evelyn might save her home.

———————

Hank reached for the doorbell right before Evelyn flung the front door open, ran out, and nearly mowed him down. He grabbed her shoulders, and when she looked up, tears had tracked down her cheeks. "What's wrong, Evie?"

"Lily went upstairs to do her homework, and now she's gone."

"Gone where?"

"That's it. I don't know. I've searched the whole house. She loves to hide, and she's good at it. I've called and called, but she won't come out."

"She's got to be in there somewhere. A child doesn't just disappear." The words escaped Hank's lips before he considered their impact.

"Yes, Hank. They do." She shivered in the early November rain. She'd been in such a hurry she hadn't grabbed a coat or umbrella. "I have to find her."

"What's your plan?"

"Just get out of my way." Evelyn pushed past him, took a few steps, and stopped.

Hank's heart broke. "You don't have one, do you?"

Evelyn's voice sounded not much older than Lily's. "No."

"She's probably still inside, warm and dry. Let me try coaxing her out." Hank reached for Evelyn's hand. "Come on. If we don't find her, we'll start a hunt."

Evelyn allowed Hank to lead her back inside. He grabbed a towel from the kitchen for Evelyn to dry her hair and began his game of cat and mouse.

Thirty minutes later, a thorough search confirmed Evelyn's fear. Evidence mounted. Lily's little pink suitcase was missing, and the clothing in her half-closed dresser drawers was mussed. Most convincing of all, Miss Persimmon was nowhere to be found.

Lily had run away.

"Sweetheart," Hank begged, "please sit down. You're wearing out the rug."

Evelyn paced the living room, and her eyes shot daggers at Hank. "While you're sitting there trying to figure this out, Lily is getting farther and farther away. She could be wet, cold, frightened, or . . ." She dropped on the sofa and put her head in her hands.

"Let's solve this with logic, not emotion."

"Well, *pardon me* for being worried, but I've already lost Jamie. I can't lose Lily too." She flung her words at Hank like a glass of cold water, and he flinched.

Hank chose not to rise to the bait. "Have you talked to Bernice?"

Evelyn jutted her chin. "I was headed there when you stopped me."

A lie. Evelyn had been too distraught. Hank raised one eyebrow and said nothing.

"Well, I would have gone there if you'd given me a minute to think."

"Does Bernice have a phone?"

"No."

Verbal ping-pong wasn't going to find Lily. Hank let the ball bounce away without a return volley. "Let's go over there. But this time, get a coat and an umbrella. We can't have you getting sick on top of everything else."

"You're not my nanny." Evelyn tugged her things out of the closet and donned them like an obstinate toddler. He'd chalk up her bad mood to worry and have fun teasing about it after they found Lily. She blew out the door like a January blizzard, and Hank had to trot to catch up. Traffic forced her to stop before crossing Capen Street.

Hank wrapped her freezing, shaky hand on the umbrella's handle with his. He sidled underneath with her, slipped his arm around her waist, and tugged her close. Evelyn stiffened but didn't push him away. When the coast was clear, he didn't allow her to put distance between them. "I'm sure she's there, sweetheart."

"Don't patronize me." Evelyn clutched the lapels of her trench coat together with hands that quivered. "Let's hope she's there."

They ran together up the concrete steps and into the apartment building's foyer. Hank lowered the umbrella and shook it off, which gave Evelyn time to escape. She flew up the terrazzo-tiled stairs to the landing, turned out of sight, and kept climbing, the patter of her footsteps keeping tempo with the falling rain.

Hank had never visited Bernice, so he scanned the rows of steel mailboxes. Neatly labeled, they listed her apartment number. 202. Hank took the stairs two at a time.

Evelyn entered without pausing to knock. Ignoring proper etiquette was yet another symptom she'd descended into panic. She also left the door ajar.

Bernice emerged from the kitchen, wiped her hands on her apron, and spoke as calmly as if people barging into her apartment were an everyday thing. "What's wrong?"

"Lily's missing." Evelyn's quaking hand brushed away a tear. "We've looked all through the house and can't find her. We thought perhaps she'd come here."

"I wish she had, dear, but I've not seen her."

The statement made Hank's stomach sour. He'd been certain they'd find her tucked in Bernice's apartment snug as a bug in a rug. All thoughts of teasing Evelyn fled as Hank's panic grew faster than dandelions in May.

"Then where could she be?" Evelyn's sentence ended on an atypical whine.

"Now, dearie. Sit down."

"I wish everyone would quit telling me to sit!" She whirled and headed for the door. "I'm going to search door to door if I have to, but I won't lose Lily."

Hank blocked her exit. "Wait a minute." Evelyn pressed her lips into a firm, straight line, but Hank offered no escape. He turned to Bernice. "I see you've been cooking."

"Baking." Bernice patted her hair, and a little cloud of white puffed out of the braid that wound neatly around her head. "I've been in the kitchen a little more than an hour, but the pie will be worth it. I planned to share—"

"More than an hour?"

"Yes, possibly." Bernice stood taller, but still her head barely reached Hank's chest. "My pie crust is delicious, but tricky."

To Evelyn, Hank asked, "When did you last see Lily?"

"About an hour ago." Evelyn chewed on her bottom lip. "I'm not certain when she left."

"Bernice, where's your bedroom?"

———————◆◆◆———————

Evelyn followed Hank down the tiny hall and pressed against him as Bernice slowly opened the door. She couldn't see in, but when Bernice smiled and put a finger to her lips, Evelyn stumbled back a step.

Hank and Bernice stepped aside, and Evelyn moved to the front of the pack. She eased the door open and spied Lily asleep on Bernice's quilt-covered bed. She lay on her side facing the door, with Miss Persimmon tucked under her chin in a tight hug. Her suitcase peeked out from under the bed, and for the first time in months, her face was relaxed in perfect, peaceful slumber.

Evelyn's knees weakened, but Hank's encircling arms steadied her. Bernice crept into the room, unfolded a crocheted coverlet which lay neatly draped over the footboard, and covered Lily. She planted a soft kiss on Lily's forehead before tiptoeing out and shutting the door so softly the latch didn't snick.

Tucking her arm through Evelyn's elbow, Bernice guided the search party back to her living room. Evelyn sat with no argument, and Bernice sidled up next to her. Hank plopped in the Victorian rocking chair with carved gooseneck swans for arms. He rocked back and wiped his hands down his face.

Bernice took Evelyn's hand and prayed, "Heavenly Father, we thank Thee that Lily is found and that Thine angels guided her here safely."

Besides running away, Lily had crossed the street against the rules. Evelyn planned to give her a good lecture when she woke up. After she hugged the stuffings out of her.

"And thank Thee, Lord," Bernice continued, "that Thee promises to guide our steps as surely as Thee guided Lily's."

Bernice's faith never ebbed, but Evelyn's lay in ashes. She wavered from day to day, wrestling with the utter devastation and balancing it against God's promises for protection and direction. Had God led Bill to the circus as he walked into a tent that would burn down half an hour later? If so, Evelyn didn't want God's guidance.

"Now, Lord, help us to seek Thy divine wisdom, for we have none in ourselves. Shine Thy light, for we know it will dispel the darkness."

Bernice prayed as if she read Evelyn's mind. She'd need supernatural help to desire to know God's will, much less do it. Darkness had swirled into her life like the tornado that struck Dorothy, plucking Evelyn from her Kansas and depositing her in the mysterious land of Oz. No familiar landmarks, no family except headstrong Lily, and now, she'd have to leave the house she loved. Could God's light overcome so much darkness?

With a little squeeze of Evelyn's hand, Bernice ended her prayer with an "Amen." Drawing both their hands into her lap, the gentle woman studied Evelyn with glittering eyes the color of emeralds but as hard as diamonds. "Now, dearie, I'll speak my piece."

"Perhaps later." Hank's compassion bone was showing.

Bernice shut him down. "No. Now. We don't have time to chase the hen around the coop again." She rubbed the back of her hand against her cheek and left a smudge of flour. "It would be a crime to pluck that little girl away from everything and everyone she's ever known just because you're too proud to accept my help."

Ouch. Chickasawhatchee might as well be Oz as far as Lily was concerned. And Aunt Clarice was no Bernice. Even in childhood, Evelyn had been terrified of her aunt's stern, demanding demeanor. How would Clarice respond to Lily's rebellious streak? Gasoline and matches. Those two would start a fire of a different kind.

But was Bernice right about the reason for her refusal to move in? When Evelyn pushed aside the curtain of practical concerns, would there be a little wizard named Pride? Possibly.

Hank opened his mouth.

Bernice shook her head and he shut it again. "I would forgive you, and so would God, but would you ever forgive yourself for inflicting more pain on a child in so much distress she ran away?"

No. She wouldn't. Evelyn bit her bottom lip.

"Far be it from me to tell you what to do, but my offer stands. Lily has already cast her vote. How about it, child? We can consider it a temporary arrangement until you get back on your feet, and I promise I'll make it as painless as possible."

How could Evelyn withstand such an assault of love? And why would she want to? Her resistance melted like a water-soaked Wicked Witch. Summoning the remnants of her resolve, Evelyn said, "Thank you, Bernice. I—no, *we*—accept."

Hank grinned like Ray Bolger's scarecrow. "Now that's settled, I do have one question."

Bernice had wrapped Evelyn in a hug, but she released her to answer. "What's that?"

Hank turned puppy dog eyes on Bernice. "The aroma from the kitchen is driving me crazy. When are you serving the pie?"

Chapter Twenty-Seven

Continued rain showers had caused misery on their trek to church even with Hank carrying Lily most of the way. They slid into their "regular" pew, far from where Evelyn had sat with Bill and Helen. She'd resigned her children's teaching position a month after the fire, unable to bear her students' incessant questions. Evelyn had no answers for herself, let alone for them.

Beside her, Hank cradled Lily. The two had grown too close for Evelyn's comfort. Was it protectiveness or jealousy? Hard to tell. She'd give anything for Lily to wrap arms around her neck or snuggle close for hugs. But her niece reserved those treasures for Hank.

Physical affection had never marked her relationship with Lily, but Jamie? Evelyn had proudly worn drool stains on her blouse, popsicle goo in her hair, and slobber on her cheek from Jamie's kisses. She ached for sensations she would never feel again—hugs from his chubby arms, the sting of an inadvertent tug on a lock of hair, the bump of a little forehead against hers during an awkward good-night kiss.

Most of all, Evelyn missed their wake-up routine. Lily's gripes and grumbles were no substitute for Jamie's pats and snuggly cuddles. If he even gave them anymore. He'd be three years old by now. It wasn't fair to compare the children, and Lily's mood had been altered by the horrors she'd witnessed. Still, Evelyn craved the feel of Jamie in her arms with a fervor that had not abated with the passage of time.

Evelyn had also chosen not to conduct a funeral for Jamie. With no body to bury, it seemed pointless. Perhaps someday she would place a memorial stone for him on Bill and Helen's grave, but her heart was still too tender.

With great irony, the music director had chosen "God Moves in a Mysterious Way" to sing this morning. Evelyn never wanted to hear it again after Bill and Helen's funeral. The ache in the back of Evelyn's throat prevented singing, but she mouthed the lyrics anyway. Folks were always watching.

> *Judge not the Lord by feeble sense,*
> *But trust Him for His grace;*
> *Behind a frowning providence*
> *He hides a smiling face.*

Had Evelyn judged God and found Him inattentive? Cruel? Her circumstances would certainly support the notion God was frowning upon her. First George's death, then Bill and Helen's, and then the mystery surrounding Jamie's disappearance and likely demise. She spent long hours at the diner in the impossible effort to make ends meet, and still foreclosure loomed like the Grim Reaper. In less than three weeks she'd move in with Bernice, and then what?

What could God do to show her His smile again? Turn back time? Resurrect Bill and Helen? Impossible. Drop thousands of dollars in her lap to pay the mortgage? Unlikely. Help her find Jamie? If he was still alive? Improbable. His trail was so cold an Eskimo couldn't find it.

The congregation continued singing, but Evelyn's lips stopped moving of their own accord.

> *Blind unbelief is sure to err*
> *And scan His work in vain;*
> *God is His own interpreter,*
> *And He will make it plain.*

Hank's rich baritone voice was so similar to Bill's. Parishioners had always cast appreciative looks her brother's way, amazed that a man with a stutter could sing so clearly and not miss a word. It would be simple to lean into Hank, close her eyes, and pretend Bill was present.

But he wasn't. Although Hank's kindness and sense of humor were reminiscent of Bill, his affection was clear. He wanted to be much more than a brother. But Evelyn held him at arm's length. She refused his every offer to help financially, trying desperately to maintain her sense of self and independence lest she rush into a rash decision because it was an easy answer to her troubles.

There could be no doubt. Not only had Evelyn judged God with feeble sense, she also had lapsed dangerously near blind unbelief. In an ironic turnabout, Hank seemed closer to God recently, while she'd walked farther away. Was she still a genuine believer? At times she doubted it. If God didn't make His presence plain, and soon, she might tumble into the abyss.

Relief flooded Evelyn when the hymn ceased. Organ music still lingered in the rafters when she dropped back into the pew. She rifled through her pocketbook for the hankie she always carried there these days, drew it out, and dabbed at her eyes.

Hank placed a proprietary arm around her shoulders, and Evelyn scooted away. One look at her expression and he withdrew it. It wouldn't do to fuel gossip about Evelyn's love life. Hank had been unable to shed his reputation, so whenever he touched her in public, she'd receive frosty glares from church members as people whispered and turned away.

One woman, a well-to-do gray-haired matron, had dared to ask the question others wanted to. "How can you take up with a circus man after what happened to your family?"

As if Hank was personally responsible for the fire. A disreputable ne'er-do-well. Bernice had shut the woman down with a none-of-your-business reply, but the words reached their target anyway. Why had Evelyn let Hank so near, not only to her but to Lily? Was she desperate enough to assuage her loneliness and grief with a man who'd led a nomadic life and was likely to return to it? She'd never recover if he abandoned her now, let alone Lily.

Reverend Archibald ascended to the pulpit and announced his text for the day. "Please open your Bibles to Isaiah 55."

Hank reached for the pew Bible because Evelyn had stopped bringing her own. The pastor read several verses before Evelyn tuned in. His words, amplified by the public address system, thudded in Evelyn's spirit like hand grenades about to explode.

> *Seek ye the LORD while he may be found, call ye upon him while he is near.*

Evelyn had sought physical shelter, financial provision, and respite from her loneliness, but she had not sought God nor believed He was near.

> *Let the wicked forsake his way, and the unrighteous man his thoughts: and let him return unto the LORD, and he will have mercy upon him; and to our God, for he will abundantly pardon.*

Even now, as the Holy Spirit challenged Evelyn with the words of scripture, she struggled to let go of her judgments against God.

> *For my thoughts are not your thoughts, neither are your ways my ways, saith the LORD.*

> *For as the heavens are higher than the earth, so are my ways higher than your ways, and my thoughts than your thoughts.*

Lily stirred, reaching for Evelyn and scooting into her lap. They sat face-to-face until Lily nuzzled Evelyn's neck and let go a deep sigh. Undone by Lily's choice to leave Hank's embrace for hers, Evelyn wound her arms tightly around her niece and rubbed her back. Soon Lily's breath evened out into a deep sleep.

A mental picture floated into Evelyn's mind on wings of a dove, seeing herself seated in God's lap in much the same way. She could almost feel His embrace, snug and comforting. She leaned into it with a new understanding. Evelyn was but a child in the universe God created. She'd never receive the answers to her questions when her capacity to understand was limited by her humanity. Evelyn would have to demonstrate to God the same trust Lily had placed in her—to guide her safely through life's circumstances, no matter how inexplicable or how much they contradicted her belief in a loving, powerful God.

Evelyn whispered a simple prayer, "I choose to trust You, God. Help me not to doubt."

A blanket of peace descended on Evelyn so heavy that she slumped against Hank's sturdy shoulder. He slid closer and placed his arm around her again. Evelyn closed her eyes, but she continued to listen to Reverend Archibald's reading.

> *For as the rain cometh down, and the snow from heaven, and returneth not thither, but watereth the earth, and maketh it bring forth and bud, that it may give seed to the sower, and bread to the eater:*
>
> *So shall my word be that goeth forth out of my mouth: it shall not return unto me void, but it shall accomplish that which I please, and it shall prosper in the thing whereto I sent it.*

Evelyn no longer cared who watched or what they thought. She rested her head on Hank's shoulder and accepted his embrace. Only one opinion mattered, and her heavenly Father understood her reasons. God had sent Hank in the time of her distress, and she soaked in his comfort like a thirsty rose drinking the morning dew. In His goodness, He'd provided solace and help, and she'd refused it because of stubborn pride.

Well, no more. The pastor's words faded to oblivion as Evelyn finally laid down the burden that was too heavy for her. *Lord, forgive my pride. Show me Your path, and I will follow wherever it may lead. Guide me, and help me as I wait for Your word to accomplish what You please in my life. Amen.*

People stared, but who cared? Not Hank. Evelyn had fallen asleep, leaning on his arm, trust and peace blanketing her expression for the first time he'd known her. Bernice leaned forward slightly and blessed him with an approving nod. That was all he needed to sit still as a statue while his shoulder served as Evelyn's pillow.

When the congregation stood for the closing hymn, Evelyn roused and blinked. Lily slept on in her arms, and Evelyn started to scoot forward. Hank shook his head and remained seated with her. She relaxed against him again.

A woman across the aisle scowled in their direction, even while she sang "It Is Well with My Soul." Absurd. Hilarious, actually. The juxtaposition of her song with her nasty expression. Hank couldn't help it. He winked at her. She stiffened and looked forward again. One biddy down, several to go. He met the gaze of every person who stared and affixed a contented smile on his lips to tell them what he thought of their opinions.

When the pastor began to voice the closing prayer and benediction, Evelyn handed Lily off to Hank. He stood, the child no heavier than a feather, and Evelyn stood with him. She slipped her hand into his, and it energized Hank like a jolt from the Hellcat's centrifugal supercharger. Come what may, even incarceration for murder, he'd make it through with God's help and the support of this woman.

But would she support him? The burden to go to Speigletown and atone for the soldier's death weighed heavier every day. Even if it cost him his budding relationship, he needed to tell her and go. Faith, family, friends. Hank's father often preached these priorities, and Hank's duty to God must supersede any notions of marriage. Yes, he planned to propose Evelyn share a future as his wife, but first he needed to settle everything in his past.

Bernice and Lily had a cookie-making date this afternoon, so he'd take Evelyn aside and tell her everything. No one spoke to them as they traversed the aisle to the exits, and Evelyn's cheeks flushed. If the heavenly Father understood why Evelyn fell asleep in church, why should His children object?

Their little troupe, including Bernice, stopped in the narthex to don their rain gear. A side door opened, and a large man collapsed his umbrella, shook off the rain, and propped it in a nearby corner. Sergeant Amato. Dressed in a spiffy suit and tie, Hank almost didn't recognize him.

"Mrs. Benson."

Amato's words echoed off the terrazzo floors, and everyone looked Evelyn's way. She completed her task of buttoning Lily's coat and spun around to greet him.

"Why, Sergeant, I almost wouldn't recognize you out of uniform." Her expression changed from cheerful to concerned as fast as a flash of lightning. "What's the matter?"

Amato strode forward and shook Hank's hand. "We need to talk. A matter of utmost importance. Is there a room nearby we could use?"

"Bernice, could you walk Lily home?"

Still half-asleep, Lily didn't yet object to Evelyn's question.

Bernice put her arm around Lily's shoulders, raised an umbrella, and scooted her toward the door. "Come on, Lily. We have cookies to make."

"This way." Evelyn headed down the hallway to classrooms, squeezing Hank's hand with a grip worthy of Joe Louis.

He hoped Amato's news wouldn't be a knockout blow.

Chapter Twenty-Eight

Evelyn perched on the edge of the folding chair and fought to maintain the peace she'd experienced only moments ago. God—present and in charge—would strengthen her to endure, no matter what the news.

Hank scooted a chair so close their thighs touched. He still held her hand and gave it an encouraging squeeze. He asked Amato, "What have you discovered?"

The sergeant's green eyes fairly glowed. "I'm not certain yet, so don't get your hopes up."

Evelyn's stomach flipped despite his admonition. "Please, Sergeant. Just get to the point."

"I've been looking for you all morning, but I couldn't find you anywhere." Amato took a deep breath and leaned forward. "It's Sunday, of course. I should have known you'd be in church."

"Amato." Hank's warning interrupted the sergeant's ramble.

"Sorry. We've looked for Jamie so long with nothing to show for it." Hank's groan brought forth another, "Sorry." Amato took Evelyn's other hand.

She gripped it and nodded for him to continue. She was as ready as she'd ever be.

"I talked last night to a woman in Middletown. She happened to be at the circus that day with a group of nurses who escaped without any casualties. They rushed to Municipal, but they were transferred to Hartford Hospital to help." Turning to Hank, he continued, "We've never thought about interviewing the people who don't regularly work there. Her name came up on a card filed away that listed volunteers from out of town."

"What does this have to do with Jamie?" Evelyn's heart might burst from the strain if Amato didn't deliver the news.

"The morning after the fire, a couple came looking for their nephew. The wife's sister and her husband were identified among the dead, but the boy wasn't. Their description matched a little boy who'd not yet been claimed."

Hank's eyes narrowed. "And no one remembered this when you asked?"

"You may forget how crazy everything was." Amato released Evelyn's hand, took out his handkerchief, and mopped his brow. "We were looking for a child who hadn't been matched with relatives. This boy had already been taken home, so no one put two and two together. It wasn't deliberate."

Evelyn wanted to hope, but this information was new and confusing. "This nurse thinks it might be Jamie?"

"The uncle had been stationed in England, so they had never met the child. They only had a picture of him as an infant, but the resemblance was proof enough to give the boy to them." Amato loosened his tie. "He was the right age, and he had blond hair and hazel eyes like Jamie. With so many people needing help, no one looked into it further."

"Why do you think it might be Jamie?"

At Evelyn's question, Amato handed her a card with a description. Her eyes seized one detail. The child was missing a shoe. A white Stride Rite high top. Hope fluttered, but she quelled its rise. Until she knew more, she couldn't allow it. "We were there the next morning. Are you telling me we missed him by a couple of hours?"

"I don't know." Amato grimaced. "It's best not to think about it too much. But we should go meet this family and see if the boy is Jamie."

Hank asked the question before Evelyn could voice it. "Where do they live, Sergeant?"

"Troy, New York. Just outside Albany."

Hank retreated so far inside himself he barely heard Amato speaking anymore. Troy. A stone's throw from home. It would be a tricky feat to manage both crises at once, but Jamie might be in Troy. Not even a possible arrest would keep Hank from going to find him. But first he had to tell Evelyn everything. That wouldn't be easy, especially after the tender moments they had shared this morning. It was simple to think of them as a family—himself, Evelyn, and Lily. And now, possibly, Jamie. That beautiful dream would never come to be if he destroyed Evelyn's budding trust by concealing his past any longer.

"How soon can we go?" Evelyn's decisive tone brooked no argument.

A sigh escaped Amato, and he mopped his forehead again. "I haven't contacted the family or local authorities. I thought the best approach might be to see if I can finagle a meeting without arousing suspicion about our true motives. If you can catch a glimpse of the boy, you'd know, right?"

Evelyn's voice quavered. "I would. It's only been four months since the fire. Surely, he hasn't changed that much."

The sergeant leaned forward and placed one hand on his knee. "I'm trying to think of a plan that will make it easiest on everyone if this is a mistake. It's always possible the child really is their nephew."

Hank needed to eliminate the rare possibility he might know them. "Who are they?"

"Dr. and Mrs. Malcolm DuMont. They live outside of town on a gated estate named Sycaway."

Hank stiffened. "*The* Malcolm DuMont? The engineer?"

"You've heard of him, then. Yes. After his stint in the military was over, he got a job teaching at Rensselaer Polytechnic Institute."

Evelyn wilted like a cut flower. "Doctor?" She turned to Hank and gripped his forearm. "What if they won't let us have him back?"

"Now, Mrs. Benson." Amato straightened and held out a steady hand. "Evelyn. If there's been a mistake, the legal system will work in your favor. Blood trumps money."

Evelyn's head still drooped.

"Listen, sweetheart." Hank infused his tone with confidence, not the shakiness he truly felt. "Let's find out if it's Jamie before we start borrowing trouble."

Amato rose from his chair, and Hank stood to shake his hand. He said, "I'll see what I can set up. It's about a two-hour drive, so let's leave tomorrow at eight o'clock in the morning."

Evelyn stood with Hank's assistance. "Thank you. I'll make arrangements with Charlie for a day off. Will you excuse me, please?" Evelyn scurried out, headed for the ladies' room.

The men stood together, stunned, like two passengers who just missed the bus as it pulled away. Finally, Amato said, "What if it isn't Jamie? I'm worried about her."

"That makes two of us."

A famous engineer? Brilliant professor and owner of an estate? What chance did Evelyn have of regaining custody of Jamie from someone so notable and wealthy? And he was married, to boot. Not a nearly broke gold star widow working at a diner and facing foreclosure.

Evelyn knelt on the ladies' room floor and hugged the commode, but breakfast was long gone. All she managed was dry heaves. She wouldn't put it past Hank to barge in and check on her, so she pulled herself to her feet and stood at the sink to freshen up. She splashed water on her face and pinched her cheeks to bring back the color. After donning and pinning her hat, she pulled down the fishnet veil. It wouldn't hide her completely, but any distraction from the redness of her eyes might help her appearance.

Who was she kidding? Her body, mind, and spirit were fractured by fear, grief, and loss. She could barely hold herself together, much less be a parent to Lily. And perhaps, Jamie. She took her frazzled thoughts in hand and spoke to the image in the mirror. "Buck up, kiddo. We'll make it."

Besides, she wasn't completely alone. She had Hank.

Hank sat alone on the sofa while Evelyn changed out of her dress into slacks. They had enjoyed lunch with Bernice, but it had been a relief to leave boisterous Lily at Bernice's apartment for the afternoon, especially in light of Amato's announcement.

The shocking news that perhaps Jamie was alive had put Evelyn on edge. She'd marched out of the ladies' room with an expression he couldn't read, but she had placed her hand in his as they left the church. She'd calmed little by little, but she still wasn't herself. He wished he could spare her more trauma, but there was no time left. He had to clear the air.

The soft tread of Evelyn's slippers descending the wooden steps snapped Hank to attention. He stood because of his mother's training, yes, but also because he feared if he sat too long, his knee would start to jiggle. Evelyn knew that nervous tic very well, and she always ferreted out the reason.

Evelyn's wan smile didn't reach her eyes. "You don't have to get up every time I enter the room."

"If I didn't, and Mother found out, I wouldn't sit down for a week."

"You seldom talk about her."

Thank You, Lord. The perfect opening. Now, give me courage. "Funny you should say that, because I have something to tell you."

She sat on the sofa and straightened the doily covering the armrest. "Do we have to talk about it now? My plate is kind of full."

"If you want me to go with you tomorrow, it can't wait."

"Why?"

"Because my hometown is less than ten miles from Troy."

Evelyn melted into the couch cushions. "What a strange coincidence. Maybe after we settle things about Jamie you can go see your parents."

"Yes. I'd like that." *Be brave.* "But I'll also need to stop at the police station before I do."

She pulled her knees up to her chest and wrapped them with her arms. "I can't take any more piecemeal revelations, Hank. I'm as wrung out as a dirty dishrag. Just tell me why you ran away from home."

RHONDA DRAGOMIR

Hank's heart tried to thrum out of his chest. His mouth went as dry as sand in the Mojave. "This is a rotten time to talk about it, what with Jamie—"

"Hank Webb." Evelyn leaned forward and put her feet back on the floor. "If you're not planning to be completely honest with me right this minute, then head out the front door and don't come back."

She didn't mean it, not after the closeness they'd felt that morning in church.

But Evelyn stood, crossed the room, and opened the door. "Talk or leave. It's your choice."

Hank met her at the door and took her in his arms. She remained stiff for only a few seconds before she buried her face in his shirt.

Her voice almost inaudible, she said, "Please."

"Sweetheart, let's sit down." Hank guided her back to the sofa, and she plopped down. He sat next to her and slipped an arm around her shoulders, desperately hoping not to lose the trust she'd just given him.

With everything to lose but so much to gain, Hank dived in. "I've told you I was 4F."

"Yes. But why did you go on the run?" Evelyn turned her face upward, and her features spoke both hope and fear.

"I got into a fight with some soldiers..." Determined to be completely forthright, he added, "...in a bar."

"You're not a drinker, are you?"

"No." Hank exhaled a deep breath. "I've never had a drop of alcohol since that day."

"Were you drunk?"

"I wish I had that excuse." Hank drew her nearer, pleased when she didn't resist. He held her securely now, but he'd let her go if she changed her mind. "I only had a couple of beers, so I didn't feel drunk. But four soldiers at the bar that day were gassed."

"Let me guess." Evelyn frowned. "They teased you for not enlisting. Soldiers did that to Bill all the time."

"You're a good guesser." Hank forged ahead. "But I took a swing at one of them. I walloped him good."

"So you're wanted for assault."

"I wish that's all it was." In a vision that often replayed in his thoughts, Hank saw the crumpled, motionless body of the man who struck his head on the corner of the bar when he went down.

Evelyn removed herself from his embrace. "What happened?"

"I think I killed him."

Chapter Twenty-Nine

Hank? A murderer? Evelyn left her spot beside him and sat in Bill's prized La-Z-Boy lounger, which she'd not done since his death. The faint aroma of Old Spice wrapped her in comfort.

Hank started to stand, but Evelyn halted him with a hand gesture. "How could you not know whether you killed him?"

"One of his buddies checked for a pulse and said, 'You killed him.'" Those three little words had hung over Hank's life like a specter of ruin, but now it was time to take him on, win or lose. He'd fight Beelzebub himself to be free to marry Evelyn. "I panicked and ran."

"Let me get this straight." Evelyn's expression betrayed her true feelings despite the calmness of her words. "You were drunk, you struck a man, and you ran away before finding out whether he was dead or not."

Hank should have listened to the little voice telling him this would be too much for her. "I said I might have been a little drunk."

"It's like saying you were a little pregnant, Hank. You either were or weren't."

"Okay. Maybe I was drunk. But I didn't mean to kill him."

"That doesn't matter." Evelyn assumed the erect posture of a self-righteous church lady. "You might be facing murder charges in Troy."

"Maybe. I plan to go and find out."

"When?" Evelyn stood and paced the floor. "Before or after I show up hand in hand with a possible felon to ask *Doctor* DuMont to give my nephew back?"

"Don't make it sound like that."

"Like what? Like the truth?" Evelyn stood still and put her hands on her hips. "Tell me one word I just said that wasn't true."

I'm sorry. Too late to be deemed sincere. *I didn't mean to.* Trite. *Please forgive me.* Forgiveness wasn't Evelyn's to give. Hank needed to face the court, accept his punishment, and ask forgiveness—beginning with his victim's family. And his own parents. Then he should follow the rising urge in his heart to run as far away from Evelyn and the children as he could. Even if it destroyed him.

Hank dragged himself to his feet and reclaimed his hat and overcoat from the peg rack behind the front door. The heat of Evelyn's gaze burned a hole in his back, but when he turned around, he could see she'd been scorched as well. How could he have imagined she'd react any other way? "I don't blame you. This is all my fault. I wish I had words to describe how sorry I am for making you believe I was a better man."

She didn't contradict him, standing braced like an oak tree determined to survive an approaching forest fire.

Hank donned his gear and tugged down the brim of his fedora. "I'll pray for you tomorrow." When Evelyn didn't respond, he added, "May I call on you after I get this straightened out?"

A fat tear coursed down her right cheek, and she brushed it away. "Please don't. We're all too fragile. I don't know how we will do living with Bernice, whether I'll have Jamie or not, where he would even sleep. . ." Evelyn's hands shook with emotions Hank was guilty of causing. When she regained her composure, she said softly, "This should just be goodbye. I need to focus on making a life for what's left of my family. Things are complicated enough without becoming entangled with your troubles."

A dagger through Hank's heart might have been less painful, but Evelyn was right. He should have listened to Darla and stayed away from her at the very beginning. But how could a moth resist a beautiful flame? It must fly near, even if it died. Intense pain consumed him as the fluttering wings of love burned to death. The best thing he could do now was leave.

Hank picked up her limp hand and kissed the back tenderly. "Goodbye, Evelyn. Please accept my apology for making this more difficult for you. That was never my intention." Hank reached for the door. Evelyn's hand lingered in the air as if she possibly wavered in her decision, but it was best for both of them if he ignored it.

He strode down the sidewalk into the pouring rain and tightened the belt of his coat. He passed through the gate, which did not creak. He had oiled it mere weeks ago while nourishing the fool's dream that he might one day live in the cozy little home with a happy wife and children. When he latched it behind him, he couldn't resist one last look at the Capen Street bungalow.

Evelyn had already closed the door.

The next morning, Evelyn answered Amato's soft knock on the front door. Eight o'clock. The sergeant was nothing if not prompt. She emerged, painfully alone.

"Where's Hank?"

Amato's question struck Evelyn like a stick against a spiderweb, leaving the remnants a tangled, sticky mess. She couldn't handle personal questions and focus on today's task, so she offered an answer that brooked no further probing. "I need to do this without him."

Amato raised his eyebrows but thankfully he asked no more. He ushered her to the passenger seat of his black 1941 Ford Super Deluxe, and soon it sped down the highway to New York.

The trip gave her more than enough time to stew. Hank—gone. For good this time. Jamie—possibly alive but in the custody of people who might not return him to her. Lily—angry and pouting because she wanted to see Hank. Evelyn couldn't bring herself to explain she'd never see him again.

After telling Bernice everything, the compassionate woman had offered to keep Lily for the next few days, ply her with sweets, and take her to school. The plan placated Lily, who never turned down the opportunity to be spoiled.

Evelyn had rifled through her closet for something appropriate to wear, but she'd lost so much weight in the past months nothing fit her too-thin frame. She had kept only one of Helen's garments, a handmade navy-blue victory suit. When she had slipped on the jacket, it buttoned as if it had been tailored for her by Helen's talented hands.

Amato tried to keep up a steady chatter, but Evelyn's one-word responses had quieted him. She smoothed down the suit's narrow lapels and reached into one of the tiny hidden pockets. To her surprise, it still contained one of Helen's hankies. She sniffed the scent of *Emeraude* and suppressed the emotion that wanted to wreck her composure.

Evelyn steeled herself against sentimentality. She wore Helen's suit, but she also needed to don her sister-in-law's devotion to her children. Fierce in their defense. Steadfast but kind. A woman who would move heaven and earth if anyone stood between her and her offspring. Evelyn crossed her arms and gripped both sleeves. She could do this. She had to. Alone.

With or without Hank Webb, she'd reclaim her nephew. *Look out, Dr. and Mrs. DuMont.* Evelyn was coming after Jamie garbed in Helen's suit of armor, a mother bear after her cub.

If they resisted giving Jamie back, they'd hear her roar.

———◦•◦———

When Amato turned into the winding driveway of the Sycaway estate, Evelyn's roar devolved to a whimper. The trooper had worn street clothing, and the car was unmarked except for a Connecticut State Police license plate and an extra antenna on the back for radio transmissions. The man at the gate only agreed to admit Amato when he flashed his badge. A burly gardener studied the car, resting his shovel over his shoulder like a soldier with a bayonet. Evelyn spotted at least two other groundskeepers, one who raked leaves from brown Bermuda grass and another who pushed a wheelbarrow of fertilizer toward an ornate, free-standing conservatory.

Amato pulled to a stop in front of a mansion built in Georgian style like a lavish Southern plantation. Two-story white columns stood like sentinels on the front porch, and a fan-shaped transom window winked above the carved mahogany doors. A man in a trim black suit emerged from the house and clambered down the front steps with a sense of urgency. He rounded the car and blocked the driver's door from opening.

Amato muttered and rolled down the window. In a voice that brooked no argument, he commanded, "Stand aside."

The butler didn't budge. "This is private property, and we are not expecting visitors."

Evelyn touched Amato's sleeve. "Perhaps we should come back—"

"I don't need an appointment." He reached into his breast pocket, pulled out his badge, and shoved it out the window. "I'm Sergeant Thomas Francis Amato of the Connecticut State Police, and I'm here on official business." He released the latch on his door and bumped the man. "I won't say it nicely again. Step aside."

The man took Amato's measure and complied.

Amato spoke in a hushed tone. "Stay here, Evelyn. Don't get out of the car unless I ask you to. Do your best to get a look at the boy to see if he's Jamie."

A thousand questions ran through Evelyn's head like foxes with their tails on fire. Her mouth felt stuffed with cotton, so she simply nodded agreement. She smoothed down her skirt, fiddled with Helen's hankie, and sneaked a peek into the house through the open door, trying not to gape at the massive hallway decorated with a sparkling crystal chandelier and checkerboard tiled floor.

The butler and Amato carried on a staccato conversation, but a heavy mantle of fear had muffled her hearing. The car closed in on her, and Evelyn rolled down her window to suck in the chilly November air. She measured her breaths and counted like the nurse had taught her so many months ago. Inhale—one, two, three. Exhale—one, two, three.

The men moved to the front porch, and the butler entered, shutting the door behind him. Amato pasted on a smile that looked more like a grimace and locked eyes with Evelyn. He mouthed, "It's okay."

After an interminable wait, a stout woman wearing a black cotton shirtwaist and a white apron emerged carrying a small blond boy. His back was to Evelyn, and his face was smushed into the nanny's fleshy neck like Jamie always did when he was frightened.

Evelyn's hand leaped to the doorhandle, and she only regained control when Amato gestured a stay. He talked calmly with the nanny and butler while he stroked the boy's fine, blond curls. He extended his arms to hold the child, but he clung tighter to the nanny. Amato rifled through his pockets and pulled out a lollipop. The boy wouldn't take it.

If Amato offered a licorice drop, Jamie couldn't resist. Evelyn grabbed her purse from the back seat and rummaged into the deep corner where she always kept Jamie's favorite treat. She couldn't put her fingers on it, so she upended the purse and dumped its contents in her lap. Her wallet, keys, and checkbook bounced off her knees and tumbled to the floorboards. A crushed, white facial tissue landed on her navy skirt, perched like a sheep under a moonless sky.

Evelyn's search captured all her attention, so Amato startled her by yanking his door open and plopping back into the driver's seat. He started the car and gunned the engine while Evelyn wrenched herself around for one last glimpse of the boy. "Why are we leaving? I never saw his face, but I'm sure that's Jamie!"

"It doesn't matter to that old battleax. She'd take on Lucifer himself before giving me a peek at Master DuMont. *Master.* Can you believe it?" Amato pounded the steering wheel with a closed fist and raced down the driveway with little heed for anyone's safety. He sped through the gate without stopping, and the rear of the car scraped the pavement when one wheel overtopped a curb on their way out.

After a few turns, Amato braked and parked. He turned to Evelyn and asked, "Are you sure that's him?"

Was she? Yes, he was the right size, although he'd grown some. His hair was shorter. Helen loved his curls long and often twirled them around her fingers when he fell asleep in her lap. His mannerisms were the same as Jamie's—

"Mrs. Benson."

Evelyn jerked her thoughts back to the moment.

"Evelyn, are you sure?"

She couldn't say for certain. Oh, God. What if it wasn't him? But what if it was? "I'm sorry. I'll need a better look to know for sure."

Amato faced front again. "Well then, we'll get one." He put the car in gear and pulled away from the curb at a more reasonable pace. "It will take a court order, but we've come too far not to know for certain if it's our boy."

Evelyn didn't overlook Amato's use of the possessive word. What a blessing to have a partner in her search who thought of Jamie as his own.

But it also made her miss the other man who had been relentless in searching. Where was Hank now? Had she done the right thing in sending him away?

With her nerves hanging by threads and her heart in her mouth, Evelyn thought not.

Regret was a cruel companion.

Chapter Thirty

Hank sat in a holding cell in the bowels of the Rensselaer County jail. He'd left Hartford immediately after Evelyn's banishment and taken an overnight bus, arriving in Troy in the wee hours of the morning. The desk officer perked up when Hank offered his real name. The rookie cop executed an outstanding warrant for the arrest of Henry Frederick Webster on the spot, and he'd been handcuffed, photographed, and fingerprinted before the cell bars clanged shut behind him—a sound he'd like never to hear again.

Thankfully, there were no other prisoners. Hank plonked himself on the hard wooden bench, rested his elbows on his knees, and covered his face with his hands. The arresting officer had kept mum despite Hank's questions, so he didn't know what charges he might face.

Even so, his thoughts congealed around only one person's troubles, and not his own. Was Evelyn at Sycaway? Was the boy Jamie? How would she react if this was another dead end? Who would comfort her? He wanted Merlin's magic wand to travel back in time and forego striking the soldier in the bar. Or back even farther and prevent his little brother's death. Or backward far enough to prevent himself from being born.

At least Hank had finally quit running. When offered his one phone call, he'd chickened out. Instead of calling his father, he contacted the only lawyer he knew—Walton Shepherd. If anyone could get him out of trouble, it would be his father's best friend. Walt would contact Dad right away, but there was no escape for any of them. He would drag his parents into the filthy muck simply because they had been unfortunate enough to bear a suicidal, angry, coward for a son. The headlines would be sickening. "Minister's Son Arrested for Soldier's Death!" Or, "Reverend Webster's Son in the Slammer!"

Tired to the bone, Hank lay down on the bench, crossed his ankles, and crooked an elbow over his eyes to keep out the light that flickered from the lone bulb dangling from the ceiling.

God, I'm in a mess. The Preacher said You love me, but I don't deserve it. Forgive me, and help me bear whatever comes. But please, God, be with Evelyn. I've messed up so bad I can't help her, but will You please take whatever good might be coming to me and credit it to her account?

Who was he kidding? What good had he ever done?

Hank wept until he fell into a fitful sleep.

———— ••• ————

"All rise." The bailiff signaled the judge's entrance, and everyone stood. The spartan furnishings in the courtroom amplified the musical jangle of Hank's handcuffs and foot shackles. "Court is now in session. The Honorable Nathaniel Kaye presiding."

A fiftyish judge with a thick mop of gray hair ascended to his chair, lifted a gavel, and struck it twice on the sounding block. Each rap zapped down Hank's spine from neck to tailbone like a jolt of electricity. The judge sat, shuffled through a stack of papers, and perused the courtroom over the top of his tortoiseshell half-eye reading glasses.

Kaye consulted briefly with the bailiff, who announced the first case of the morning. "The judge will now hear a motion concerning the custody of Ronald Herbert DuMont, nephew and ward of Malcolm and Edith DuMont. The petitioners may approach the bench."

DuMont? It couldn't be! But without looking left or right, Evelyn strode down the aisle, her heels clacking on the highly polished oak floors. Escorted by Amato, looking frail, she sported dark circles under her eyes, which Hank had caused. Her hair glistened like dark honey, pinned up into a victory roll underneath a navy pillbox hat, and a white ruffled collar was buttoned under the lapel of her suit. Escaped curls framed her face like an ethereal angel.

Amato—ever vigilant—scanned the occupants of the courtroom. When he spotted Hank sitting on the bench for prisoners, his eyebrows shot up. Hank dropped his gaze, hoping Amato wouldn't draw attention to his connection with Evelyn. She shouldn't admit any acquaintance with him given the trouble he was in. It was best for everyone if they were supposed strangers.

The judge finished reading a paper and looked up to appraise Evelyn and Amato. "This motion contends that the child now in custody of the DuMonts is not their nephew, but yours, Mrs. Benson. On what basis do you make that allegation?"

Evelyn didn't respond, and Hank couldn't see her face. She reached out to Amato, who offered, "Mrs. Benson believes the boy's identity might have been confused during the aftermath of the Hartford circus fire."

The judge's face betrayed no emotion. "And you are . . ."

"Sergeant Thomas Francis Amato of the Connecticut State Police."

"What is your role in this inquiry?"

"I've been assisting Mrs. Benson with the search for her nephew since the day after the fire. We've tracked down every lead without finding the boy. I recently discovered the connection to the DuMonts, and I believe he may be the child we are looking for."

The judge scrutinized Evelyn again. "Do you have a voice of your own?"

Hank wanted to wallop the judge for his insensitivity, but that wouldn't help anyone.

"I do, Your Honor." Evelyn blotted her lips with a hankie. Hank perceived the exact moment she found her grit. She straightened, returned the hankie to her coat pocket, and spoke with conviction. "I represent the parents of James William Halstead. My brother Bill and his wife, Helen, lost their lives in the fire, but their blood runs through their son's veins. I won't stop looking for him until I find him or lie dead in my grave."

An inspired woman in the gallery clapped her support until the judge stopped her with a rap of his gavel. "I'll have order in my court, young lady." Speaking to Evelyn, he continued. "Have you spoken to the child to ascertain he is your nephew?"

"No, Your Honor. We visited Sycaway yesterday, but the servants turned us away before I got a good look at him. But he's the right size, and he had some of Jamie's mannerisms."

"Did you speak to Edith—" The judge coughed into his hand. "Did you speak to Mrs. DuMont?"

Unfair. The judge knew the DuMonts. How could he be impartial? Hank hadn't spoken yet to Walt, but maybe he could intervene.

"Judge Kaye." Amato stood taller. "With all due respect, perhaps we should petition another judge since you are acquainted with the DuMonts."

Judge Kaye removed his glasses and leaned forward. "Are you impugning my honor?"

"No, sir." Evelyn's interruption likely saved Amato's badge. "Whether he's Ronald DuMont or James Halstead, I'm certain everyone wants to know the boy's true identity. All I ask is an opportunity to see him, talk to him, and find out if he is my nephew. If he's not, there's no cause to upset him. But if he is, I want him returned to my custody."

The judge donned his glasses but left them perched on the end of his nose. "Custody of a child is for the court to decide. I will rule in the child's best interest, and that's that." Kaye pinned Amato with a look that could have frozen a coal furnace. "Right, Sergeant?"

"Yes, sir." Amato acquiesced, bowing his head.

"I hereby order Malcolm and Edith DuMont to bring the boy and appear in my courtroom tomorrow morning to settle this matter." He beckoned the bailiff. "Have the clerk of courts issue a summons and arrange for it to be served as soon as possible." Kaye pushed up his glasses. "Is that acceptable to you, Sergeant Amato?" The judge raised an eyebrow.

"Yes, sir." When the judge rapped his gavel, Amato offered his elbow to Evelyn. She put her hand in the crook, and when they turned around,

Hank bent at the waist as if to tie his shoe. He watched Evelyn's black faux-velvet Mary Janes walk past—attached to shapely calves adorned with silk stockings—and he swallowed hard. But not before savoring the scent of Evelyn. Dove soap, White Shoulders, and everything fresh and good.

When her footfalls decreased in volume, Hank sat up.

The bailiff cried, "The judge will now hear case 81978, the people versus Henry Webster."

How could his case be heard when Walt wasn't here yet? Hank turned and cast a desperate look toward the double doors at the rear of the courtroom. When he did, he locked eyes with Evelyn, who hadn't exited yet. Her face drained of all color, and her wide eyes resembled those of Scarlett O'Hara facing the flames of Atlanta. Amato none-too-gently tugged her into the hallway and out of sight.

The officer who had escorted Hank to the courtroom jerked him to his feet. His first step, hampered by the shackles Hank had forgotten he wore, nearly caused him to sprawl on the floor. He regained his balance and did the convict's shuffle to stand before the judge's bench.

"Bailiff, read the charges."

At Kaye's command, the bailiff read, "Henry Frederick Webster is accused of assault in the third degree under New York Penal Code 120.00. On September 5th, 1942, the accused intentionally or recklessly caused physical injury to Private First Class Paul Stuckey, of Albany, New York, striking him with a fist to the jaw and knocking him unconscious when the victim struck his head on a table."

The soldier didn't die? Woozy-headed, Hank sagged against the officer holding him. Not murder then. Or homicide. Assault. Still bleak, but perhaps not a life sentence.

"Mr. Webster. Your attention, please." Judge Kaye peered down from the bench. "Assault in the third degree carries a penalty of a maximum of one year in jail, a fine, or both. How do you plead?"

How should he answer? Hank couldn't form a thought, much less words.

"If you don't have an attorney, the court will appoint one for you." The judge's words seemed to echo down a tunnel before they reached Hank's hearing.

A commotion commenced at the rear of the courtroom, and Walton Shepherd hustled forward, chucked his briefcase on the defense attorney's table, and took Hank by the elbow. Without the sturdy support of both men, Hank feared he might crumple. Walt said, "I'd like to present a motion to dismiss charges."

The district attorney, who'd been silent until that moment, leaped to his feet. "Objection. There is sufficient evidence to bring this case to trial and no legal basis for dismissal."

"No need for so much drama." Judge Kaye read through the documents, paused a moment, and said, "Motion denied. Mr. Webster, what is your plea?"

Guilty. Hank had taken a swing at the man, and even if he wasn't dead, he might still suffer effects from it. He opened his mouth to speak when Shepherd spoke for him.

"Not guilty."

"Very well. So entered." Kaye studied Hank for a moment and said, "The facts seem very straightforward. I see no reason to prolong this matter any further. It's been more than two years since the incident, and I want to clear it from my docket. Trial is set to begin tomorrow morning at nine o'clock."

Shepherd's grip on Hank's elbow tightened. "I'd like to request bail for my client."

Judge Kaye chuckled. "Really? The defendant ran from the scene and hasn't been seen since. Bail is denied. He can cool his heels in jail until morning." Speaking to the bailiff he said, "Next."

Hank's escort shoved him toward the side door through which he'd entered the courtroom. Shepherd followed, saying quietly, "We need to talk. Just keep your head down right now and look very, very meek." He whispered, "Don't worry. We'll get this ironed out."

Chains clanked matching the rhythm of Hank's every step. At least he wouldn't have to face Evelyn.

Or so he thought.

When he passed through the doorway, a fleeting look down the hallway revealed Evelyn standing in the cross hall clinging to Amato's arm like a drowning woman clutching a floating board. She stepped Hank's direction, but Amato restrained her.

Hank took a hard left, turning his back on the woman he loved. Walt mumbled he had something to do, and he turned the opposite direction. Hank descended the stairs to the basement cells as quickly as he could, followed by the hulking officer who hopefully blocked Evelyn's view.

He'd had almost twenty-four hours to stanch the bleeding of his heart. But the wounds would be ripped open again in the morning.

Chapter Thirty-One

Evelyn tugged her arm out of Amato's grip and strode toward the front desk. "I can't just leave. I'm going to see if I can visit him."

"Not if you want to get Jamie back."

Reality crashed upon Evelyn like a rowdy wave on the shore, sweeping the debris out to sea. No matter how much she loved Hank, and she truly did. No matter that she wanted to stand by him through his trouble like he'd stood with her. No, reality demanded she had to put regaining custody of Jamie at the top of her priorities.

Amato tossed aside his professionalism and hugged her like a sister. "I promise, I'll do everything I can to help Hank. But in the meantime, you need to stay out of it."

Evelyn permitted Amato's comfort to seep through his embrace. "Sergeant, I've never asked. Are you married?"

"Yes, I've been happily married for forty-two years to the same wonderful woman."

"What would she say if she saw you hugging me?"

"She'd say, '*Cosa pensi di fare, testa di cavolo?*'"

"What does that mean?"

"What are you doing, cabbagehead?"

Evelyn exploded with giddy laughter. "Is that all she'd do?"

"And then she'd invite you to the best Italian dinner you've ever eaten. Sometime during the evening you'd get a gentle but firm message to leave your mitts off her man."

"Thank you. I needed a laugh." Evelyn put proper distance between them again. "She's a lucky woman."

"I tell her that every night, but I'm not sure she's convinced." Amato's friendly smile faded. "If I take you back to your hotel, can you manage the rest of the day without company?"

"Yes. I'm exhausted." Evelyn took stock of her physical wellness. She was a big bundle of nerves and fatigue. "I think I'll take a nap, get dinner in the hotel restaurant, and turn in early. Tomorrow is a big day."

"The biggest." Amato scrunched his eyebrows together, making them look like a giant caterpillar perched on his forehead. "I have a little investigating to do."

"What more is there to find out? We will simply have to see if the boy is Jamie."

"Not about Jamie. About Hank."

Evelyn's hope soared. Hank wasn't a murderer. Maybe if he were exonerated, they could resume their romance. But what if he were jailed? Could she accept a man convicted of assault as a suitor, or perhaps, a husband? A flash of heat leaped to Evelyn's cheeks and burned.

Heavens. Could she allow Hank to become Lily and Jamie's father?

———————⋯———————

His escort had barely locked the door when a familiar, hearty voice spoke to the officer who climbed the stairs. "Walton Shepherd. I'm here to visit my client."

The jailer said, "You can go, but not him."

The officer's statement revved Hank's heart like a dragster when the light blinked green. It could only be one "him." Could Hank bear a reunion with his father while he was sitting in jail?

"He's with me." Walt was a natural leader, commanding and firm in his purpose. The officer let them pass.

Two sets of feet descended, and Hank knew his father by his highly polished wingtips. They appeared first, then his immaculate suit, and finally his wide shoulders. When his father's head came into view, Hank took in his expression of worry, fear, and—wait. Was there also joy?

"Son, is it really you?" Dad rushed to the bars, extended both arms through them, and said, "Come here."

Hank stumbled from the bench and held out his hand for a shake, which was more than he deserved.

Dad grasped his hand and pulled Hank forward so forcefully that Hank nearly clonked his head. The two men embraced with the bars between them. An immediate rush of fatherly love engulfed Hank, bringing so much relief all his breath left his body. He inhaled and said, "I'm no longer worthy to be called your son. I'll only bring shame to you and Mother."

Dad's preacher voice boomed through the empty cells. "My son has come home. It's time to celebrate your return."

A fracas erupted upstairs, out of view but not out of hearing, accompanied by Mother's stern words. "I don't care if the rule is only two visitors at a time. Just try to stop me, Oliver Parsons. Remember, your mother is on my women's committee at church."

Mother appeared, spotlessly dressed in the height of style, but her coiffed hair, which had been coal black, was almost completely white. "Where's my boy? Hank?" She blinked as her vision adjusted to the lack of light.

When their eyes locked, Hank was whisked back in time to the day he'd stolen a shepherd's pie from mean Old Lady Winterton's porch and given it to their neighbors who'd lost everything in the Depression. His mother's softly rounded face wore the same expression. Reprimand? Yes, but also fathomless love—the kind only a mother could give, a reflection of God's love.

She dropped her pocketbook and sprinted to Dad's side, her hand reaching through the bars to caress Hank's cheek and ruffle his hair. "Look at you. So much taller, and all filled out! But you could still put on a few pounds. Who's been feeding you?" She twittered like a little bird, running her inspection from head to toe. "Oh, Henry. Please tell me you didn't appear in court wearing *that*." She tried to brush a spot from his shirt, but it was a stain, not lint.

Leave it to Mother to want him perfectly attired. "I have a change of clothing in a suitcase, but I wasn't allowed to have it in. . .here." His mouth and throat felt like he'd swallowed a glob of molasses. He could barely get words out. "Mother. Mama—I'm so sorry."

"Pishposh. There will be time for a proper apology when this mess is behind us. And believe me, son, I'm going to milk it for all it's worth." Mother's eyes twinkled as she leaned forward and pressed her face to the bars. "Come on, now. Give your mother a kiss. I've waited two years for it, so make it a good one."

Hank angled his head just right and bussed her dear cheek. How could he have left his parents without a word? And how could they ever forgive him?

"I hate to interrupt this reunion, but we have business to discuss. Mildred," Walton said, speaking to Mother, "leave us men alone to sort this out."

"You are such a killjoy, Walt." Turning to Hank, she said, "I don't know if your gray suit will fit you anymore, but I'll have your father bring it tonight along with a fresh white shirt. I can't have my boy sitting in the courtroom dressed like a vagabond. And I'll come knot your tie. You never were any good at that." A tear escaped the outer corner of her right eye, and she whisked it away. "I love you, Henry, and I'm glad you're home, no matter what."

Mother retrieved her purse and pulled the handle up to her elbow before ascending the stairs with the grace and posture of a queen. Although she was out of sight, he still heard her say to the jailer, "And you, Oliver— you treat my boy right or I'll forget talking to your mother. I'll take it straight to the Almighty."

"She's a marvel," Walt said.

"A powerful force of nature, and don't you forget it." Dad's voice broke. Hank imagined his parents had drawn strength from each other when he had left so abruptly. Dad often preached at weddings, "A strand of three is not easily broken." Dad, Mother, and God. Maybe if they were united behind him, everything might work out.

"Now, Henry." Walt's sternness returned. "We need to talk."

───────●●●───────

"All rise."

At the bailiff's order, Hank scooted back his chair and stood. In a complete turnabout from the previous day, he wore his gray worsted suit with a matching silk handkerchief peeking out from the breast pocket, its four points creased in Mother's distinctive Cagney fold. With the neat Windsor knot in his burgundy tie, he was as well dressed as Walt. He'd put on some muscles in his shoulders in the past two years, so it was snug, but acceptable.

And he wore no handcuffs or leg shackles. Walt had blistered the jailer for treating Hank like a desperado when he was only accused of a misdemeanor. Thus, to his great relief, no jangling chains today. He couldn't bear for Mother to see him that way.

The bailiff intoned, "The judge will now hear the case of the State of New York versus Henry Webster."

What? Jamie's case should have been first. He'd spoken nothing of it to his parents, but he'd bent Walt's ear late last night about helping Evelyn today, and to his great relief, Walt had agreed. What if he were sent back to jail? How would he bear not knowing the outcome?

"Henry." Walt tapped his shoulder. "The judge asked you a question."

What? His thoughts had wandered far from his own fate. He cleared his throat. "I'm sorry, sir. Could you repeat the question?"

"Mr. Webster, don't try the patience of the court today." Judge Kaye scowled and leaned forward. "Is this not a serious matter to you?"

"No. Er, I mean—yes, Your Honor. I know how serious it is." Hank stuck his forefinger between his neck and the tie and tugged.

"I asked you to tell me the events of September 5th, 1942, as you remember them." The judge scanned the brief in front of him. "I have affidavits from other eyewitnesses, but I'd like to hear your side of what happened. Will you answer questions directly from me and waive your right not to incriminate yourself?"

"Yes." Hank wanted to put this behind him. Today.

"No." Walt grasped Hank by the sleeve of his jacket. "That's not a smart move."

Hank shook off Walt's hand. "Yes, Your Honor. I agree to your questioning."

Kaye grinned, but was it friendly or malicious? "Bailiff, swear him in."

Hank repeated the oath to tell the truth, and breathed a prayer he'd be smart enough not to botch this. He took a quick glance at Father, who sat directly behind him, and his nod affirmed Hank had made the right choice.

Judge Kaye leaned back in his chair, removed his glasses, and set them on the desk. "Now, Mr. Webster, in your own words, tell me the events of that night."

"Well, Your Honor…" Hank's vocal cords went AWOL. He'd prayed long and hard about what to say, and now the opportunity was his, all his prepared speeches seemed inadequate. He glanced to his right, and there, in the front row beside his mother, sat Evelyn. Strength poured from her smoky eyes directly to Hank's, and it warmed him to his toes. She nodded and smiled.

Facing the judge again, Hank spoke the simple words God had given him last night. "Your Honor, nothing good happens when a man drinks."

"On that we agree, young man." The judge laid the papers on his desk. "Go on."

"The soldiers and I had all been drinking. They were drunk." Nudged by his conscience, Hank added, "I don't think I was drunk, but it's all a little hazy."

The quick intake of breath from his mother nearly derailed him, but Hank got back on track. "They called me a coward for not enlisting to fight the Nazis."

The judge folded his hands in front of him. "Why didn't you?"

Time for naked facts. The truth, and only the truth, as he'd said when sworn in. "I tried to, but they labeled me 4F because I received psychiatric care as a teenager."

Out of the corner of his eye, he spotted Mother retrieving her hankie from her purse. When she wiped her eyes and snapped the latch shut, Hank flinched. She and Dad had worked hard to keep that secret, and now it was exposed for all to hear.

"Reverend Webster's statement has already informed the court about this matter."

He did? Father admitted his son's biggest failure?

Judge Kaye then asked a surprising question. "When the soldiers teased you about not enlisting, how did that make you feel?"

"Embarrassed." Hank's answer was no louder than a whisper.

The judge asked louder, "And ashamed?"

Hank matched his volume. "Yes."

"Angry?" The judge fairly shouted the question.

"Yes!" Hank's hand formed a fist without his permission.

"So you struck Private Stuckey."

"Yes."

Kaye eyed Walt like a cat that caught a canary. "Would you like to change his plea, Mr. Shepherd?"

Walt whispered into Hank's ear. "What are you doing?"

"Telling the whole truth." The moment Hank spoke the words, a weight lifted from his soul. Speaking for himself, he said, "Yes, Your Honor. I want to change my plea. I struck Private Stuckey. I'm guilty." A year in jail, the consequences of a conviction on his record, even possible separation from Evelyn forever—nothing else mattered. Hank would never be a free man unless he freed himself with the truth.

"Good. Now we're getting somewhere." Judge Kaye leaned back in his chair. "Henry Frederick Webster, I find you guilty of assault in the fourth degree."

The prosecutor's face reddened, and he stood to his feet. "Why the reduction in charges?"

"You overreached. These reports"—the judge fluttered through the documents with his thumb—"show the injured man only received a bump to his head. There were no serious physical injuries, and he went straight back to his base with no request for sick time. Neither did he seek medical attention."

Hank shook his head to be certain his hearing wasn't impaired. He'd run because the soldier's buddy said he was dead. It had all been a lie. Almost three years of his life—wasted—because a stupid, drunk soldier pranked him.

A peek toward Evelyn and his mother showed both women wearing hopeful expressions. They clasped hands. Wait—how did they know each other? It didn't matter, truly, because his path had been guided by the Almighty. It had led him straight to Evelyn. He still didn't deserve her love, but he was thankful to have basked in it before he'd destroyed her trust. He was a better man because of it.

The prosecutor dared a challenge. "But, Your Honor—"

Kaye interrupted again. "No buts, Mr. Sanders. The facts speak for themselves." He folded his hands over his generous girth and interlocked his fingers. "Besides, Mr. Webster was provoked."

"Hear, hear." Dad bellowed before silenced by a stern look from the judge.

"I'll let you in on a secret, son." The judge leaned forward and rested his arms on his elbows. His eyes gleamed. "My brother was 4F in the Great War because of a heart murmur. When a loudmouthed soldier did what Private Stuckey did, he got a lot more than a bump on the head."

Had the judge defended his brother with a fist? The wise man didn't divulge all the facts, but Hank got the message, and it was welcome.

"Before I hand down my sentence, the court will hear testimony from Sergeant Thomas Amato."

Hank hadn't spied the sergeant in the gallery. When he turned to look, Amato, attired in his dress uniform, made his way swiftly to stand before the judge.

"I understand you have testimony about the character of the man I'm about to sentence. The court will hear you now."

"I've spoken to my fellow officers who were present when the Hartford fire raged full force. They were trying to rescue as many people as they could from certain death." Amato pointed at Hank. "This man, at great risk to his own life, helped hundreds of people get out of that tent. Without his heroism, many more people would now be dead."

Yes, but Hank hadn't been able to save the two that now mattered the most to him because of Evelyn. Bill and Helen. His stomach clenched, and his eyes stung.

Mother released an audible cry, and Dad tapped Hank's forearm. He leaned forward and whispered, "I am proud of you, son. Greater love hath no man than this. . ."

That a man lay down his life for his friends. Hank could finish the familiar verse without a prompt. Evelyn's brother had done that to the utmost, and if he were free to marry her, Hank would make sure Bill's children didn't grow up without a father.

"A hero, eh?" Judge Kaye gazed intently at Hank. "I hereby sentence the defendant to time already served in jail and a fine of fifty dollars payable to the Red Cross."

Was he really free? Hank checked Evelyn's expression, and she offered him a bright smile.

The bailiff cried, "The court will now hear the case regarding custody of Ronald Herbert DuMont, ward of Malcolm and Edith DuMont."

Evelyn sobered immediately.

*God moves in His mysterious way, His wonders to perform. He plants His footsteps in the sea. . .*Cowper's hymn. God had moved in His providence to plant Hank and Evelyn's footsteps beside His in the sea of distress.

A sharp rap of Kaye's gavel yanked Hank's thoughts back to the courtroom.

And rides upon the storm. Lightning and thunder crashed, but Hank put his trust in the God who rides with His children.

Chapter Thirty-Two

Hank had been escorted from the courtroom following the judge's unexpected verdict. Sergeant Amato had located Hank's parents yesterday, and from the bubbly welcome Evelyn had received from Hank's mother today, he'd also disclosed their special relationship. Although she felt a little embarrassed, Mrs. Webster's stalwart presence during Hank's proceedings had been very welcome.

Evelyn made her way to the plaintiff's stand, where Amato welcomed her, along with Mr. Shepherd. The lawyer pulled out her chair, but before she sat, he said, "Hank asked me to help you today, and it's my privilege to do so. Just follow my lead."

Evelyn leaned forward and placed both hands on the table to steady herself. She'd wondered how she would navigate this process without legal advice, and like manna from heaven, here it was.

Familiar wails of distress emanated from the rear of the courtroom. That was Jamie's cry! She'd know it anywhere. She turned around to see a well-dressed couple proceeding down the aisle, followed by the nanny carrying a squirming child. He fought and kicked so much Evelyn couldn't get a glimpse of his face.

The DuMonts took a seat at the defendant's table with a haughty-looking lawyer wearing horn-rimmed glasses, and the nanny sat behind them. The boy again burrowed his face against her neck so tightly it was a wonder he could breathe. He whimpered and sobbed, but the woman did nothing to comfort him. She held him like an iron clamp on a piece of lumber. Cold. Immovable. His wails heightened to shrieks.

Evelyn pushed herself to her feet.

Shepherd tugged her back down. "You can't approach until the judge okays it." Softening, he said, "I know this is difficult for you, Mrs. Benson. Keep it together for a few more minutes. Henry tells me you have a spine of steel. Now's the time to prove him right."

Henry? Oh yes—Hank. She'd have to get used to hearing him called by his legal name. Despite Shepherd's admonition, she glared at the nanny. The nanny glared back.

"Mrs. DuMont." The judge rubbed the back of his neck. "It will be impossible to conduct this proceeding if the child doesn't calm down."

Edith DuMont scurried around the banister and sat beside the nanny. She tried to wrest the child from her arms, but the boy's shrieks escalated to screams.

Evelyn reached into her purse for a licorice drop, placed last night in a particular pocket so she could locate it, and gave it to Amato. She'd not be permitted to approach, but he would. The screams tap-danced on her spine like Jimmy Cagney. If the child didn't stop soon, she'd cry too.

Amato offered the drop to Mrs. DuMont, who unwrapped it and shoved it under the boy's nose. He grabbed it, stuffed it in his mouth, and wiped his forearm under a nose that ran like a sieve. But he quieted.

Dear Lord above. It IS Jamie. Evelyn rode a roller coaster to the highest high she'd experienced in months, but it careened over the top and down to the lowest valley. Would the judge rule in her favor? A single, nearly broke waitress living like a hobo in someone else's apartment? Jamie could stay with the DuMonts and enjoy a wealth of benefits because of their riches. She felt like a mountain climber standing at the base of El Capitan without any ropes or pitons. Ascending would be impossible.

"Steady, Evelyn."

Was Amato a mind reader? No. Evelyn's shaking hands and shallow breathing had given her away. He was a detective, after all.

After everyone was sworn in, Judge Kaye commanded, "Mr. and Mrs. DuMont, please bring the child and approach the bench."

Mrs. DuMont tried again to claim the child from the nanny, but Jamie clung to her like a barnacle on a sailboat's hull. Mr. DuMont pushed her out of the way, grabbed Jamie's arm, and yanked. The nanny rose as well, and after some furious whispering, all three adults stood before the bench with Jamie still in the nanny's arms.

The judge removed his half glasses and chewed on the wand before saying, "I must say, Mal—er, Mr. DuMont, the child doesn't seem fond of you or your wife."

Mrs. DuMont interjected. "We've only had him for four months, and he endured a terrible trauma. You see, my husband and I were in Europe, and we'd not met—"

"I'm well aware of the circumstances. Don't waste my time with explanations I don't need. It's clear that in four months you've not yet been able to form an attachment with the child." The judge asked the nanny, "How many hours a day is the child in your custody?"

The nanny lifted her chin, shifted Jamie to the other hip, and stood taller. "He's never out of my sight."

The judge rested himself against the back of his massive black leather chair.

Spots of red colored Mr. DuMont's cheeks. "Ronnie is our ward, not our son. We are doing everything in our power to create a stable home for my wife's sister's son. We're not here to determine our suitability for that task, but to settle the ruckus that woman"—DuMont pointed to Evelyn—"is stirring up. This is a simple case, Nate. Either the child is her nephew or my wife's. Let's get on with this circus."

"Objection, Your Honor." Mr. Shepherd scooted back his chair and stood. "Mrs. Benson's claim is not a circus, and that's a very insensitive comment given the considerable pain she has endured. There is ample evidence to believe a mistake might have been made, and this court has the obligation to sort out the truth."

"You want to lecture me too, Walt?" Judge Kaye peered down from the bench at both men.

Evelyn's hopes rose slightly as her coaster car clacked up the next hill. Since the judge knew both Mr. DuMont and Hank's lawyer, perhaps he could be impartial. She sneaked a peek toward Mrs. Webster, who was already looking her way. She mouthed, "Have faith."

Kaye took in a slow breath and exhaled. "Today I represent the State of New York. I'm on the side of truth, and I'll render my verdict without any advice from either of you." He tapped his finger on the massive, antique oak desk. "Mrs. DuMont, let Mrs. Benson hold the boy."

Just the thought of holding Jamie again caused Evelyn's eyes to flood. The nanny stepped forward, and Evelyn grasped Jamie under the shoulders. He didn't cry out, but he tightened his grip on the nanny. The only way to wrest him from the nanny's arms would be a tug-of-war. No matter how much she wanted to, it would only cause Jamie more distress.

"See. I told you, Your Honor." Mrs. DuMont rubbed Jamie's back, and he swatted her hand away. "Ronnie is having trouble with relationships because he's so traumatized. I want to be a mother to him, but these things take time."

"Four months is a long time, Edith." The judge pursed his lips. After a pause, he said, "Mrs. Benson. Is this boy your nephew?"

Evelyn turned and spoke to Jamie directly. "Jamie?"

At his name, his little blond head popped up, and the boy wiped away a spot of black drool with the back of his pudgy hand. Evelyn's heart swelled. There could be no more doubt. His beloved features struck her soul like the clang of a church bell. Jamie was alive, well, and only five feet away. "Yes, Your Honor. It's Jamie."

"That's a positive sign, but I'll need more proof. Unless you can demonstrate to the court some attachment to the boy, I will have no choice but to rule in favor of the DuMonts."

Lord, how can I make him remember me? A wave of nausea crashed over Evelyn. Then an idea arrived on angels' wings. Evelyn asked, "Will the judge allow something a little unconventional?"

Judge Kaye raised one eyebrow. "If it will help resolve this issue, I'll be indulgent, but make it quick."

Evelyn corralled her skirt tightly against her legs, knelt, and lay on the floor facing Jamie. She tucked her arms under her head like a pillow.

"I say, Mrs. Benson. What are you doing?"

Evelyn ignored the judge's question. She said to Amato, "Take off your coat and cover me."

Amato complied, but the coat only covered her to her hips. He whispered, "What are you doing?"

Evelyn ignored him too. *This has to work. Please, God, help Jamie remember.* She closed her eyes and commenced snoring like a bear.

"This is ridiculous—"

"Be quiet, Malcolm, or I'll have you removed from the courtroom."

With her eyes closed, Evelyn was in agony as silence reigned for a few moments. Then it was broken by a rustle of taffeta and the patter of soft footfalls. Soon a little hand touched her shoulder and warm puffs of air came from sweet nostrils mere inches away from her face.

"Not yet, Jamie. I'm still sleeping." Evelyn scooted out of his reach, turned her back to him, and resumed snoring.

Jamie giggled. He toddled around her feet, squatted beside her, and patted her cheek in the most wonderful sensation Evelyn had ever felt. He said, "Wake up."

Evelyn's heart leaped. Her boy was remembering her. She opened her eyes to the most beautiful sight—Jamie's smiling face. She said, "No, Jay-Jay. Just a few more minutes."

Jamie's eyes sparkled with mischief. "Uh-uh, Aunt Evie." He lifted the lapel of Amato's coat, lay down with his back to her, and wriggled so close Evelyn thought her heart would stop beating.

She hugged him tightly and sobbed. Mrs. Webster cried out, and sniffles could be heard from spectators in the gallery.

Jamie turned to face her and wrapped his arms around Evelyn's neck. She gave him an Eskimo kiss, and he rubbed her nose so hard it flattened against her damp cheeks. "I wanna go home, Aunt Evie. Please take me home."

Amato reclaimed his jacket. Evelyn brushed dirt from her skirt, which now needed a good wash. She stood, and Jamie reached for her. She picked him up, and true to form, Jamie nuzzled his face into her neck.

Mrs. DuMont, who had tucked herself under her husband's arm, clutched a fancy embroidered hankie and wiped her eyes while black streaks of mascara striped her cheeks.

Evelyn's roller coaster car topped another peak and swooped down again. Her triumph spelled tragedy for Mrs. DuMont. Her sister's son was likely dead. A devastating feeling, one Evelyn knew well.

Everyone looked to Judge Kaye, who wiped the side of his face and sighed again. "Edith, I'm sorry for your loss. I know you don't have children of your own, and I had hoped this boy was your nephew. However, I cannot ignore what just happened."

Mrs. DuMont whimpered.

To Evelyn, he said, "This boy is undeniably your nephew, but it is my responsibility to rule in the best interests of the child." He asked, "Sergeant Amato, can you testify that Mrs. Benson is prepared and able to provide a suitable home for this boy?"

Amato cleared his throat and turned troubled eyes to Evelyn. "Your Honor, Mrs. Benson is a fine woman, an upstanding citizen, and she loves this child with all her heart."

"That's not what I asked." Judge Kaye hardened. "Sergeant, do I need to swear you in?"

"No, Your Honor."

"Then answer the question. Can Mrs. Benson provide a stable home for this boy or not?"

Evelyn needed to relieve her friend from telling the odious truth. "Judge Kaye, I'm a widow, and I lived with my brother and his wife. I don't have the funds to catch up on the mortgage, and the house will be foreclosed on the thirtieth of this month."

The DuMont's lawyer found his voice. "Your Honor, the DuMonts are willing to keep the child and rear him as their own—"

"Shut it, Arthur." The judge's order silenced him. "Mrs. Benson, where are you employed?"

"Charlie's Diner."

Mrs. DuMont muttered, "A waitress—"

Evelyn brushed a speck of dust from the floor off her lapel. Helen's lapel. Her mama bear roared. Jamie's head stayed pressed to her neck, and she kissed the top of his head. "Yes, Mrs. DuMont. I'm a waitress. I may not be able to keep Bill's house, but I *will* make a home for Jamie." To the judge she said, "I'm not rich. I can't give Jamie a fancy house or a private education. What I can give him is the love of a mother instead of a nanny, knowledge of his parents and how much they loved him, and the mixed blessing of a big sister as stubborn as he is."

The corner of the judge's mouth twitched before he regained control. "And you have not remarried?"

The question slapped a muzzle on the bear. "No."

"So the child would grow up without a father?"

"I will do my best—"

Evelyn's reply was cut off by the judge. "The court will hear testimony from Henry Webster."

"I'm here, sir."

Hank? His deep baritone voice flooded Evelyn with relief. She whirled, and there he stood in his Sunday best. So very handsome. Strength personified.

Judge Kaye commanded, "Please approach the bench."

Evelyn's relief turned to dismay. No. It would tip the scales in favor of the DuMonts. She turned to Mr. Shepherd. "Please—"

Hank's lawyer grinned like a Cheshire cat. "Have faith, Mrs. Benson."

Why did everyone keep telling her that?

Chapter Thirty-Three

Evelyn's head tried to float away from her body, and the breathing exercises taught by the nurse didn't help. When Hank reached her side, he supported her with a hand under her elbow. She leaned against his steady, sturdy frame. If the judge hadn't known their relationship before, he certainly could see it now for himself.

"Mr. Webster." The judge's expression gave no clue whether he was pleased or not. "You are still under oath."

"Yes, sir."

Judge Kaye leaned forward and removed his spectacles. "Are you acquainted with Mrs. Benson?"

Hank put his hand atop Evelyn's. "No, Your Honor."

What? He'd perjure himself? Evelyn whispered, "Hank—"

Hank continued, "She's more than an acquaintance. She's a very dear friend."

"I see." The judge paused long enough that everyone fidgeted. "Are you in love with her?"

At the startling question, Evelyn detected the smallest twitch of Hank's bicep.

Hank looked down at her, and his eyes telegraphed his answer. "I love this woman with all my heart."

DuMont's lawyer smacked the table and stood. "Nate, what does this have to do with custody of the child?"

The question might as well have been a peashooter firing on a Sherman tank. Kaye said to him, "One more outburst, and I'll hold you in contempt of court. Sit down." The judge's expression softened when he turned his attention to Evelyn. "Mrs. Benson. Do you return his love?"

Evelyn didn't look at Hank. How could she escape this impossible situation? "I don't know."

"Under oath." The crease between the judge's eyebrows eased for the first time this morning. "Tell me. Do you love him?"

Hank slipped his arm around Evelyn's waist and turned her to face him. He asked, softly, "Do you love me, Evie?"

Evelyn could gaze into those eyes for the rest of her life and never grow tired of the love, the steadiness, and yes—the faith in God she saw there. "I do. I love you, Hank."

The judge cleared his throat. "A little louder for the court, please."

Recklessly, passionately, eternally—Evelyn could deny it no longer. "Yes. I love him."

"Hallelujah!" Hank's mother clapped her enthusiasm. Soon the whole gallery joined her.

"So, Mr. Webster. Is there something you'd like to ask Mrs. Benson?" Kaye preempted the DuMont lawyer's expected objection with a stern glare. The man took a sudden interest in the floor.

Hank dropped to one knee and looked up at Evelyn with such earnestness her heart fluttered like butterfly wings. "Evie. This isn't how I'd planned it, and I don't have a ring, but—"

"Wait. Wait! This has to be perfect." Mrs. Webster scurried to Hank's side and handed him a ring. "Use this."

"Mama, where did you get that?"

"It was my mother's, and a little birdie told me you might need it today." She flicked her fingers in the air as if shooing a fly. "Now, get on with it."

Reverend Webster beamed and nodded.

Hank took the ring, a single diamond set in Victorian filigree, and slipped it on Evelyn's finger. It hung like a St. Bernard's collar on a dachshund. She moved it to her middle finger where it fit better.

He whispered, "We'll have it resized." In full voice, he said, "Evie, will you marry me?"

With Jamie still in her arms, Evelyn joined Hank and knelt before him. "Yes." She could only speak the single word—others were swept away by the tidal wave of love that crashed on her shore.

More applause from the spectators accompanied Evelyn's one-armed hug. It hadn't died down before Jamie thumped Hank on top of his head twice with a pudgy hand and said, "Go away. *My* Aunt Evie."

"Jamie!" Evelyn broke her hug and removed her nephew from striking distance of her new fiancé.

Hank chuckled, and in a man's no-nonsense way, he took Jamie from her arms. Jamie gaped at him but didn't struggle. "No, little man. *Our* Evie, and don't you forget it."

After indulgent laughter at the precocious boy, Judge Kaye sobered. Speaking to the DuMonts, he said. "Malcolm. Edith. The court is sorry for your loss. But in light of all the facts, we must return Jamie to his birth family."

Edith clutched her husband's lapels and sobbed. He put a strong arm around her and replied, "Your Honor has made the right decision. In her more unguarded moments, Edith has admitted her difficulty in feeling close to the boy. I think on some level she knew he wasn't our Ronnie."

Jamie's nanny abandoned the courtroom. Her rubber-soled shoes made no noise as her footfalls faded, allowing everyone to hear her sniffles. She'd lost not only a child she might have been fond of but likely also her job.

The thought diminished Evelyn's joy but only somewhat. She'd found Jamie, and somehow, by God's grace, He'd walked upon the waves of the storm-tossed sea to join her to Hank. If the DuMonts turned to Him, they would also be comforted.

Exclamations of surprise rippled through the courtroom, but the rap of the judge's gavel quieted them. "Custody of the child in question is hereby awarded to Mrs. Evelyn Benson." He whispered something to the bailiff and pounded his gavel yet again.

The bailiff's stentorian tone was devoid of emotion. "All rise. This court is now in recess for thirty minutes." As the spectators began to converse, he approached Evelyn's little group. He waited respectfully until the Websters and Sergeant Amato finished their congratulations and hugs before saying, "The judge would like all of you to join him in his chambers."

"In a moment." Hank's audacity startled Evelyn, but she'd learn his ways as the years passed. He still held Jamie, who seemed unusually content, and he grasped Evelyn's hand with his free one before crossing the aisle to speak to the DuMonts.

"Sir. Ma'am." Hank released Evelyn's hand and extended it to Mr. DuMont. "We are sincerely sorry for the confusion that raised your hopes. We are familiar with your feelings, because we've both experienced the highs and lows of grief every day since the fire."

Mrs. DuMont clung tighter to her husband and didn't respond.

Mr. DuMont shook Hank's hand. "Thank you, Webster." His thick voice betrayed his emotions.

Evelyn hadn't thought he had any. She touched Edith DuMont's shoulder. "Would you like to say goodbye?"

The woman lifted her tear-stained face and stared at Jamie for a moment, before shaking her head and turning back to her husband.

"A goodbye is more than we can manage right now, but perhaps in a few months we'll come to Hartford for a visit. We will have our own questions to ask the authorities." DuMont looked to Amato for affirmation.

The sergeant replied, "I'd be glad to help in any way I can."

"Very well." DuMont offered a feeble smile. "Perhaps we could visit then."

"You're welcome any time." Evelyn surprised herself by meaning the words.

The bailiff cleared his throat. "Judge Kaye is waiting."

Walt Shepherd stuck out his hand to Malcolm DuMont, whose disgruntled lawyer had fled right after the ruling. "Sorry, Malcolm. I just wanted the child to grow up with the right family."

DuMont replied, "He will." He herded his wife down the aisle, and

Hank guided Evelyn toward the side door. Amato, Mr. Shepherd, and Hank's parents followed.

Whatever could Judge Kaye want now?

———————•◦•———————

Kaye seemed much less imposing sitting behind his office desk. He smiled when the group entered, easing Hank's nervousness. A little.

Pointing to two well-padded armchairs, Kaye said, "Take a seat, Fred. Mildred, sit down before you float away."

Was anyone involved in the custody hearing who wasn't already acquainted? Hank still carried Jamie, who now squirmed and wriggled to get down.

Mother scooped him into her arms, and her comforting ways mesmerized the little man. "Let's see what is in my purse, eh?"

Jamie brightened. What toddler could resist rummaging through a woman's pocketbook? They sat together, and Mother lost herself in the wonder of meeting her new grandchild.

The judge pulled out a cigar from a desk drawer, clipped the end, and lit it before taking a long puff. He exhaled a grayish-white cloud. "Would you like one, Walt?"

Shepherd snatched it before the judge changed his mind.

Kaye puffed out another smoke-filled breath. "Henry. Mrs. Benson, please forgive me for putting you on the spot in public. I'd never have done so were I not sure of your answers."

Dad's cheeks flushed, and Mother turned her chair slightly aside. The dickens they were! Amato and Walt also wouldn't meet Hank's questioning look. "So all of you were in on this. Co-conspirators, eh?"

Everyone except Mother nodded. He'd pin her down later. For a hug and a kiss.

Evelyn's cheeks bloomed color like a summer rose. "I, for one, owe each of you a debt of gratitude for my happiness. Thank you." She looked expectantly at Hank and nudged him with an elbow.

"My bride-to-be just took the words out of my mouth." Hank hardly knew what to think. He simply enjoyed the camaraderie of being surrounded by friends.

"I'm a judge, you know." Kaye smiled. "There's no need to wait. I could perform the ceremony right now."

Mother hadn't seemed to pay attention, but she cried, "No!" She patted her snowy hair and said, "I mean, we'd rather have a church wedding, right, Hank?"

Evelyn said, "No worries, Mother Webster, I'd never get married without Lily here. She'd never let me forget it if she couldn't dress up as a flower girl."

"I can't wait to meet her." Mother's eyes shone.

More conversation ensued, but Hank's thoughts leaped from topic to topic like a trapeze artist. Where would they live? How could he provide for his new family? And what—oh, what—had he done to deserve such a blessing?

Cowper's hymn sang in his thoughts again, the words ringing with truth.

> *Ye fearful saints, fresh courage take;*
> *The clouds ye so much dread*
> *Are big with mercy and shall break*
> *In blessings on your head.*

The dark clouds in Hank's mind rolled away, a brilliant sunray broke through, and it seemed to Hank as if the Lord Himself rested a hand of blessing upon his head.

Epilogue

⤳

One more day, and Hank would be her husband. Lily and Jamie, joyful at their first reunion, now acted fully like the little terrors they were. Evelyn loved every minute of the normalcy she thought would never return. Shrieks and thumps, tears and bumps—all welcome—along with snuggles, cuddles, and bedtime stories.

Evelyn sat on the sofa in a rare respite from the hullabaloo of family life. Bernice had offered to sit with the children at her place, so Evelyn sipped a cup of coffee and enjoyed the soft lights adorning the Christmas tree. She'd never envisioned a Christmas Eve wedding, but all the world seemed decorated with her joy. Compliments of the season.

An early wedding gift had arrived from Sarasota. Inside the brown paper wrapping was a box wrapped again with brightly colored paper. A card addressed, "To Fraidy Freddie and his poor bride" left no doubt as to who it was from. Hank's eyes had twinkled when he handed the gift to Evelyn to open. When she lifted the flap, a coiled spring shot out of the box. Evelyn had shrieked so loudly the children came running. Hank had been smart enough not to open it himself, saying, "Ringling clowns always get the last laugh."

But the laughter of her family would soon fade from inside this dear home. When the general public had learned Evelyn and the children would be forced to vacate their home by the end of November, the bank suffered from bad press. A one-month stay had been granted, enough for the children to celebrate their last Christmas on Capen Street. They must have decided the furor would have died down by then, and they were correct.

Hank had already led the daunting task of searching for a little place of their own. With their two incomes they could only afford an apartment which had opened in Bernice's building, but it had just two bedrooms. Jamie and Lily would have to share a room, which would make Evelyn have to find a referee's uniform. It was only a temporary fix, one they'd decided they could live with until Evelyn finished night school and earned her teacher's certificate. Hank had urged her to follow her dream—another sign of the depth of his love for her.

A rap on the door summoned her, and Evelyn peeped out the window before answering. A horde of reporters had descended after they returned from Troy, wanting interviews and "inside information" about the search for Jamie. The world loved a happy ending, especially during the holidays.

Two familiar figures stood on the porch. Mr. Viller and Mr. Gooden from Hampshire Bank. Buzzards. Couldn't they wait another week? The house would be empty by then.

Mr. Gooden spoke first. "Hello, Mrs. Benson."

For one more day, yes. But Mrs. Webster by tomorrow this time. She could manage one last crisis on her own. "Hello. And hello, Mr. Viller."

"Please pardon this intrusion, but we have urgent business of a personal nature." Mr. Gooden licked his chapped lips and attempted a smile.

Mr. Viller flipped up the collar of his wool coat. "It's very cold out here. May we come in?"

Evelyn experienced a sudden, inhospitable urge to turn them away, but she said, "Of course. Please come in."

Neither man removed his coat, and Evelyn didn't offer to take them.

"This is a highly unusual situation, ma'am." Mr. Gooden offered a genuine smile. Perhaps his cold heart was thawed by the scent of freshly baked gingersnaps and coffee. Without ceremony, he handed her an envelope.

A quick surge of dread flipped Evelyn's stomach. Her hand trembling, she reached for it and ran her finger under the flap.

"No. You don't need to open it now." Mr. Viller's Adam's apple bobbed up and down. "On behalf of Hampshire Bank, I apologize for the distress we've caused during an already difficult time."

They were sorry. Ha. Evelyn didn't believe in Santa Claus, either. "Thank you." Her rote response was the best she could manage under the circumstances.

"When your story of finding your nephew caught the imagination of the city—in fact the nation—people wanted to help." Mr. Viller paused. "*I* wanted to help. I know I wasn't the friendliest person in the months after the fire, but we were under tremendous pressure from our stockholders. I am truly, deeply sorry."

Well. Maybe Santa was real, after all. She'd been certain Mr. Viller would only find a lump of coal in his stocking this year. "Thank you. I accept your apology."

Mr. Viller held out his hand, and Evelyn took it. He then added his other hand, covering hers. "The envelope holds the deed to this house, Mrs. Benson."

Evelyn wobbled, and the gentlemen helped her sit in the nearest chair.

"We received contributions from all across the country. From pennies to hundred-dollar donations, they arrived in a continuous stream until the house was paid off."

Mr. Gooden added his wide smile to that of Mr. Viller. "And there was cash left over. The envelope contains not only the deed, but a passbook for a savings account in the lad's name. If more donations arrive, we'll deposit them there in a fund for his future education."

Evelyn opened the passbook, but stars in her eyes prevented her from seeing the amount clearly.

Mr. Viller chuckled. He rotated the book. "It helps if you read it right-side-up."

The amount was staggering. Evelyn fumbled for what to say. "Gentlemen, I can't find words . . ." She swallowed and murmured, "Thank you."

"Mr. Viller wanted to wait until Christmas, but then we discovered you're to be married tomorrow. Consider it an early gift from Hampshire Bank." Mr. Gooden positively beamed.

"We know you're busy, so we will be on our way. Merry Christmas, Mrs. Benson." Mr. Viller knotted his worsted wool scarf below his neck and buttoned his coat again. Mr. Gooden did the same.

Evelyn stood and walked to the door with wooden steps. She opened it, the men passed through, and she overheard Mr. Gooden say, "I love being a Christmas elf." Mr. Viller gave him a hefty shove.

After shutting the door, Evelyn leaned against it and stared at the deed. No. Not Santa Claus. But she'd wager Bill Halstead had something to do with this since he had the ear of the Almighty.

With Lily as the all-eyes-had-better-be-on-me flower girl, and Jamie as the most adorable—if rambunctious—ring bearer, Evelyn Benson walked down the aisle of South Congregational Church on the arm of her boss, Charlie Reynolds, to become Mrs. Henry Webster.

Charlie, wearing a spiffy Brooks Brothers suit, ushered Evelyn with the posture and bearing of a medieval knight. An aging, potbellied knight, but a noble one. Some folks gasped and whispered as he passed. Others seemed not to recognize him at all.

They passed the pew where Evelyn sat during Bill and Helen's funeral, but not even that memory could diminish her joy. Evelyn allowed herself to scan the dear faces of friends in attendance, some new, some old. Mr. Viller and Mr. Gooden had been invited, and Evelyn welcomed their presence as representatives of God's miracle in keeping the Capen Street home.

Bernice sat in the position of honor as mother of the bride, joined by the Amatos, and Hank's friend, Phil, beamed at her from his seat beside Mother Webster. Without the wisdom and spiritual maturity of those two amazing friends, Hank and Evelyn might not have enjoyed this happy ending today.

Then, Evelyn had eyes only for Hank—her soon-to-be husband, yes, but also her best friend. The waitress and circus clown had been transformed by the wand of wedding magic into a couple that might have been the models for the bride and groom cake topper Darla found. The light in Hank's eyes at his candid perusal head-to-toe was followed by words he whispered when she arrived at the altar. "You're gorgeous."

Mother Webster had insisted on buying the lovely cream-colored suit she wore, and Helen's ruffle under the collar and lapels added the perfect, feminine touch, wrapping Evelyn with a lacy hug from her sister-in-law. An off-white velvet half hat with a net covering her eyes and a nosegay of red roses completed her ensemble. Evelyn had never felt lovelier.

The ceremony passed in a haze of joy, and Evelyn feared she might giggle like a lovestruck teenager when Hank said, "I do." The word *handsome* didn't begin to describe her groom, suave and as devastatingly charming as Clark Gable. Evelyn felt as if she were the starlet in a moving picture.

Hank's father struggled to keep his composure, at one moment whispering, "Pay attention, you two." When he finally arrived at "You may now kiss your bride," Evelyn lost touch with every reality except Hank's strong embrace and his soft lips pressed against her own.

For a moment too long, evidently, because titters of laughter and applause swept the congregation before Darla, who pretended to be the grumpiest matron of honor in the history of weddings, said with fake sternness, "That's enough, circus man."

Hank broke the kiss and winked at Darla before pouring his love into Evelyn through his sky-blue eyes. He said, "I love you, Mrs. Webster."

"Thank you, son! I love you too!" Hank's mother called out the joke from the front pew and chortled, very pleased with herself for joining the mischief.

"Us too," cried Lily, puckering up. Hank scooped Lily and Miss Persimmon—the doll Lily had insisted needed to be dressed in a matching outfit—into his arms and planted a big, sloppy kiss right on his new daughter's rosy cheek. "I love you, Miss Lily."

Jamie threw down his pillow and cried. Evelyn handed her bouquet to Darla and swept Jamie up for a new-family hug. She peppered his face with kisses until he pushed her away. Bride and groom both still held the children when Reverend Webster said, "Ladies and gentlemen, may I present to you Mr. and Mrs. Henry Webster."

The magnificent strains of the organ played, "God Moves in a Mysterious Way," for the recessional march, and Evelyn sang the words softly as she smiled at friends and congregants.

> *Blind unbelief is sure to err*
> *And scan His work in vain;*
> *God is His own interpreter,*
> *And He will make it plain.*

After a glorious wedding night in their bungalow—he could still hardly believe the generosity that made it theirs—Hank and Evelyn rose when the stars still twinkled against a navy-blue sky. The children were tucked safely across the street with Bernice—not awake yet, surely. He and Evelyn planned to do it themselves in a little while to begin their first Christmas Day as a family.

Bundled up to her pert little nose, which he couldn't help but kiss, she said, "Dress warm and meet me on the porch."

Hank had no idea what his new bride was up to, but he'd have a lifetime to enjoy her spontaneity. He felt like a teenager up to mischief while everyone else slept. The frostbitten trees glittered under the streetlights, but Evelyn lit the way with a flashlight down the sidewalk to the gate in the backyard that opened to the cemetery.

Snow crunched under their feet, and huge flakes fell to earth like sparkling confetti. Even the frozen tombstones wore mantles of white like hugs from heaven, and the city sounds vanished, muffled by the wondrous hush of Christmas morning.

Hank guessed their destination but not the purpose of the visit. They stopped at Bill and Helen's graves. A newly installed stone was engraved with both names, united in death as in life, with lilies of the valley carved in relief around the chiseled edges.

Evelyn brushed away the light coating of snow that obscured the words. She knelt on the frozen ground as if it were a church altar. Hank joined her, placing his arm around her shoulders. She looked up, and tiny tears had frozen on her lush eyelashes next to the snowflakes. "It haunts me that no one ever faced the consequences for causing the fire."

It haunted Hank too. No one had heard from Russell since he fled, but God knew where he was. Someday he'd be found. If he didn't face trial on earth, he surely would on Judgment Day.

Evelyn said, "I miss them so much. But without what happened that horrible day, we wouldn't be here now."

Hank's throat contained a lump he couldn't swallow. Nor could he reply. His heart was too full of God's goodness.

"Did you see, Hank?"

Hank coughed. "See what?"

Evelyn brushed away the blanket of white that obscured the words carved across the bottom. She shone her flashlight on flowing script with a doublet written by William Cowper that perfectly captured their separate journeys and the one they had just begun as man and wife.

> *The bud may have a bitter taste,*
> *But sweet will be the flow'r.*

Hank embraced Evelyn, and from her honeyed lips he savored another taste from the sweetest flower under heaven.

Acknowledgments

No one who launches a book into the turbulent skies of the publishing world is a solo pilot. This debut novel would never have left the hangar without the encouragement and prayers of exceptional supporters behind the scenes.

Dale, my dear husband, you are the hero in every novel I will ever write. I forgive you for boisterous cheering at award ceremonies, and my best-kept secret is that I enjoy it. A little. Your steady, constant encouragement and advice has kept me airborne.

Jana and Chris, my daughter and son-in-love, thank you for the best writer's retreat ever inhabited by an author. The opportunity to live near you and your family 24/7 brings joy that speeds my journey.

Thank you to all my family members who refueled me with gallons of love, sympathy, and patient listening. Sophia, dear niece-in-love, when my tanks of inspiration and motivation were nearly empty, your support was high-octane.

Linda Glaz, I could never ask for a better agent/navigator than you. Thank you for keeping me on course and believing in me when I didn't believe in myself.

Rick L. Brunner, Esq., thank you for helping me pilot my aircraft out of a pop-up legal thunderstorm.

Gregg Bridgeman, thank you for prodding me to go full throttle. I'm not stalling anymore.

Thank you to all my friends at Serious Writer, Inc. You gave me pilot's wings in 2019, and I'd never have had the confidence to get in the cockpit except for you.

My critique partners at the KCW Mentoring Group all deserve thanks for putting wrenches and screwdrivers to my manuscript. Your oily coveralls prove you're the best maintenance crew ever. Tracy Crump, you are an outstanding chief engineer. From the earliest moments I dreamed of taking this flight, you have been my stalwart friend and advisor. I'm deeply grateful.

DiAnn Mills, Deborah Maxey, Candy Arrington, PeggySue Wells,

Chris Manion, and Marva Southall, when I think of all the high-tech writing gadgets you installed in my cockpit, I can only say, "WOW." I fly higher and farther because of you.

To the team flying with me—the professionals at Barbour Publishing— thank you for creating the flight plan. Rebecca Germany, thank you for understanding that some writer-pilots cry over their characters. JoAnne Simmons, thank you for operating the editing levers and flaps that give this book a smoother flight.

Thank you to the typesetting team at Barbour Publishing that made my aircraft look so shiny and sleek.

Mom and Dad, writers are supposed to avoid clichés, but I think I'll be forgiven for breaking the rules in the acknowledgments. You may be witnessing this flight from heaven, but you and Jesus are the wind beneath my wings, and you always will be.

Jesus, You are the true pilot. Thank You for allowing me to be Your copilot. I'll fly anywhere with You.

Author's Notes

Shortly after this book's debut, Hartford will commemorate the eightieth anniversary of the 1944 circus fire. Barbour Publishing named this series A Day to Remember, but many people have never read the accounts of that horrific day. While researching the gripping stories of the fire's victims and survivors, I gasped, cheered, and wept.

This book is fiction, and I have used literary license to imagine the thoughts, words, and actions of circus, police, and city officials during the catastrophe. However, the agony of real people swept up in the fire is beyond description. I hope readers will experience some degree of the shock and terror of that day through the eyes of my characters.

I read several well-researched books, and I recommend them to anyone who would like to learn more about the events of July 6, 1944. *A Matter of Degree*, by Don Massey and Rick Davey (Willow Brook Press, 2001) features the story of Little Miss 1565, who is briefly mentioned in this manuscript. The mystery of this little girl, who the authors identify as Eleanor Emily Cook, gripped the city and the nation as forensic scientists and detectives struggled to identify her body. The book also contains a timeline, historic photographs, and a detailed index of names, dates, and events pertaining to the fire.

The Circus Fire: A True Story of an American Tragedy, by Stewart O'Nan (Anchor Books, a Division of Random House, Inc., 2001), is another exhaustive account of the fire. The author's style of literary storytelling makes it a gripping, thrilling, heart-wrenching read.

The Hartford Circus Fire: Tragedy Under the Big Top, by Michael Skidgell (The History Press, 2014), contains not only an account of the fire and its aftermath but also a brief biography of all 168 victims. That tally includes the collective body parts of one unidentified victim, whose story I used to explain why Evelyn believed Jamie was dead. Photos of many of the victims are included in the book, and their poignant stories deeply affected me. They served as inspiration for the composite characters I devised for this book, which I hope does honor to their memories.

One such victim was six-year-old Raymond A. Erickson, Jr. He attended the circus accompanied by his mother, Sophie, and several family members. When panic ensued, Raymond's uncle, Stanley, herded the group to attempt escape over the infamous animal chute tended by my fictional hero, Hank. When he was separated from several family members, including Raymond, Stanley rushed back inside the tent to search before he was forced to flee from the intense heat.

Stanley eventually located Raymond, burned but alive, and took him to Municipal Hospital. He placed his nephew on a cot in the hospital corridor and asked a priest to perform last rites. Then he resumed his frantic efforts to locate the rest of his family. Hartford police offered their assistance and finally urged Stanley to seek treatment for his own burns. He spent two weeks in the hospital recovering.

But to everyone's surprise and horror, Raymond had vanished from the hospital. Investigators thought perhaps another family had taken custody of the boy in error, and urgent inquiries were made to try to locate him. Sophie Erickson found her son's shoes—with a broken, knotted lace—at the hospital, the only clue he might have survived the fire. Jamie's character and the search for him is based on Raymond's story, and I included this heartbreaking detail, weeping as I wrote.

Unlike Jamie, Raymond was never heard from again. Sophie eventually called off the search, in part because she didn't want to inflict further trauma on other parents. When I imagined the horror of Sophie's life sentence in a prison of grief and uncertainty, I knew I had to write a happier ending for Jamie. How I wish it were more than fiction.

Bill Curlee was the inspiration for strapping, lovable, heroic Bill Halstead. A resident of Euclid, Ohio, he attended the circus with his son, David, while his family visited relatives in Hartford. Curlee helped David escape over the animal chute but after commanding him to flee, Bill remained behind to attempt the rescue of other frantic people trapped there. Witnesses attested to his heroic actions, which resulted in Bill's death when the tent collapsed on him.

Official investigations of the fire resulted in conflicting and confusing information. Culpability was attributed to circus officials for lapses in safety measures, and five circus officials were convicted on a variety of charges. Ringling hamstringed their future profits to set up a victim's compensation fund, and eventually they settled all legal claims, including one payment to a woman who had suffered burns but only requested a refund for the price of her ticket.

A report of the original investigators alleged the fire was caused by a stray cigarette butt carelessly tossed in the grass under the bleachers. However, assisted by knowledge gleaned from post-fire events, many people firmly believe the fire was the result of arson by a man named Robert Segee, who suffered brutal child abuse which resulted in deep psychological wounds. Segee's story is the factual basis for my fictional character Russell Segal. Jailed numerous times and convicted in other cases of arson, Segee confessed in 1950 to having set the Hartford fire but later recanted, claiming investigators coerced him into it.

A new investigation on the origin of the fire was opened in March 1991 by Connecticut's Department of Public Safety commissioner based on findings by Lieutenant Rick Davey of the Hartford Fire Marshal's office (a coauthor of *A Matter of Degree*, in which he lays out his case that Segee set the fire). Tests run by Connecticut's State Forensic Lab did not support the idea of the fire's ignition by a cigarette butt, but neither did they discover signs of arson. Without conclusive evidence, the investigation closed in 1993 finding that the source of the fire was "undetermined."

Interest in the events of that tragic Thursday has not waned. Current comments, family tributes, and memorable photographs are accessible on a website dedicated to helping us remember what happened that fateful day at this URL: https://www.circusfire1944.com.

While nonfiction books about the fire chronicle the physical and emotional trauma of this tragedy, I have chosen to focus upon its spiritual implications. Most of us will never live through a historic disaster like this one, but other, smaller catastrophes are a universal experience. Thank you for exploring with me the questions we all have during those times about God's power and goodness. I've said a prayer that God will help readers of this book navigate their own crises without losing faith and hope in His love. Like my heroine and hero, Evelyn and Hank, we are left to ponder the impact of God's mysterious ways.

Questions for Discussion

1. Sometimes mankind's simple choices contribute to experiencing a disaster or avoiding it. How do we reconcile this with the providence of God?

2. Since God knows in advance that tragic events happen, what responsibility does He bear for the outcome, and why doesn't He stop it?

3. Can Christians expect more divine protection than non-Christians in a disastrous event? Why?

4. How should survivors process the information that a loved one made a fatal choice they could have avoided? What should we do when we feel angry about it?

5. How does it affect your relationship with God when tragedy strikes you or a loved one?

6. How would you comfort someone like Evelyn, who seems to bear an unusually heavy load of grief?

Rhonda Dragomir is a multimedia creative who treasures her fairy-tale life in Central Kentucky, insisting her home is her castle even if her prince refuses to dig a moat. She has multiple published works in anthologies and periodicals, along with Bible lessons studied weekly by more than 10,000 women around the world. Rhonda has garnered numerous writing awards for both fiction and nonfiction, including her selection as 2019 Writer of the Year by Serious Writer, Inc. In 2020 she was also a finalist in ACFW's Genesis Contest for her first novel, a 16th century historical romance. View her published works and read excerpts of her works in progress at www.RhondaDragomir.com.

A Day to Remember

A new series of exciting novels featuring historic American disasters that changed landscapes and multiple lives. Whether by nature or by man, these disasters changed history and were days to be remembered.

When the Waters Came
By Candice Sue Patterson
May 31, 1889

Pastor Montgomery Childs struggles to tend his humble flock in Johnstown, Pennsylvania, while seething at the evil practices among the rich and privileged on Lake Conemaugh. Like Noah, Monty prays for justice, but he never expects God to send a flood. Annamae Worthington comes to help the newly formed Red Cross deal with the aftermath of the failure of South Fork Dam, never imagining the horrors she will encounter. As Monty and Annamae work together distributing supplies, housing survivors, and preparing the dead, a kinship forms between them. But when an investigation into the collapsed dam points to the South Fork Fishing and Hunting Club, secrets emerge that may tear them apart.

Paperback / 978–1–63609–758–9

When Hope Sank
By Denise Weimer
April 27, 1865

The Civil War has taken everything from Lily Livingston, leaving her to work for her uncle at a squalid inn along the Arkansas riverfront that is overrun by spies and bushwhackers. Her only hope of escape is a marriage promise she is uncertain will be fulfilled. When on April 27, 1865, the steamboat *Sultana*, overloaded with soldiers, explodes and sinks, Lily does all she can to help the victims, including Lieutenant Cade Palmer. But what would the wounded surgeon think of her if he knew she could have prevented the disaster—and may have knowledge of another in the making?

Paperback / 978–1–63609–829–6

JOIN US ONLINE!

Christian Fiction for Women

Christian Fiction for Women is your online home for the latest in Christian fiction.

Check us out online for:

- Giveaways
- Recipes
- Info about Upcoming Releases
- Book Trailers
- News and More!

Find Christian Fiction for Women at Your Favorite Social Media Site:

 Search "Christian Fiction for Women"

 @fictionforwomen